My Dying Breath

Clare Connelly

First published 2023 (c) Clare Connelly

http://www.clareconnelly.com Blog: http://clarewriteslove.wordpress.com/ Email: clare@clareconnelly.co.uk

Follow Clare Connelly on facebook for all the latest.

Join Clare's Newsletter to stay up to date on all the latest CC news. www.clareconnelly.com

About the Author

Clare Connelly grew up in a small country town in Australia. Surrounded by rainforests, and rickety old timber houses, magic was thick in the air, and stories and storytelling were a huge part of her childhood.

From early on in life, Clare realised her favourite books were romance stories, and read voraciously. Anything from Jane Austen to Georgette Heyer, to Mills & Boon and (more recently) 50 Shades, Clare is a romance devotee. She first turned her hand to penning a novel at fifteen (if memory serves, it was something about a glamorous fashion model who fell foul of a high-end designer. Sparks flew, clothes flew faster, and love was born.)

Clare has a small family and a bungalow near the sea. When she isn't chasing after energetic little toddlers, or wiping fingerprints off furniture, she's writing, thinking about writing, or wishing she were writing.

Clare loves connecting with her readers. Head to **www.clareconnelly. co.uk** to sign up to her newsletter, or join her official facebook page.

PROLOGUE

He watches her almost as closely as I do. She cannot lift a hand without his eyes following the gesture, it is a silent ballet: her gestures create an echo in him that he seems unable to control. He watches her always – but I am watching him.

I have waited years to find her and now I have, but I cannot act when he is there.

He is a complication I had not anticipated.

Life is full of complications though and rewards come to those who wait.

I will wait and I will watch and soon this will be over. For I have found The Sole Survivor and I intend to right the wrongs of that night, finally.

ONE
THUNDER ON A STORMY NIGHT

I'm dying to tell him the truth. Of course I am. Lying to this guy is like peeling off my skin, layer by layer. But if I tell him? It will be the end. Not just of 'us', but of the delicate tightrope I must walk. Maybe even the end of me. The secret I carry is not just my own: all the people I love most are wrapped up in its silence and so I hold onto it earnestly, even when I would wish to divulge the truth of who and what I am.

But I don't.

I sit across from him, watching the way his hair flops forward a little over his brow as he reaches for his coffee, already his fourth despite the fact it's still early in the day; the way his symmetrical, determined face scans The Guardian on his Tablet, taking in the facts printed and those that aren't. The way his lips curl with that particularly derisive scowl of his as he sees one of his business rivals appear on the pages.

And I imagine how it would feel if he looked at me like that. If his eyes filled with that legendary coldness and he turned that famously ruthless disdain on me.

Alex isn't an ordinary man. He didn't get to own one of the biggest tech companies in the world by being compassionate and patient. He's rough. And he's demanding. Impossibly determined to get what he wants, and from the minute he saw me, he made it obvious he wanted me. I was his latest obsession and he hunted me mercilessly, in that way he has that makes it almost impossible to say no.

I could have though, and a part of me wanted to. I saw danger in Alex from the first moment I met him, and I'm usually very good at avoiding danger (I've learned to be, naturally). It's not his darkness that terrifies me though, but how much I crave it—how much I crave him.

He knows nothing about me beyond the construct I have allowed him to see and now I find I want him to know all of me. The real me. It defies logic and it breaks every rule we've agreed to. Sex and no-strings is the promise we've made and there are so many strings around the truth of my being that I am tied into a thousand knots.

Could he unravel me? Would he want to?

A curse fills my mind, tearing through me like thunder on a stormy night.

"You're frowning."

As far as I can tell, he hasn't even looked my way, but I make an effort to rearrange my features. I purse my lips, lifting the corners into a smile he once told me was the sexiest thing he'd ever seen. "Wrong."

"Really?" He flicks his eyes to mine, and his scepticism sears me. "What is it?"

I shake my head and a curl of dark brown hair drops in front of my eyes. I push it away, tucking it behind my ear at the same time he reaches for it. Our fingers brush and it's there. *Zap.* Electricity and awareness. It scorches me. Does he feel it? It's hard to tell. In the privacy of his apartment he's a veritable sex-god. But he can fold that side of himself away when we're out, presenting a cool, untouchable façade to the world even when he's so not like that. Passion runs deep with Alex and it is his passion that drives me to the point of distraction.

I tap my fingers against my knee, wondering at the charge of desire that's making my stomach churn.

"What's what?"

It's an infinitesimal change in body language but I'm attuned to every single detail of his. He shifts his weight forward slightly and his shoulders are tense beneath his custom ten-thousand pound-suit. "If you're worried about something, I want to fix it."

But haven't I had enough of that in my life? People reaching in and rearranging the pieces of my existence because they think I can't look after myself? "Fine. Take me to bed."

His eyes flicker just enough to show that I've hit a nerve. "That's on my agenda, believe me."

"Now."

His laugh pours over me like warm caramel. "You are impossible."

I am. I didn't used to be, but meeting Alex LaMar has shown me that I am desirable and powerful. I guess I'm a little high on that power, even though I inherently understand how fleeting it is in nature. I am his latest obsession, but I am not foolish enough to think I will obsess him for long —we've agreed as much. This is temporary. But right here and now, I have him, and I love that.

"Impossible to resist?" I tease, flexing that power, feeling it spread through me as beneath the table I let my toe shuffle over his calf, inching it higher and higher until it's between his legs. He doesn't betray so much as a flicker of response, except in the depths of his eyes, where he can't quite control his reactions, there is a darkening of colour, a flash of recognition.

His hand curls around my ankle and I'm reminded for the millionth time of how strong he is. Half-man, half-beast, I often think to myself, barely contained by the stitching of his suit. Broad shouldered, a chest that ripples with bulked muscles and dark eyes that see so much more than I show anyone else. He removes my foot easily, but instead of dropping it to the floor like I expect, he lifts it higher into his lap. He removes my shoe and beneath the table, he rubs the sole of my foot, his eyes snatched to mine with a slightly mocking air.

His skin on mine feels so good that I shudder in my seat. "Let's go back to your place."

His lips twist with regret. "Not possible. I have to work."

"Don't you own the company?"

"Yes. And over thirty-thousand people around the world count on me doing my job so they can keep doing theirs."

I pull my foot away but his fingers don't release me. Instead, they travel higher along my leg, teasing my calf now and then the sensitive flesh behind my knee.

"What about me?" I ask breathily.

"You'll wait."

"What if I won't?" I whisper, dropping my eyes so he won't see the desperation gathering there, like storm clouds on the horizon. Power is fleeting; one minute I am high and the next I am waiting for the wave to crash. Frustration gnaws at me.

He doesn't pretend to misunderstand and I'm glad. He's not like other guys I've known, or dated. Not that we're dating, I guess. We're sleeping together. That's about the most he's promised me, and even though I agreed with his terms, because they suited me too, you'll probably have guessed by now that I'm in way over my head. I never knew it would be like this. He is intoxicating. "Then that's your choice."

Non-committal. Putting the ball back in my court, as he is so talented at doing. I should be gratified, but I'm not.

I swallow back my frustration.

Four weeks this has been going on. Four weeks since we met, since he fundamentally changed a part of me, four weeks since I first learned the pleasure of life with Alex LaMar in it. On the one hand, that doesn't seem like long, on the other, I cannot remember ever not knowing him.

I know that soon my life will swallow me back into it, making it almost impossible to accommodate the demands of this relationship. University is back, and though it's early in the term, I can already feel the risks of inattention. My focus isn't where it should be and my grades will suffer if I don't take care.

"Meet me in the back," he says, placing his tablet and phone into a small leather bag he carries.

My stomach is filled with butterflies; that's what he does to me. I weave through the tables and no longer see the other diners. It's just him and me and the ravishing I hope he's about to give me. I slip through the doors to the back corridor of this cafe and I watch as he pays the bill and strides across the room, oblivious to the way heads turn in his direction—Alex never notices that, but I do. I'm someone who's spent a lifetime learning how *not* to be noticed, and he's the opposite—so meteoric and blindingly handsome and yet he barely realises what kind of impression he makes. Or perhaps he simply doesn't care.

He doesn't waste a second. Away from prying eyes at last, his body crushes me to the cold, tiled wall and his mouth possesses mine; his tongue is punishing me and pleading with me and I know then that he's as desperate as I am. He's hard against my gut but he's too disciplined to do more than kiss me. My knees are weak and my shoulders sag; without the strength of his body holding me to the wall I know I'll slip to the floor.

And when I moan a little into his mouth he grinds his cock against me. "It's an IOU," he explains, breaking the kiss and putting horrible, aching distance between us.

I nod, completely torn apart by fire and flame.

The bathroom door bangs shut and a woman emerges. She looks at us quizzically and Alex instantly changes. He's cool and calm, his smile perfectly banal as he reaches into his pocket. I've seen him do this enough times to know what the gesture means. He slips his key into my hand. "Text and let me know when you get there."

Frustration spirals inside me. "One of these days I'll get sick of waiting for you, you know."

His laugh is like melted butter over my spine. "We'll see."

I roll my eyes, but smile, because I can't help it. "You're an arrogant bastard, you know?"

"I have been told."

And he's right to be so cocky, pardon the pun. Maybe if I'd lived a normal life, I'd have had some idea how to deal with a man like Alex. But I'm flying blind. I've dated a couple of guys, neither of them anything special. The truth is, until meeting Alex, I had no idea I was even a sexual person, really. But I am hooked on him and the way he makes me feel, and I can't imagine myself closing the door on this in a million years. But at some point I must. To protect my secret, I keep people away, and Alex isn't someone who will be happy knowing only part of me. Eventually, he'll ask. He'll see the way I evade questions, he'll realise there are whole chunks of me I keep buried, and he'll want to know, because that's just who he is.

I sense his gaze burning into me, watching me, all the way to the front of the restaurant. But I don't feel the other set of eyes, though they follow me with exactly the same degree of interest. They're still watching me when I pull the heavy glass door inwards and emerge onto the blustery Soho street. They watch me as I clip away, and I have no clue. I don't find out about them until much, much later. But for now? I still believe the biggest danger that faces me is the total cluster-fuck of lust I feel for a guy who may disappear from my life any day now.

———

He arrives late. It's almost midnight when I hear him open the door. And I'm a little bit pissed off. The anger lasts precisely as long as it takes my eyes to settle on the details of his face. So handsome, so rugged, and so tired. I ache to run my hands over his shoulders and kiss him tenderly, pressing away the fatigue. But that's not who we are.

"You're still up."

"Yeah." And I walk towards him so slowly that I'm practically pausing between each step. The lights are off except for the lamp near him. As I draw closer, he realises I'm only wearing a skimpy negligee, and that my fingers are toying with the spaghetti straps. When I'm close, but not so close that he can touch me, I slide them down my arms.

I'm naked beneath. The silk pools at my feet. I step out of it. "You wrote me an IOU, remember?"

His lip twists like a coil. "I've been thinking about little else all day."

I make a tsk-ing sound. "What a shame you weren't here sooner then. I'm a little tired now."

His eyes probe mine. "Too tired?"

A small smirk tilts my lips because so much is revealed in his question. His concern for my welfare—if I say 'yes', he'll tuck me into bed with a chaste kiss, because he is caring like that. But I hear his desperation too, that I say 'no', and allow him to fulfil his promise.

"Not too tired," I offer after silence has stretched for about as long as I can let it.

His breath expels in a soft whoosh of relief, and his hands are reverent as they run along my sides, cupping breasts I weeks ago ceased to think of as mine. They are his, as is all of me.

"Where the hell did you come from, Sash?" He mutters, and for a second I freeze. Fear trickles down my spine as one of the questions I most fear comes out of his beautiful mouth. But he doesn't mean anything by it, I'm almost sure of it. Not in the way I worry about. This is just one of those things; a question intended to flatter. My past holds little interest to him—there's no danger here.

"Your imagination?" My heart beats fast against my ribs for a plethora of reasons.

"My imagination isn't this good," he denies, dropping his hands to grip my wrist. He pulls me hard, so that I jerk against him and my breath snatches loudly across the empty room.

"What does this say?" He strokes the word tattooed across my inner forearm. It has been written in a curling script, making it difficult to distinguish the individual letters. "Monachopsis."

His laugh is loud in the sensually charged silence of the room. "Mona-what?"

I shake my head. "Long story." I want him so badly I feel a little bit nauseous. Having never known desire like this, I have no concept if this is normal, but I do know I'm not willing to give it up.

His fingers drop to his belt. His eyes are burning through my soul as he pulls it quickly from his pants then undoes the button and zip. He steps out of them and grabs my wrists; his fingers are firm around my flesh and I suck a breath in that shakes with pleasure. It's going to happen. And soon. "All day I've thought of you. Of this. All day."

He wraps the belt around my wrists, curling it in and out of my skin until almost the whole belt has been used. He buckles it and pulls it tight so that breaking free is impossible for anyone but Houdini. I'm not Houdini; nor do I want to escape. "Where?" I say breathlessly, ignoring the fact I should be worried by the depth of need I feel for this man.

And now he scoops down and picks me up, and though I've had years knowing just how well I can take care of myself, I'm not ashamed to say how good it feels to be held by him like this; how safe I feel with him.

He's big and I'm small and still I wonder at the way he lifts me so easily. He carries me through the apartment to the guest room we always use. His room I've only seen occasionally—when he's not in the apartment and I'm free to roam around and wonder at the parts of his life he keeps completely separate to me. You'd spy too, wouldn't you?

He shoulders the door and then puts me on my feet near the foot of the bed. There's a hook low down on the frame; I've seen it before and always presumed it was something decorative. But he pulls on the belt around my wrists and clips a thick velvet chord through them. I'm tied to the bed and because of where the loop is, I'm bent over at more than a ninety degree angle.

His hands spread my legs from behind and I imagine what my arse must look like, pale and round in the milky moonlight that slices through the window.

I can't see him but I can hear the whisper of clothes as he undresses and I'm so wet that I can already feel myself coming a little. I'm on the brink of begging when he reaches down and runs his touch over my long hair. He pushes it aside so that his hands can stroke my neck. "I will never get over how beautiful you are."

I shake my head, ready to push aside the compliment as form rather than fact. He doesn't give me a chance. His dick, sheathed in a condom and huge and hard pushes to the core of my being. I writhe in surprise and relief and gratitude. His fingers dig into my hips, holding me steady as he thrusts into me hard, so hard that my head hits the bed frame at one point and I laugh a little. He swears and issues a gruff apology but I shake my head. I don't care. I love it when he's desperate for me. I don't want him to stop.

He understands and even though I feel him throbbing he slows down, refusing to own his climax yet. But me? Oh, I'm there. I sail over the edge, screaming into the room as my whole body begins to shake and I pull at my hands. And when I think I can't handle anymore, he leans forward, cupping my breasts and moving deeper inside me. He's twisting my nipples—he knows I love it.

I want all of him, more than this. I want to feel his weight on me. I want his kisses. And I know that will come, because Alex is never satisfied with just once.

This is the necessity of our relationship. The first coming together that is mandated by a day's distance. It's no-frills sex.

Sure enough, he feels me come apart and he holds me, waiting for the frantic breathing to subside before pulling out of me.

"Untie me," I moan, wanting so much more.

I don't see him shake his head. "No way."

I angle my head to meet his eyes but he nods towards the bed. "Lie down."

I frown. "I can't ..."

"Yes, you can."

And he's right, but there's nothing elegant about the way I scramble onto the bed and my cheeks are pink when finally, I'm lying on my stomach on the thick mattress. I stare at him mutinously, wondering if he gets a kick out of my awkward ministrations, but he doesn't notice apparently.

"No, no," he murmurs. "On your back."

"I'm not a contortionist," I snap.

With a grunt, he rolls me over, and my wrists form an X that I can't unravel. "I have had a shit of a day, Sasha. I could do without the smar-tassery."

"You don't think my arse is smart?" I grumble and his lips flicker in a tight smile.

"I think your arse is heaven," he contradicts. "And that I want you a thousand times tonight."

"Even you don't have that kind of stamina."

"Where you're concerned, I wouldn't be so sure." And finally he's kissing me, and thrusting into me, his body weight on mine and every-thing is perfect, just as I knew it would be. It's perfect as I orgasm again and he kisses me and whispers in my ear, platitudes that I don't even know I need to hear.

He pushes into me and he's coming, every muscle in his body flinches as he crosses his threshold and explodes. And I smile, because he's mine. Not forever. Maybe not even for much longer. But for tonight.

I'm not going to waste a moment thinking about the future, even though it scares the hell out of me.

Two

Creatures and their habits

I should be tired but I'm not. My body is deliciously sore and my eyes are heavy but my mind is filled with memories that breathe fire and zest into my being. I tap my pen against the desk, angling my head to study Dr Carlton, hoping I look interested in tortious law when really all I can think about is Alex.

But Dr Carlton isn't easily fooled. Maybe because he's young enough to still remember what it's like to be at university. He looks at me and his lips hint at a smile before he carries on with the lecture. I smile back on autopilot and focus more firmly on the notes that are being projected onto the screen.

It's not like I don't care about my degree.

I do, passionately. When I was ten years old and my world tipped on its head, I swore I'd work out a way to make everything better. The power of those who practise law had been, until then, something I understood in a very abstract way. But when I was at trial, and I saw for myself how that power can be wielded, it locked into place my own need to master the law and use it to my advantage.

It has been my sole life ambition, all that matters to me. Until I met Alex. I shiver as I remember the way we fell asleep, his body wrapped around mine, his hands holding me so close that our breath was synchronised. I'm not a calm sleeper. I thrash about and toss and turn, by virtue of the terrors that still course through my blood, so we never stay like that for long, but to fall asleep so cherished is new to me.

Is it new for him?

The question brings bitterness to my mouth because I know the answer and it's not pleasing. Nothing about what we're doing is new for him. He has had many lovers, or so I presume, and each has been discarded no matter how cherished they might have felt for a period in his life.

He told me as much the first time we slept together. *This isn't a prelude to love, Sasha. I'm not looking for Happily Ever After. I'm not offering romance. If you want those things then you should go now, before we begin.*

I should have left.

The spell had been cast though and I was already unable to break free of it.

"Sasha? Your essay had some interesting points on this. Do you want to elaborate?"

Damn it. Carlton knows I'm not listening. I shake my head, my cheeks flaming, and he grins again, a rakish smile that reminds me I used to think he was pretty damn hot. B.A. Before Alex.

He's a visiting lecturer, over from the States, and he has that rich, honeyed accent and a Californian sun-tan. His hair is blonde and long; he wears it in a fashionably dishevelled bun and his face is covered in spiky golden stubble. He made a name for himself when he was straight out of college defending an innocent black man who'd been set up by a crooked cop for murder. It was a huge case and made headlines around the world. Carlton alone had believed the man's version of events. He'd used his own money to run all of the tests and double check all of the evidence at private laboratories and when his money had run out he crowd-funded a huge amount to keep the case going. He's been heralded as a sort of modern-day David to the establishment's Goliath and everything he has touched since has turned to gold.

"Come on, guys! You're all so quiet today. What's going on?"

There's a collective spasm of chairs and desks as we snap to attention, leaning forward and re-engaging. Carlton laughs. "That's better, I guess."

He runs his hand over the back of his neck and turns to look up at the clock. "You've got to understand the real-world implications of what we're doing here. You're fourth years. You're this close to getting out there and practising. Why are you sitting here?" He pivots to the front row, pointing at a girl whose name I can never remember.

"Umm," she mumbles, flicking her eyes around the room, too shy to speak so she shrugs.

"'Umm,' isn't an answer!" He shakes his head. He's being kind though. He moves along. "Clint?"

"Yeah?"

"You enrolled in law at one of the finest schools in the UK. Why? What does this mean to you?"

"I want to be a barrister."

"Right." The steam of frustration rising from Carlton's head is practically visible, even though his face is calm and his shoulders aren't bunched together. I don't know how I got so good at reading people's emotions.

Yes, I do, actually. I just don't like to dwell on that. When your very survival depends on knowing how someone feels and assessing if they're a threat, you become a swift and adept judge of character.

"The law isn't theoretical, guys, but a moving feast. It's not just... something you study. It's something you *are*. Something you feel. It changes you and you should want to change it."

We all nod, though I wonder if anyone else has the same understanding of his words as I do.

"Sasha? You look like you've got something to add."

He looks at me like he knows me, but he doesn't. I think maybe he's just great at reading people, too. He's right, though. I was driven to this degree for a reason, and that reason resonates as strongly in my soul now as it did way back when I first chose this path. "People who know the law, who speak its language, hold all the power in this world." It's just Carlton and me. I tune out my classmates and their speculative glances. "More power than money, more power than politics. The law, in our country at least, emboldens those who have no hope. To speak the language of law enables us to speak for those who face unthinkable cruelty and loss. Not just the wrongly and unjustly accused," I murmur, thinking of his case.

"But refugees and children and others weakened by society and circumstance."

He brings his hands together in three slow claps. "Now, that's an answer." He looks at the clock once more. "We're almost done here anyway. Go home. Next week my first question for each of you is going to be this: *Why are you here?* I want an answer like Sasha's from each of you. And if you can't come up with one you might need to seriously consider your choice of degree because if you think the workload is tough, wait until you're out there in the real world with clients and cases and court systems to navigate."

There's a raucous noise as books are slammed onto desks and then stuffed into backpacks and handbags. I don't have my textbook because it's at my flat, and I haven't spent proper time there in weeks. I slide my notebook away with the hastily photocopied pages of someone else's text jutting out of the sides. Carlton catches me as I come down the aisle, ready to leave.

"That was a good answer," he says, smiling like we're old friends.

I like him. I feel comfortable with him. And he makes a nice difference from my other lecturers who are uniformly stuffy and old-fashioned. "Thanks."

"You feel injustice like a personal responsibility." His eyes linger on my face.

"Shouldn't we all?"

His laugh is nice; soft and gentle. "Yeah, but in reality, most people don't give a shit unless it directly impacts them."

I arch a brow, surprised by the curse.

He must see my reaction because he shrugs. "I'm not talking to you now as your teacher. I'm talking to you as … a friend."

A friend? That's interesting. "I didn't know we were friends," I can't resist saying, my tone light and teasing.

"All friendships start somewhere. Have you got time for a coffee?"

I'm tempted. This guy is really interesting but all my spare time is invested elsewhere. And I'm desperate to get home and reacquaint myself with my own apartment, before Alex is finished work. "Rain check?" I say with true regret.

"You got some other place to be?"

I nod.

"Let me at least grab you a takeaway then," he offers. "You looked like you could hardly keep your eyes open."

I grimace. "Was I that obvious?"

"You're just usually more of a live-wire in my class."

I smile at the description; it weakens my resolve. "There's a place just around the corner."

"Great. Let's go." He scoops up his own books and pushes the door, holding it open for me. The hallway is packed but we weave through the crowds and emerge onto the steps soon enough. It's a grim London day. The sky is grey and menacing.

"Menacing?"

I didn't realise I'd spoken the words out loud but I nod. "I always think it's like the clouds are sinking down, ready to squash me." I shake my head at the foolish description.

"I like it." He digs one hand into his pocket as he walks. Outside of the classroom, he looks more like my contemporary than a lecturer.

"I would have thought you'd hate the weather here, given that you're from somewhere perennially sunny?"

"On the contrary, I love change."

"I hate it." I shiver unconsciously. I've known too much change.

"Do you?"

I shrug, reminding myself to be careful. I don't really need the reminder; after so many years of hiding, this is who I am now, but around people I am comfortable with I am most at risk of forgetting myself.

"I'm a creature-of-habits girl I guess." I point to the line of shops across the street. "See that bookstore?"

He nods.

"I've worked there for the last four years."

He grins. "That is definitely a habit."

"It's convenient," I say in a voice that is jokingly defensive. "Plus I get to talk about books for hours on end. It's brilliant."

"Did you grow up around here?"

Specificity is the devil. I keep my response casual. "Not far. I moved to a little studio flat around the corner, when I started university." I pan my hand around the grim skies and low-lying buildings. "This is my village now."

"Cheery," he replies with a shake of his head.

"How are you finding London? Besides loving our gloomy weather."

"I always think you guys give your weather a bad rap. The summer was pretty good."

"Yeah. All three days of it."

"Fair point." We turn the corner and the white star heralding my favourite cafe comes into sight. "I love the history here. The culture. I think I saw just about every theatre show playing in my first month."

"Geek," I grin.

"Theatre buff," he corrects, smiling down at me in a way that should inspire caution. I feel a *frisson* of guilt, as though I'm doing something wrong. Which is completely stupid. I'm not flirting with my lecturer – I'd never do anything so stupid. And Alex? My heart accelerates when I imagine him. Would he be jealous? That's hard to say. Possessiveness is different to jealousy. The fact he feels the former in no way suggests he'd experience the latter.

"What's been your favourite?"

"Nuh uh," he says. "Not after that 'geek' comment. I'm not sharing."

"Oh, come on. Tell me yours, I'll tell you mine."

He considers it a moment. "Okay, deal. Matilda."

"You're kidding?"

"Why?"

"It's just, I love it too. I've seen it six times."

"Six? That's just showing off."

"It's utterly brilliant," I enthuse, warming to one of my favourite subjects. "That song about being naughty? That's me to a tee."

"I can see that." And again a *frisson* dances along my spine.

But I ignore it. "I mean it. I just love the idea of it. So many rules exist and some are important, some of them just hamstring us. You've got to move with your conscience."

"You're passionate about this."

Again I need to deflect. "As are you." We stop walking. We're outside the cafe, and it's busy. "You took on a case that, if you'd lost, would have made you unemployable. No one would have wanted a bar of you."

"He was innocent."

"How did you know?" The sun pokes out from behind the clouds for a second and I squint looking up at him.

"A lot of reasons."

I narrow my eyes. He's doing my trick—keeping something secret. "You're evading."

"Very good, counsellor."

"Why?"

He leans closer towards me. I can smell something salty on his breath and wonder if he's had hot chips for lunch. "Because it's more airy-fairy than legally relevant."

"I like airy-fairy."

He straightens and grins. "Coffee."

I make a sound of complaint as we push into the busy café. "That's not fair."

"Haven't we just been saying that? What are you having?"

"Piccolo latte."

He joins a line and I move to the sandwiches out of habit. I'm not hungry but I love to browse.

A heap of people are working behind the counter so the service is speedy. Carlton is by my side within minutes brandishing a tiny coffee for me and a huge one for him. "The American habit of thinking bigger is better," I chastise, wrapping my hand around the smaller cup.

"You're welcome."

I shake my head in smiling apology. "Thank you."

He grins. "I'm going to go for a walk. I like to drink as I go."

"You'll be walking for miles before you finish that."

"Good." We step back into the cool afternoon. "Which way?"

"Oh." I hadn't expected this. But then again, I am walking home, it's no hardship to go some of the way with him. I nod towards my usual route and we're moving again. "Where are you living?"

"The University rented a place for me in Clerkenwell."

"Nice."

"Yeah. It's central."

"So, you were telling me how you knew he was innocent."

"Ah! And tenacious. Another excellent quality, Miss Lewis."

"Thank you, Carlton."

"Dr Carlton."

"Nope. I like Carlton. And if you don't answer my question I'll downgrade you to Carl."

We turn a corner and he's quiet; I wonder if he's thinking about something else.

"Have you ever met someone and just known?"

Now it's my turn to be quiet. I need to mull that one over a little. I mean, of course I have. I met Alex and just knew I would do anything he wanted, go anywhere he wanted, even though there was danger inherent in that decision. There have been a handful of other people, too, throughout the course of my life. Meera, my best—possibly my only— friend. I met her and I knew I could trust her. Not with my secret, but with my secrecy. She knows there's a big black hole of information in my past and she doesn't push it. I love her for that.

I can't answer his question so I don't. "Is that how you felt?"

"Yeah." He sends me a look of embarrassment. "So the case of the century was really based on my hunch."

"Don't be ashamed of that. That simply means you've got great intuition, doesn't it?"

"Clayton was so obviously terrified. He'd confessed. It should have been a simple defence aimed at getting him a reduced sentence. But none of it added up. Least of all how this gentle, quiet and polite man could have murdered two old women in their beds."

I shiver at the gruesome detail. "Who did it?"

"The victims were grandmothers of rival gang members; their murders were retaliatory. Can you believe that?"

I know all about the things bad men can do to the families of their enemies. I shiver and sip my coffee to hide the gesture. "And the cop?"

"Was paid off by the gangs. It should have been easy to pin it on Clayton—he had access, needed money, and as a teenager he'd been involved in an armed robbery, only he hadn't really. He'd been in with a bad crowd and had agreed to keep watch while they did a job. None- theless, on paper, he looked like a good fit for it."

"He would have been, if you weren't assigned to the case."

"Yeah, I guess so." He's quiet again and I'm wondering what he's thinking about when he says, "The first time I met him, I just knew. He stood when I entered the room, called me 'sir' unfailingly, and answered all my questions in full. There was no attitude. He's not an educated man, and he's huge and tattooed—the kind of looks that a jury would eat for breakfast. But he's not a killer."

"He must love you."

"Yeah. Kinda." Carlton pauses at the corner, waiting for me to direct him. But we're getting closer to my home now and that's a barrier only Meera has breached.

So I flash him a smile and shake my head. "This is where we part ways."

He looks up at the buildings that surround us. "You're home?"

"No." The sun breaks through the thick cloud cover for a moment, making me squint.

"What is it? Don't want me to see your drug lab or something?"

I nod, pretending to be serious. "Damn it, I knew I'd get discovered one day. Was it the lingering smell of chemicals?"

His laugh is nice. Deep and husky. "That, and the suspicious white powder that's always on your nose." He reaches over and wipes at the powder we both know isn't there. It's strange for him to touch me, but he's just playing out a joke. Nonetheless, I step backwards a little guiltily.

"Thanks for the coffee."

He doesn't push it and I'm glad. "Any time. See you 'round."

My apartment is nothing special. My parents—and I don't mean my real parents, they're dead—but Ally and Rick, who took me in and raised me, hate this place. Compared to their mansion in Buckinghamshire with its millions of windows and liveried history as long as your arm, river views, strawberry patches and apple orchards, this is incredibly low-rent. And it *is* low-rent. Totally affordable for a uni student like me. I think of the bank account they've set up in my name, stockpiling a small fortune in the allowance they provide that I don't access. I plan to give it all back to them one day. A sort of thank you for loving me when you didn't have to.

My neighbours are loud—so loud that they drown out the dark thoughts which haunt my dreams. I never worry here that I am alone.

How can I be when they throw parties almost every evening? They've invited me often enough but I have created an image of the studious anti-social book-worm. I smile apologetically and slip into my apartment, happy to be alone but to know that they are there. My upstairs neighbour is the polar opposite. From time to time, I wonder if she is my future. A spinster, alone, just her and a cat and an addiction to hand-blending tea.

My flat is thick with a dank stench. I spy the culprit of malodour: a bunch of tulips purchased around the time I met Alex that have turned into sludge in a vase. The water is now brown goo and the petals litter the bench top, along with stamen pollen that might have been yellow once but is now a brownish gold. "Ugh." I would leave them if there was any chance someone else would come along and clean the vase out for me but sadly, that's the price of living alone.

I think of Ally again with a grimace. Her immaculate home is always groaning under the weight of cut flowers and growing up she impressed on me again and again the importance of maintaining a bunch. Regularly trimming the stems and changing the water is theoretically great, but I appear to be more of a 'set and forget' flower lover.

I wonder what the best way is to dispose of them? Too much liquid to put in the bin. Too much flower to put down the sink. Could I flush them? I stand there wondering about the advantages of each plan before opting for the bin. Happily, in another win for my terrible house-care skills, the bin is half-full still and I realise I've been a little unfair to the tulips. Surely this putrid waste has something to do with the smell? I add the tulips and wretch as I quickly tie the bag.

My phone rings and I know even before I pull it from my handbag that it's going to be Alex. Maybe I'm not the only one who's fallen down the rabbit hole.

"Hello." Blood washes through my veins.

"Where are you?"

I frown, eyeing my apartment. "In the place where things go to die."

I think I hear his smile in his question. "Meaning?"

"My flat."

This inspires silence. He's curious. He doesn't think of me in those terms; as a person who has a life and a home. "I see." He's grappling with it. I wonder where he's going to go, what he's going to say.

"Where are you?" I say finally, every fibre of my body alert and humming.

"At my place."

I look at my wristwatch in surprise. "It's just gone five. Why are you home so early?"

More silence. I'm nervous suddenly. An air of discontent has shrouded me, dogging my steps since I parted ways with Carlton, like I did something wrong, something I shouldn't have done.

"Are you still there?"

"Yeah. I'm here." I can hear his cogs turning. "I can come to you though."

"No." Too fast. I wince. *Be cool.* I've been lying for almost as long as I can remember and usually it comes second-nature, as easily as breathing and walking. Then again, around Alex my breath burns and my body shakes. He robs me of all my usual skills. "My place is definitely not fit for human habitation."

"I'd like to see it," he says at the same time, so our words mesh over the phone line.

It surprises me. I put it in the back of my mind, to ponder later. "Another time. Maybe." I furrow my brow. "What are you doing home so early?"

He pauses. I stub my toe along the line of tiles, tracing the grout, waiting for him to speak.

"I have to work late tonight. I thought I could see you now."

I frown but my heart is soaring. "You work late most nights."

"Yeah." I'm already reaching for clothes and stuffing them into a bag I got at the Borough Markets a couple of years back. It's a far from suitable vessel for clothes and makeup but it's all I can lay my hands on quickly. "I'll send a car."

"Not necessary." *TOO FAST.* I smile, even though he can't see it. "I'll be there soon."

"How soon?"

"An hour?"

His voice is gravelly. "Get here faster."

THREE
DARKNESS AND LIGHT

We are darkness and light; ash and sand. We shouldn't mix but we do, perfectly. It's all I can think as I lie pressed against him, in the early hours of the morning. He got in about twenty minutes ago. I heard the door, even though I was asleep.

Was I always like this? Or is it a by-product of That Night?

By the time I realised it was Alex and not an intruder, I was wide awake. I listened while he showered, and when he came to bed, I rolled over to kiss him. We'd made love that evening. I'd come back to his place, as instructed, and he had taken me in the lounge room and then the kitchen, and then he'd gone away again. I'd stayed... His schedule is demanding but I think I am more so, for only hours later I want him again.

"Hey." He had kissed me back, but it was a kiss of exhaustion. My beautiful, usually tireless lover was fatigued beyond belief. I pressed my head against his shoulder while he stroked my hair and then rolled onto my side. He spooned behind me, his hand transferred to my hip, moving lightly in time with his breath.

"How was your day?"

My eyes flutter open. The moon is casting a lovely creamy line into the room. It's not like we don't talk. It's just that we don't talk much. At least, not with words. God, that's so cheesy, but it's true. I've told him nothing about who I am yet I believe he knows me intimately. "Good. And yours?"

"Were you working?"

He does know I have a job, even though he seems to find it hugely inconvenient when it means I'm not available to be at his beck and call.

"No." I reach down and squeeze his hand. "Go to sleep."

I feel him tense and wonder if he takes exception to being told what to do. "I thought you were coming straight here." He nuzzles into my shoulder and I'm so, so awake now. But compassion for him and his exhaustion keeps me still, despite the stirrings of lust.

"Why?"

"You didn't set the alarm when you left this morning. I presumed you were here. When I got back this afternoon and found you were gone, I was concerned." He says it without a hint of admonishment but I sit bolt upright anyway.

"Oh my God." I turn to face him. He's watching me, those intelligent eyes of his cloaked in curiosity. I must look strange because he's scanning me and processing whatever it is he reads in my features. "I'm so sorry, Alex."

"It doesn't matter," he's quick to reassure me. But I know the truth. Alarms are there for a reason. I'm *always* careful.

"I was in a hurry," I say, even more apologetically. "I wasn't concentrating."

"It's fine," he promises.

"I feel like such an idiot."

"Over an alarm?" He pushes up on his elbows and the sheet falls lower down his body. I can't help it. I stare at his abs. He's so beautiful it hurts. "It was just an accident."

"Yeah, but accidents are..." I zip my lips. I have to deal with my guilt on my own time. He's too attentive; too watchful and if I'm not careful I'll reveal my own hang ups about security and alarms. Accidents are how they find you. I am careful, always.

"I wanted to see you. I expected you to be here, that's all." He changes the subject and the compliment, as vague as it is, does funny things to me. I can't hide my smile. I don't want to.

"I wish I'd been here."

"So you weren't at work." He puts an arm out, forming a void that I am only too happy to fill.

"No." I know it doesn't seem like a big deal, but to me, it is. I'm used to keeping secrets, remember? Separating one part of my life from another is more than a habit; it's a survival technique. "Uni's back now; I had a lecture."

I've surprised him. I hear it in the words he doesn't say. His fingers run over my back while he digests this statement. Does he think it's strange that we've been sleeping together for a month and he didn't know I'm a student?

His question is measured, calm. "I see. What do you study?"

I prop my chin on his chest, so our eyes lock. "What do you think?"

His smile makes my tummy flop. "That's a hard one. I gather burlesque isn't a tertiary subject?"

I punch him jokingly but perhaps he thinks I'm offended, because he catches my fist and lifts it to his mouth. His kiss is an apology. "I was kidding." He laces his fingers through mine, tangling them in a way that makes my heart burst. "If all my fortune were riding on this guess, I would say something like law."

I lift my brows, breath-taken by his acuity. "Oh? What makes you say that?"

"You're smart. Inquisitive. Ever-cautious about what you say, as though you need to weigh every word before it leaves your perfect, delectable lips." He kisses my lips, lips he finds perfect and delectable, and I kiss him back hungrily even though my heart is hammering in my chest at the danger inherent in his perceptiveness. He shifts away. "The only people I know who are so reserved with how they phrase answers are lawyers."

"And me."

"So? Am I right?"

My voice emerges a little strangled. He's so perceptive. It's a red flag; a warning. I must be more careful or secrets will spill, lives will be ruined. "Fourth year."

"And I was your summer project."

"Yeah. Kinda."

He grins. "And now that you're back?"

I wait, not quite understanding.

"I presume you'll be a lot busier. Maybe there won't be the time for this?"

A pit opens before me. Is this how it starts? The beginning of the end? A casual suggestion that perhaps things might have changed, and the relationship might no longer work? Does he want me to end it? Is that why he's asking?

My doubts are a fast-running river, swallowing and churning me and I am directionless suddenly. I've never been with someone like Alex, but I can imagine he'd have a bulletproof way to end relationships without causing drama. A way of almost making it seem like it had been his lover's idea, rather than his. Is he doing that now? The worry comes out of nowhere. He needs me like I need him. But for how long? The feeling that this relationship is a time-bomb hounds me. I take a breath. I need to calm down.

"Actually, I don't know," I say, sounding him out. I'm rewarded by a narrowing of his gaze that speaks of deep displeasure. Relief leads to courage and daring. "It's a pretty full-on schedule and I'm very, very dedicated to my studies."

It's not a lie, either. Though I'm saying it to get to the bottom of how he feels about me, and where he wants me in his life, I am being truthful about my dedication. Until I met Alex, university occupied almost all of my thoughts. Will loving him derail that? Can I find space in my life for him and law?

He catches my wrists and rolls me onto my back. He's straddling me, pinning my arms to my side. "Perhaps you should consider giving up your job then."

I shake my head from side to side. "Can't. Need rent money."

"Then you're going to have to work out how to juggle a job, university, and me."

In terms of what I want him to say it's not even one-hundredth of the way there, but it's a start. It assuages the nasty doubts that were drowning me a moment ago. "You might prove detrimental to my studies."

"I won't be." His kiss now is a warning and I heed it. He's not finished with me, and I'm nowhere close to finished with him. Certainty brings with it relief. The end is nowhere in sight. There is a force that ties us and it is unrelenting.

My hands are ripping at his boxers, pushing them away with a desperation he creates in me. I ache to feel him and his own need is as just as marked. I'm only wearing a silk nightie and he doesn't bother to remove it. He just pushes it up, balling it in his hands at my side. God, I need him. "Condom," I whisper, surprised I'm able to remember such a detail when I'm flicking with fire.

He swears—I love the way he does that. It's so animalistic and dark. When finally he enters me I'm so ready that I cry out on an actual sob of relief. I wrap my legs around his waist; he's so deep, I can already feel myself losing control. He moves quickly, and I throw my head back, crying out into the stillness of his apartment while pleasure engulfs me. It is everywhere. It is the air I breathe; the coldness I feel. It haunts me with his touch.

We make love like that until finally his control wavers and I have no comprehension of how many times I come. The concept of multiple orgasms was foreign to me until I met Alex and now I feel ripped off if I don't climax three times, at least. How could I possibly give that up?

The next morning, I wake up smiling, but he's gone. Disappointment is a pit in my stomach when I reach for him and find only expensive organic cotton sheets. I run my nails higher and they hit a card. I blink my eyes open, swallowing my furry morning breath.

Send me your uni timetable. A.

I flop back against the mattress. It's so like him. And yet, it's a concession of sorts. An agreement to work within the confines of my life. But I don't have any intention of falling in with his plans so easily. The card is thick and expensive, printed on good-quality card stock. His whole apartment is luxe. But I am sick of being here without him. It's as though, with university resuming, I'm remembering that I'm my own person. That I have a life and that I need to pursue it. Another survival technique? Definitely. On some deeply instinctual level I've become terrified of how much I'm willing to give of myself to this man.

I shower, lathering myself in his beautiful bath products and spending time blowing dry my hair. It's the wrong thing to do though because I smell like him all over. He's going to be on my mind all day.

And he is. I have two subjects at uni and a short shift to cover lunch breaks at the bookshop, and all day I think of Alex. He's under my skin, in my blood, and God, I'm hungry for him. I get a break sometime around three o'clock and, holed up in the back of the store, I check my phone. There are three emails from him. Rather, there are three subjects from him, because he writes nothing in the body of the emails.

11.23 am. Did you get my note?

1.45 pm. I want to see your schedule, Sasha.

I smile at that. He's chastising me. I can just hear the way he's saying my name.

2.57pm. Not playing, huh? I need to speak re tonight. Call me.

Call me. The invitation was there but I have to read it a few times to believe that it's real. I've never done that before. He's called me, but only sparingly. My finger hovers over his name in my phone, ambivalent to make the final press.

"Sash? I know you're on break but we're slammed out here. Do you mind....?"

"Of course not." My manager Annie is a total doll. "I'll be right there."

I open the last email and begin to type: *No time to talk. Can you email me?*

I send it with a smile, imagining his scowl when he sees it. Why do I enjoy provoking him so much?

Annie hasn't exaggerated. The store is flat out. I help an eight-year-old pick the perfect David Walliams book and an eighty-two-year-old find the Royal Horticulture Society calendar she's been looking for. There's a man hovering around the self-help section and when I offer him assistance his lip begins to quiver. Turns out, he's in the midst of divorce and wants books on starting over. I find what looks like a good one and hand it to him but he's evidently decided I'm more helpful than a book and begins using me as free therapy. I nod and make sympathetic noises until I can extricate myself. I do feel sorry for him, and when he shuffles to the counter ten minutes later, his nose pink and eyes red-rimmed, I go so far as to offer him a tissue. I think he's holding out for a hug so it's a slightly awkward exchange.

Being on the register is what I need. It makes the time go fast. My eyes creep to the clock several times and I wonder if Alex has written back. It's on my eyes' perhaps tenth foray to the timepiece when a familiar face looms into view.

Holy Shit. My heart is about to beat its last. Alex is here. He's scowling. I laughed earlier when I thought he would react like that, but seeing his face now I feel a little bit remorseful. To my surprise, he joins the back of the queue. I smile at the customer I'm serving and mumble my way through the transaction, and then serve the next customer, and the next. By the time he reaches the counter, there are four people behind him. "Yes, sir?"

His expression is deliciously stern. "I'm looking for a book. Can you help me?"

I'm tempted to tell him to shove off, but I can see he's trying to talk about something important and I'm more than a little bit interested. "Sure."

The woman behind him huffs loudly and I send her a saccharine smile. "If you'll just wait over there, I'll be with you as soon as I can."

I really don't get any pleasure out of keeping him waiting now. Especially not when I can feel his eyes on me the whole time. I can't tell if he's impatient or cross, but his expression is dark—at least, to me it is: I'm good at reading people, remember, and Alex isn't just 'people'. "Annie?" I flag her attention just when I worry he might lose patience altogether and leave. "Can you take over?"

She's more frazzled than I've seen her outside of December and the pre-Christmas mayhem, but to her credit she comes right over. "Thank you," I whisper, squeezing past and making my way to Alex.

"I don't know why we're so busy today," I mutter.

He says nothing, which is not, in my limited experience, a good sign.

I try another tack. "What book are you after, sir?"

His eyes are staring at my lips. God. He's going to kiss me. And I'm desperate for him to. That alone scares me so I step away a bit, but he immediately brings a hand around my back, holding me where I am.

"What time do you finish?"

I scan his face, trying to understand why he's in such a foul mood. Even for Alex he seems weirdly pissed. Surely this isn't about my uni schedule? "Um, I don't know. I'm here for as long as they need me." I cross my arms, a sure sign of defensiveness, I know.

He expels a short, sharp breath, his nostrils flare, and inexplicably, my temper rises.

"Why are you being so weird?"

"What about me is weird?"

"Everything." At night, in his apartment, I know where I stand and what we both need, but this encounter throws me. "Look, I have to get back to work. Are you just here to be all grouchy?"

His smile is a perfect example of how unpredictable he is; it is beautiful and rewarding, lightning flashing through the darkness of a storm, and my gut aches for more. "I have a thing tonight."

"A thing?" I prompt.

"It's a cocktail party at this place in the West End. Will you come with me?"

I'm staring at him, hoping his words will start to make sense. But they don't. Because that's not what we are. Besides the occasional coffee at the place around the corner from his apartment, we don't do 'out'. "Um...why?"

He grins. My skin prickles all over. "Because of your wit and conversational skills, obviously."

I'm tempted to punch his arm but Annie's already sending us curious looks which I think she believes to be covert. "On a Wednesday night?"

"Yes, Sasha. Believe it or not, people do go out through the week."

My heart is rabbiting angrily. "But ... why?"

He's not expecting that. He was sure I'd jump at the chance to go on a date. Is that what this would be? A date? A normal couple thing? Is it a threshold I can bring us across that will infinitesimally yet vitally change who and what we are? *Say yes*! But self-preservation is my stock in trade, remember, and nothing about dating Alex LaMar is safe nor wise.

"It's a cocktail party," he says softly, and his fingers move over the curve in my back. "Food, wine, music. It's supposed to be fun. You'll enjoy it."

"I'm familiar with the concept." I can feel myself furrowing my brow in a way that my mum (my real mum) used to tell me, even as a child, would lead to wrinkles and premature ageing. *Always rub your sunscreen UP, Bianca, not down. You don't want to drag your face to your ankles at your age.* "I mean, why now?"

"Because it's tonight."

I shake my head. Annie's got a queue forming and the teenager she hired a few weeks ago is barely capable of scanning a book without asking for help.

"I mean why are you asking me now? You've had heaps of these things since I met you."

"True." His eyes narrow, giving nothing away. "So?"

I'm quiet, thinking this through a moment.

Apparently he takes my non-response as a 'yes'. "I'll pick you up at eight."

It's instinctive to reject that idea. "I'll come to you."

His eyes flash with the searing pleasure of victory and I realise he's out-manoeuvred me. I'm so keen to avoid him knowing where I live that I've acquiesced to the party invitation when I had no intention of doing so. He nods, confident once more. "It's black tie."

"Black tie?" My disapproval is contained in the tone in my voice.

He nods. "You have clothes that are suitable?"

I bite back a smile. "Yes. Why? Are you going to go all Edward Lewis Pretty Woman on me and give me a credit card to take on a shopping spree?"

I suspect he has no idea who Edward Lewis is and what Pretty Woman means. But he shrugs. "Do you want that?"

I gape for a moment, surprised he would think for a second I was serious. "Like a hole in the head," I mutter, shuddering as I say it because I know just what holes in heads look like. "I have lots of suitable dresses."

"Good." He lifts a finger then and runs it down my cheek, as though he can't not touch me. "Wear one."

I lift my hand to my forehead in a mock military salute which brings a smile to his face.

He leans close to my ear. "Forget your underwear."

I blush to the roots of my hair. I can feel my face burning.

"I want to imagine you naked beneath your dress. I want to know that I can touch you any time I want to."

A shiver runs down my spine. I find some inner-strength. "Don't push it. You're lucky I'm even coming to this thing."

"But you will be coming." It's an intentional double *entendre* and it serves its purpose. I'm speechless.

He straightens and smiles.

That's it.

He's walking away just as quickly as he arrived. I stare after him, knowing I must look like a bemused buffoon. It takes a good ten seconds before a customer realises I'm free and approaches me for aid. She's getting divorced, and she hopes if I can recommend a self-help book on rebuilding her life. Absentmindedly, I wonder if she's the other half of the customer I dealt with earlier. If not, perhaps I should introduce them?

I smile at the thought as I lift a book out for her and turn back to the registers. I practically float through the rest of my shift. Alex has asked me on a date. And it *is* a date.

What does it mean? If anything? And how long can I let this go on before I really absolutely have to cut him free?

Even here, he is with her. Amongst the books and the browsers there is Bianca and there is him. Does he know that I am watching? Does he know about the professor she spends time with? Will he care when she is gone?

Four
The Air I Breathe

I'm not vain. And I'm not someone who goes in for false-modesty either. I know that I can make myself look pretty good with a bit of effort and tonight I've gone to more than that. I've straightened my hair so it's glossy brown, then pinned it into a fashionably awkward-to-construct ballerina bun high on the top of my head; I've chosen one of the dresses that my mother (Ally) gave me. It's vintage couture. Have you seen the original Sabrina with Audrey Hepburn? That dress she wears on the tennis court, when she's waiting to meet David Larrabee? Well, this dress is a bit like that. It's black though, cut straight across the breasts and nipped in at the waist before falling in a tiny pencil skirt to just above the knees. It's embellished with stunning lead grey embroidery, forming a floral peacock pattern along the edges.

Despite his instructions, or perhaps because of them, I wear silk lingerie and team the dress with killer black heels.

My tummy is filled with a kaleidoscope of butterflies. I hail a cab easily enough—usually I'd take the tube—I mean, I'm a girl on a budget *but* this dress is definitely not public-transport-friendly—and before I know it I'm cruising through Mayfair, towards his Knightsbridge flat.

The butterflies don't abate. The whole trip they flutter away furiously so that when I step onto the kerb and stare up at his elegant building I feel as though I could pass out. It's ridiculous, and I'm ashamed of the sentimentality and weakness that has made me hesitate on the footpath. My finger presses his button imperiously as if by jabbing my finger at the small circle I can dispel this odd cloud of apprehension. "Well?"

"Well?" His disembodied voice returns mine and I press my lips together.

"I'm waiting."

"Downstairs?"

"Evidently," I murmur, wishing I'd thought to ask for his key, surprised he forgot to give it. I never keep the key he hands me. Every time I leave his place, I put it on the front hall stand. It's a small, likely meaningless gesture—a sign of my independence, proof that I don't want anything from him, so that when this ends, when he ends it, he doesn't know how badly I care.

The buzzer sounds and I slip through the door gratefully, in from the cold. My nerves are understandable. Despite the fact I met Alex at an incredibly sophisticated magazine party, this sort of thing is not how I ordinarily roll. I had only gone to that as a favour to my best friend and she'd had to promise me a dozen of her sinfully good cupcakes before I'd even considered it. Meera knows how much I hate these events, but she'd been desperate and had, alongside baked-goods bribery, invoked the mandatory-attendance clause of our friendship contract. So, I went, and there was Alex.

Everyone had worn suits or tuxedos—it was that kind of thing—but his had been different. *He'd* been different. Tall, well-built, with tanned skin and watchful eyes, he'd commanded attention effortlessly, and had been constantly surrounded by people—different people, drawn to him in a way I understood, because I too had found my gaze travelling to him without intending it. He was like a magnet.

I didn't know until we were almost ready to leave that I was also a magnet to him.

He'd been watching me, he said. He wanted to buy me a drink. But he said it in such a way where we both knew my acceptance was a foregone conclusion. I nodded anyway. He put a hand in the small of my back and my eyes had jerked to his because awareness almost knocked me sideways, and *I'd known.* I would go home with him, I would walk through the fires of hell if he asked me to.

I fear I still would.

I'm just about to head to the bank of elevators when my phone rings. I slip it out of my clutch and see mum's face smiling back at me. The photo was taken last Christmas, in the lounge room of their home. I can just see the fronds of the enormous tree to the right of shot. Despite the fact I arrived a few minutes late, I don't even think about not answering.

"Hey."

"Rick! It's a miracle. She's alive."

I smile. "Oh, the dramatics, mother."

"Well, Sasha, darling, you've been harder to catch than a fly in space. We haven't seen you in the longest time."

"I was at Buckinghamshire, like, a month ago."

"It was far longer than that, and please refrain from using 'like' as a placeholder."

I grin. "But it's like, so totally, like, convenient."

She shudders – I know it. "When are we seeing you again?" Her voice is clipped, rich with disapproval and I get that squeezing ache of vulnerability for her. It's the deepest love, isn't it, that can make you adore someone when they're being a bit of a pain in the arse?

I think of Alex and shake my head gently. "That's a good question."

"I know university is very demanding, but you could give up that job anytime, and then you'd have more time for us."

I feel him enter the foyer before I see him. I turn slowly, phone pinned to my ear, and every single atom of air whooshes out of my lungs.

I thought *I* looked good!

But Alex LaMar in full-blown black tie should come with a health warning. He's a total hazard; there's no other way to explain it. The suit is jet black, as though coated with onyx and his shirt is the polar opposite, white like fresh-fallen snow. His bowtie is one of those incredibly fancy double knot contraptions, and he's slicked his hair back from his face revealing a high forehead and symmetrical features. I am used to seeing his hair flop a little forward and I miss that debonair dishevelment but God, this James-Bond-meets-Thor is a stunning substitute.

He's looking at me, but the phone tucked under my ear causes him to frown analytically, as though he's wondering who I'm talking to, who in my life I have space for besides him.

Mum continues. "You don't need the money, after all. We're more than happy to support you while you finish your degree."

"I know that. And it's very generous of you …"

"You know I hate it when you do that."

"Do what?"

"Make it sound as though we're strangers. You're our daughter; generosity doesn't enter the equation. What we have is yours. So take it now. We just want to spend time with you. Don't you see that?"

"I do, I really do. And I promise I'll get there soon."

"When?"

I try to bring my calendar to mind but Alex has sent all of my senses into a state of overdrive. I can barely file my words in the right order given the sight before me. He was like this the night we met and yet still I am knocked sideways. I want to skip the party and go straight upstairs. He has become the air I breathe. "Um," I cringe, knowing Ally hates 'um' more than 'like'. "I'll see if I can drive out this weekend. Or next. Soon, I promise."

"And you'll stay over?" She seems to think better of schooling my grammar.

"I'll try." There is something in her insistence that gives me pause. I have been a bad version of myself lately. A bad friend to Meera, a bad daughter to Ally and Rick, a distracted employee, a less than invested student. And it's Alex's fault. Well, and mine, too, because I've been complicit in all of this. I turn away from my magnet, conscious now that I haven't been upholding my end of our relationship. "Is everything okay?"

"Perfectly. But you know, we worry."

I suppress a sigh; their concern is familiar to me. It has dogged us all the time we've lived together as a family. Though I'm ostensibly free from the shadow of danger, it is nonetheless ever-present. The knowledge of what almost happened and the certainty that some of those culpable are still out there, and undoubtedly still looking for me. The Sole Survivor. "I know. But I'm fine." I lower my voice to a whisper. "I love you. Give daddy a hug from me."

I disconnect the call and slip the phone away. I feel like tears are about to sparkle in my eyes. Not good. I blink quickly and then spin around.

"My mother."

His brow lifts in undisguised interest. "You have a mother?"

I nod, my smile distracted and dismissive all at once.

His eyes narrow thoughtfully. "Tell me about her."

It's a command. I respond with a question.

"Why?"

He holds out a hand, and I place mine in it. "Because I want to know."

"Why?"

"Why not?"

"She's not relevant to us."

"Isn't she?" We glide through the door together, like a real couple. But we aren't. I have to remember that. More importantly, I have to remember that we can *never* be that. Not because he's closed off and has told me it's not what he wants, but because a real relationship brings with it the potential of danger to him, and me. The conversation with Ally has been a timely reminder of why I have to keep my shields up.

"You're close to her?"

I relent, because I have no need to hide everything from him and it's a relief to give him something that resembles the truth. "Yes. Mostly."

"Meaning?"

I angle my face to his. "That we fight from time to time."

"About?"

A car is waiting. It's sleek and black; I think it's the same one he drove me home in the night we met but I can't remember because I'd been slightly overawed by Alex. I have a vague recollection of telling Meera I had a headache and her telling me she'd dock two of the cupcakes for my early departure before I skipped out and met him on the street. I kept the fact I was going home with Alex secret—not because Meera would care. If anything, she would have loved to think of me finally doing something random and spontaneous. But somehow even then I shied away from discussing Alex and me, even when there was nothing to discuss.

My mind has wandered but Alex's is rapier sharp. He is staring at me, waiting for me to continue and I drag myself back to the present with effort. "Clothes. Boys. Curfew. The usual."

He holds the door open but before I can move past him and take a seat in the luxurious back of the car, he pulls me against his chest. His kiss is passion and possession; and if possession is truly nine-tenths of the law then I am utterly, legally his.

My hands have a life of their own. They're slipping into his jacket, pressing against the warmth of his back and his tongue is duelling with mine. I don't want to win though. I relish his dominance.

There are stars in my eyes when he lifts his head. "And were boys something you fought about often?"

I don't understand the question at first. It seems to come out of nowhere. Belatedly I recall my last throwaway line about my mother and my arguments. "Oh." I shake my head. "No."

"Sure they weren't." Scepticism colours his words.

I slide into the backseat, my eyes trained on his figure as he takes the seat right beside mine. No, he partly takes mine too. He reaches for the seatbelt and pulls it firm across my abdomen. When he clicks it in, he simply drops one hand to the hem of my dress and snakes his fingers between my legs. I look frantically to the driver at which point Alex presses a button and a dark screen lifts between us and the front of the car.

"I'm disappointed," he chastises gently when his fingers encounter a barrier.

"Why?"

"I told you. No underwear."

"That's not really my style."

"Even when your lover asks it of you?"

"Is that what you are?" He moves from his seat as the car pulls out, crouching on the generous floor in front of me. His fingers dig into my thighs as he loosens the frothy, lace-edged G-string and slides it down my legs and all the way off. He lifts it to his mouth and kisses it (I almost come) then he tucks it into his pocket. I think it's over. That we're done. But hadn't I learned by now? Alex LaMar will always, always take more than you think you're prepared to give.

"This dress is nice," he says thickly, pushing it up higher around my hips. I have to wiggle a bit and when it still catches on the seat he groans and pulls at my legs sharply so that I'm further forward into the car. My legs are now on either side of him and he spreads them wider, before bringing his mouth towards me. My soul. My core. My wet, aching, pulsing heat. God. His tongue is in me, running along my sex, finding my throbbing need and teasing it. I press my fingers into the car's roof and bite down on my lip to stop from screaming out. It's intense, I'm not going to lie to you. London is a blur I cannot fathom.

"I want you," I groan, writhing on the seat as the feelings begin to engulf me.

"You want to come," he corrects, breathing warmth against me.

I nod. Yes. I do want that. "Please."

And with his mouth and his tongue he drives me to a fierce orgasm; a silent explosion of sexual release that shocks me for its strength and desperation. I'm shaking when he finishes. I'm quivering from head to toe, partly from sensual arousal and partly from shock and shame. Did I really just let a man go down on me in the back of a car?

I straighten in the seat and push my dress down around my knees, feeling like a prim school teacher found with her hand around a dildo. He has no such concern. He takes his seat beside me as though he's just done nothing more complex than tying my shoes.

"You are amazing when you come."

It only heightens my embarrassment. I send him a glare that must speak volumes and turn to look out the window. But my breath won't slow down and my pulse is firing.

His hand reaches for mine as he comes to sit at my side. "I'm sorry."

The words catch me totally off-guard. He's not someone I've heard apologise. It grabs my attention at least. "What for?"

"For not being able to resist you. And for enjoying it when you're awkward."

"You should be." I'm grouching for no reason. "I don't know if I know how to be that person you want me to be."

"I want you as you are."

Those words! Those sweet, sweet words. If only I could believe them. If only I could let them in. But then what? If I take them to be true, does that make us more than I think we are? And to what end? I know I can never be with someone like him. Too much is at stake; too much rides on the secret I'm protecting.

"You just look so beautifully elegant. Untouchable." It's a gruff admission. "I had to make sure you're still my sexy, ready-for-anything Sasha."

I am, I am, but oh, it's too tangled. I smile brightly and the effort costs me. I don't want to think about him and me and the hold he has over me. I try to remember the confidence in my own free-will. That buzz of independence that reverberated through me when university went back and my life returned to something more like its normal pattern.

"May I have my underwear back?"

He studies me thoughtfully. The car is slowing to a stop. The idea of going into some fancy club without knickers makes me feel as though I might as well be naked.

"I like you without." But he hands them to me. He's watching me, waiting to see what I'll do and I'm high on the power, or the illusion of it at least. For him I could almost be tempted to throw caution to the wind and leave them in my bag. But I'm just not that kind of girl. I pull them on as though they're a coat of armour.

We're stopped completely now but I don't have my bearings. I haven't been paying attention to anything but the man beside me and the way his body makes mine snap to attention.

"So is that what the women you usually sleep with do? Go out pantyless?"

Shit. As soon as the words leave my mouth I want to swallow them back. It's opening a door I really don't want to see beyond. He's experienced. He must have had loads of women in his life before me. And I hate each and every one of them with that blind rage only a possessive lover can feel.

"I'm more interested in where this prudish side of you has come from."

"I'm not a prude," I deny vehemently. "And the car seems to have stopped."

"So it has." He makes no attempt to move, though. "You do anything I ask of you in the bedroom."

I feel heat flush through my cheeks. "That's different and you know it."

"Why?"

"Because it's private."

His smile is indulgent. "How many people are you planning to let see up your skirt? Isn't it also private? Or at least for my eyes only?"

"What is this thing?" I grumble, nodding to the window. I hope the conversation change will appease him but it earns me a throaty laugh.

"You shouldn't let me see this side of you, all shy and prim. It's too tempting to tease you in public now."

"I'll find a way to tease you right back," I grumble.

The car is buzzing; atmosphere swirls around us. Tension is a spark and it's throbbing with intensity. Neither of us wants to leave the confines of his limo.

"This is going to be torture." Did I say that? Or did he?

"Only a few hours," he promises me, wrapping my wrists together and pulling them hard against his chest. "And then we'll make up for lost time." But I'm throbbing all over. I want him to cancel this party and just take me to bed.

"I have an early morning lecture," I drop my eyes a little lower, hoping he won't realise that I'm playing a card from my diminishing deck.

I barely register the way a muscle jerks in the side of his jaw. "If I had your schedule I would know that."

I feel the polite apology flicking against my tongue but I keep my mouth resolutely shut.

"What's your point?"

"I don't know if I should stay over."

It's a challenge and a threat. The first I am to issue him. There's silence as the chess pieces of our game shift a little. I risk a look at him but his expression gives little away.

"If we're here long, I mean, I should probably just go straight home. Afterwards."

He cups my face and it's sweet and gentle and I shut my eyes on the sensation of falling deep down the rabbit hole of no return. "I'm not going to ask you to jeopardise your university for what we are."

Ouch. For what we are is not defined, but it's clear from his sentence that it's not important enough to jeopardise anything. And isn't that good? Don't I feel that way too? Nonetheless, I can't help asking, "And what are we, Alex?"

His eyes probe mine; my breath snags. "Late."

FIVE
WHERE FEARS FIND THEIR FEET

As we step out a couple of flashes go off in my face and instantly my blood is raging through my body. I'm an idiot. An absolute idiot. I'm sleeping with a guy who's pretty high profile, he's going to some private member event and it doesn't even occur to me until now that the combination of these factors might lead to me getting my photo taken? Worse, published? I dip my head lower, and lean towards his chest.

I don't know if it's because he notices but he wraps an arm around me holding me tight to him, so that by the time we reach the door I have forgotten about the photographers and begun to worry that I've left a dusting of makeup on his immaculate suit.

We're in. Like being sucked through a vacuum everything changes. The noise of the street and the paparazzi fades, only to be replaced by the subdued strains of elegant jazz music and clinking glasses.

"Good evening, Mr LaMar." A woman who should surely be swanning around on a glossy magazine photo-shoot is looking at Alex as though he's just done to her what he did to me. I can practically see the drool creeping out of the corner of her very plump, very eager lips.

Jealousy spears me sharply.

"Heidi." He's stepping away from me a little and I risk a glance at his jacket. No make-up. "This is Miss Lewis."

Heidi (of course that's her name) looks at me in a way that only women get. It's barbed and feline, and despite her smile I can feel the frost wrapping around me. "Welcome to the club."

"Thank you," I purr back but her comment's unsettled me. Is she speaking in code? Is there a club for women like me? Alex's lovers, ex-lovers now, who all meet for commiseration cocktails and talk about how great he is? I sneak my arm into the crook of Alex's. I enjoy it a little too much when her arctic blue eyes drop to the intimate gesture.

Alex is impatient. "Will you organise a bottle of ..."

"Your usual, sir?" She interrupts him in a way that I don't and he smiles. Fascinating.

"Thanks, Heidi."

"What's your usual?" I murmur as he leads me deeper into the venue. I think I've heard of it. No, I've seen it. In a Harpers & Queen magazine I was reading at the hairdresser. It listed six of the best private members' clubs in London and this was one of them. With its decadent yet traditional furnishings, blacked out windows, soft lighting, exceptional security and a cellar that boasts hundreds of thousands of pounds worth of alcohol, this is the place everyone wants to be. And I'm in it. With him. And about a hundred other people. There's a sign in the corner; perhaps it will tell me what the party's for. I can't make it out from here.

"You'll like it," he promises.

He thinks he knows me so well. "And if I don't?"

"Then I'll get you something else." His eyes are searching mine. Is he trying to read me, or feed me information? Or am I just a complete fantasist to believe we communicate silently like that?

"What was with this, out there?" He imitates my head-burial and I laugh, because it's so absurd to see a man like him try to hide his face against my shoulder. For a start, I'm almost a foot shorter. And in a street fight I'd last about three seconds, despite having watched all the Jason Bourne movies about a hundred times each and been sent to martial arts classes by Ally and Rick for years and years.

"I don't like photographers."

He is so far from convinced. Why does he let it drop? I have seen him do this time and time again. I say something that doesn't placate him and he doesn't pursue it. It reminds me of a circling shark because I know he will not let it go until he's satisfied; he just lets me think I'm free of the line of questioning. It is an illusion.

He puts a hand in the small of my back and guides me to a table. Despite the group of people milling, this table is empty and when I slide into the plush leather booth I spy the 'reserved' plaque at its centre.

"Aren't we meant to be going to a party?" I murmur, my eyes drifting to the other side of the room.

He nods. "We will. Soon."

"This table is reserved."

His lips lift into a smile. "I had it reserved."

"Why?"

He turns around, his expression impatience personified. "So many questions?" He responds, his eyes dropping to my lips in a way that makes me suck in a quiet breath. Is he going to kiss me?

"I just ... you said we were going to an event."

"And so we will," he nods to the well-dressed group and then flicks his eyes back to me. "All I want right now is to sit here and talk to you. Just you. No one else in the room. The party can wait."

He is an enigma; I will never understand him. I let the matter drop; after all, I want what he does. My eyes meet his—they mark my acquiescence. "Do you come here often?"

A man appears in a suit and at first I mistake him for a business acquaintance of Alex's before realising he's holding an ice bucket and two glasses. I recognise the Perrier-Jouet floral markings when he lifts it from the bottle but there are extra embellishments that signify this is a particularly unique bottle.

The man pours two glasses and then nestles the champagne in the ice bucket and leaves.

"It's a good place to conduct business."

I mull on that. Why do I care that it's probably not true? Because I do. I'm a fact-seeker. A truth-finder. My life has depended on both those traits. "And you drink expensive champagne with your ... business ... dates?"

He arches a brow. "Ask what you really mean." It's a directive, not a question.

"It doesn't matter." And I try not to let it.

"What doesn't?"

"The fact that you obviously come here often, and presumably with whomever you're sleeping with at the time."

"And that bothers you." Trust Alex! He finds the weakness in my argument and pushes it wide open.

"It interests me," I lie unconvincingly.

"Is your sexual history relevant to what we're doing?" He pushes, scanning my face.

"No." But then again, my sexual history reads like a who's who of boring, with most of the players MIA.

"Then nor is mine."

But I can't stop thinking about them. The women who've sat opposite him here. Who've been in that bed in his apartment. Who've been bent over and taken like I was the other night. My heartbeat ratchets up painfully. "What's this party for?"

"It's a fundraiser."

I arch a brow in disbelief. "What for? The underprivileged billionaires of Canary Wharf?"

"For child refugees," he speaks softly, though his lips are twisting at the corners to show he appreciates my snappy remark.

"Oh."

"You're even more smart-arsey than usual this evening."

It's on the tip of my tongue to apologise but I stop myself. Instead I lift my shoulders in what I hope passes for a wordless, wry acknowledgement of his assessment.

He lifts his glass of champagne and holds it towards me, indicating I should do the same. I cheers him, then sip. It's delicious, of course, but I only have a little before placing it back on the table. My eyes skim the room. I know no one, and no one knows me. At least, that's my firm hope. What would mum say if she knew I was somewhere like this? Would this be the kind of place that *they* would come? My parents (the dead ones) had liked this sort of event. The big house, the fancy clubs, the jewellery, cars, the works. They worked hard, and played harder.

But I don't want to think about them.

"What are your parents like?"

He almost spits his champagne out, the question comes so completely from left-field.

"My parents?"

I blink. "What's the matter? Do your usual business dates not ask about your parents?"

"No," he says honestly.

"You don't want to talk about them?"

He shrugs but I sense it's practiced. "There's not a lot to talk about."

"Do they live in London?"

He shakes his head slowly from side to side, apparently still bemused I'm pursuing this. It makes me more intent to mine the information I want.

"My mother moved to Bath and my father Kent."

"Divorced?"

"When I was twelve."

"I'm sorry," I murmur.

He lifts one shoulder, as though it doesn't matter. But if it doesn't now it would have then, I'm sure of it.

"They weren't a good couple."

"No?" Most people would have regarded that as a question but he only confirms it with a small shake of his head.

"Why not?" I push harder. And in my defence, I could have had no idea that I wasn't the only one with a fucked up background sitting at the impossibly lovely table in the middle of this fancy pants bar.

He's closing up though, and that should have given me a hint to slow down. To leave it. "A million reasons."

But I am the mistress of deflection and I recognise my own bag of tricks being pushed into service. "Such as?"

His eyes don't leave my face as he drinks once more. "Such as being badly suited."

"It upsets you to talk about," I murmur.

"Not at all. It serves no purpose to talk about."

"I don't believe that." I lean forward, my voice husky.

He slides his champagne away and leans back in his seat. Beneath the table his knees brush mine but it's an accident, I think.

"My father was a drunk."

"Was?"

"Is," he corrects with a nod. "Surely only a few cheap gin bottles away from finally ending his miserable existence."

I reach under the table and put my hand on his knee. He doesn't react. I'm not sure he even notices. "That must have been hard on you when you were younger."

"I spent a lot of time out of the house."

"Where did you go?"

He laughed. "The computer lab at school. The football fields. Anywhere. I signed up for everything. Chess club. Math club. Latin club. Football. Tennis. I was the definition of a joiner."

"Your mum wasn't able to help him stop?"

His eyes are pushing hard against mine, somehow, miraculously, robbing me of breath at the same time. "My mum was a little too busy trying to keep her eyes in their sockets and her jawbone from breaking to give a shit what I was doing."

Sympathy rips through me. "He hit her."

"Yeah." He grinds his teeth together, containing an anger that is dark and desperate. "That's one word for it. Eviscerated would be more appropriate. Demolished, even."

"God, Alex. I'm sorry. I had no idea…"

"How could you? I have a great PR team who do an excellent job keeping the press away from my private life. For the most part."

"Your mum…is she…did she meet someone else?"

"No." He runs his finger around the rim of his glass. "She had a stroke about a year after they broke up."

"She's dead?"

"Worse. She's a ghost. In a nursing home."

"God." I feel pity storming all of my defences. What can I say? What can I do? "Alex…"

"*C'est la Vie*. Other people have it worse."

"Really?" I bite down on my lip, hoping the pain will stop me from crying. "What did you do when she…"

"When her lights went out? That's what it's like, you know. It's the most oddly surreal thing you can imagine. She's breathing and her eyes open but there's nothing there. No one's home."

A shiver runs menacingly down my spine. "You must hate seeing her like that."

"Yes."

"Did you move in with your dad?"

"With that prick? Are you kidding? I'd have killed him. I was bigger. In the year since they split puberty hit and I could have knocked him out in one punch. I was safer to stay away."

I don't for a second doubt the truth of his words. I'd felt his strength for myself, but only in the best possible ways.

"I stayed with a friend. His mum knew the whole sordid history and took pity on me, though I think she was always a little afraid that I might start brawling and drinking. I'm a lot like my dad. To look at, at least."

"But you're nothing like him in other ways." I don't know how I know, but I do. That's his biggest fear. The weakness that wakes him in those middle hours, when night has turned fears to reality and the impossible and improbable seem likely.

"Aren't I?" His smile is sinister and my gut churns. Not out of fear for myself but for him.

"Of course you're not. Look at what you've done with your life. You're a self-made success story. You're incredibly smart..."

"He was ruthlessly brilliant." He reaches beneath the table and puts his hand on mine. I shiver as electricity flows through my veins. "A genius, really. The alcohol numbed the crazy edges of that. The hitting was a control thing."

"But you would never be like that."

"He might have said the same thing at one time in his life." His eyes lock to mine; it is a fierce entanglement, as though we are being meshed together. "Don't you understand? I'm as fucked up as he was. I don't drink but I have other addictions that I struggle to manage."

"Oh yeah? Like what?"

His smile is grim. "What do you think?"

It dawns on me then that the darkness of his lovemaking is dependency. And mine is just the same. My need for him is a curse; a remnant of a childhood that has become characterised by violence and loss.

His eyes lock to mine as he drinks champagne. It is strange; I see him as a spirits man, not a fine wine connoisseur. Only Alex LaMar could make a goblet of champagne look masculine.

"How was your shift today?"

It takes me a while to remember that he came to the bookstore. It feels like an age ago. I resent the change of topic, but I get that he needs it. Conversation is an ocean, a rolling tide of topics, and for now, this one must ebb. "Busy." I smile softly. "Everyone seemed to be looking for a book." I drink my champagne. The bubbles are little bombs of delight exploding inside of me.

"You've worked there for a while?"

I nod. It's small talk and it's strange because we don't really do that. "Four years." I run my finger down the condensed liquid on the side of the glass. His eyes follow my finger and his jaw clenches. What is he thinking?

"Why books?"

"Why not?" I smile at him, and my heart slips strangely in my chest at the answering look. "You don't approve?"

His laugh is warm honey. "I neither approve nor disapprove."

"The shop is near my flat," I say with a shrug, reaching for my glass once more. But his fingers meet mine, lacing through them, and he stares at our entwined hands—his darker than mine, his fingers long and commanding. My pulse ratchets up a notch.

"And close to uni. It's convenient."

He nods thoughtfully. He is always doing this—looking for something more in what I have said.

"LaMar." The voice comes from a long way off. We both look towards it at the same time, and Alex retracts his hand from mine. The absence of touch is coldness and ice. I miss it. I miss him. The reaction makes me angry at myself. I drink the rest of my champagne without thinking. The hit of alcohol zips straight through me.

It feels good. I feel lighter. My thoughts are less pressing in my mind.

"Tom." He nods, his smile a small flicker on his handsome features. He stands. God, he is beautiful. A specimen of utter gorgeousness. How can his body be so firm and strong? Heat colours my cheeks, remembering the ways he has used that body to possess me.

They shake hands. Alex stands a head taller than the other man. I watch, happy to stay where I am, but Alex waves a hand in my direction. "This is Sasha; a friend of mine."

A friend? I arch a brow but I am too adept at pretending to be what I am not to react in any other way. I smile easily, standing but keeping a small distance between myself and Alex.

"Nice to meet you." I extend my hand and Tom shakes it, his eyes running over me in a way that makes my skin crawl. In my opinion, men look at you like that for two reasons. They're either sleazy and think that putting it out there is a great way to get a woman into bed. Or they're seriously inexperienced and can't help the trajectory of their eyes. They see breasts and are magnetically drawn to them, staring because they don't know how not to. I would put Tom in the former camp. His smile is a study in interest and I wonder if Alex notices.

"Likewise."

Ally and Rick often attended elegant parties like this, though they only took me once or twice. I think they worried that somehow, someone, might link me to her, just as I had when I'd walked into this bar tonight. But I have met enough of their well-heeled acquaintances to know how to speak to men like Tom as though I move in this sphere all the time.

"You're missing the fun," he grins at me, and now I feel Alex stiffen, as though every bone in his body is ready to snap.

"We're having our own fun first," I return.

He laughs then turns back to Alex. "Mitchell and Rose are here," he says. The names mean nothing to me but Alex nods, his eyes lifting past Tom to survey the crowd.

"I invited them."

Tom shows surprise. "I thought negotiations were bitter between the two of you?"

Alex's smile reminds me of a wolf. It is menacing and wild. "They are."

Tom shrugs. "I was surprised to see them."

"There is no point adding insult to injury," he says quietly, turning to our table and refilling my champagne glass. He hands it to me and there is something in his eyes that floods me with curiosity. I wonder what the backstory is. Who are Mitchell and Rose and what dispute is Alex in with them?

"Did you see the report –,"

"Tom," Alex speaks over him, his eyes not leaving my face. "Not now."

Tom nods, and laughs. "Sorry. Business, business, business. You coming over?"

Alex is reluctant. I don't understand it. We are here to attend this party so why is he acting as though there is an invisible barrier holding him back? But he nods after a moment; a curt tick of his chin.

His hand on the small of my back is perfect. I want to move closer, I want to crush my body to his side, to feel more of him; all of him. But he is no longer mine. There are many people here and they all want to speak to Alex. Though he is a perfect gentleman and takes every effort to keep me close and involved, I fade away from him eventually. His world makes my head spin. He is smart and successful but until tonight I had no comprehension of how absolutely brilliant he is.

I take my glass of champagne, now almost empty, and move through the milling guests. They are London's elite. I recognise many of the faces from the newspaper. Politicians, actors, finance types. There are works of art on the wall and I gravitate to them, curious about the bold colours. I don't know the name of the artist but that doesn't mean anything—despite Ally's best efforts, I'm not really much of an art aficionado.

"Having fun?"

It's Tom and his pervy eyes. I hope my cold smile will send a message of disinterest to him. But Alex is three deep in suits, his focus on the conversation he's in. I watch him and figure there's no harm in passing time with this guy he introduced me to.

"Have you known him long?"

Straight to it. I shake my head. "No."

There is a silence I find to be uncomfortable. "You?"

He takes a sip from his drink then catches an errant drop of alcohol from the corner of his mouth with the back of his hand. "Yeah. Years. I worked at one of the first companies he bought out."

"Oh?" I am curious. There is so much about Alex I don't know.

"He's a bastard." His smile makes my skin crawl. "But I suspect you already know that."

I swallow, my eyes drawn to Alex's dark head. His autocratic face is serious. What is he talking about?

"He's not so bad," I murmur, sipping my champagne before remembering it's empty. I cradle the glass in my hands.

"He's certainly good at convincing women he's worth spending time with," Tom laughed. "Never short of someone like you to bring to these things."

His eyes are on me again and they're lascivious. I shiver involuntarily and lift my empty glass at him. "Excuse me. I'm going to get a refill."

I don't wait for a reply. Suddenly I feel dirty. I don't like being compared to Alex's other lovers, and I don't like being looked at as though I'm a piece of meat that Alex just happens to have procured first. I weave through the crowds again, this time, towards the ladies' room.

Alex is waiting for me when I step out a few minutes later, my frayed mood calmed after some time alone. I smile at him, concealing the fact I've been pissed off by his mate.

Alex sees through it. Somehow, I don't know how, he knows what I'm not saying; what I do not want him to see.

"Want to go?"

I don't bother lying. "Yep." I am full of need for him. He is the only man I want to look at me as though I am desirable and sexy. Just Alex. Only ever Alex.

"Have you had a good night?" I watch him as I ask the question.

"We shouldn't have come."

He's angry! Beneath his prefect veneer of social grace he is spitting chips. It's enough to push my own mood aside; the mystery of Alex deepens.

"To be fair, we only stayed like an hour," I point out reasonably. "We were barely here."

He holds the door for me and as I pass through it his fingers grip my wrist. I look up, but as soon as our eyes meet I look away again. What is this between us? How does he set me alight with a single look?

"I don't want to share you," he mutters, and I can't tell if he's angry with me or himself, or someone else.

"That's good. I have no intention of being shared," I quip, attempting to lighten the mood. But it's a match to gas.

"I didn't like the way he looked at you."

He's talking about Tom and I can't resist saying, "Perhaps if you'd introduced me as something other than your friend he would have considered me off limits."

It is a fair point but it doesn't help. "Men like him need no encouragement."

I pause, knowing I need him to understand this point. "I gave him none, believe me."

"I do." A gravelled admission torn from the fabric of his being. His eyes don't leave my face and I understand the fear there. If I am terrified of how much I need him then it's mutual. He is a control freak—different to me. I have learned to exercise control over the years to save myself from slipping up. Slip ups, for me, could be deadly. But Alex is just like this. He is a control freak by nature and what's happening between us is impossible to control. If I had known it would be like this, would I have resisted him, and this, on that first night?

He steps back, allowing me to pass out of the elite club. This time, I'm braced for photographers, but they're gone now, happy that they've got their photos, or moved onto another club.

It's cold out, but I don't feel it; I am being burned by flame, remember? I can't get into the car soon enough. Only, we don't touch in the vehicle. It's as though we both know the fire's too big now; too hot. We can't ignite it in a confined space.

But as soon as the elevator reaches his floor and we are in his apartment, alone, he makes a guttural grunt and rips his belt from his pants. "God, Sasha—this is—,"

He shakes his head, frustration clipping at him. He frees his erection without taking his pants off and lifts me easily. Damn my underpants! They're a barrier I don't want but with my legs around his waist, he has no time for them. He pushes them aside; the fabric digs into my hips but I relish the pain.

"I know," I say simply, because I do.

He takes me hard, so hard I cry out and arch backwards. He spins me in the air, pushing me against the fridge. Magnets fall to the tiled kitchen floor. We don't notice. He's thrusting fiercely inside of me and I'm ripping my hands through his hair. I'm screaming. I can't believe how perfect this feels.

It's the first time we come simultaneously. The first time he explodes when I do, without waiting for me to come again and again. And his loss of controls is the ultimate aphrodisiac. I hold him tight, my head pressed into his neck, my arms around his shoulders and my legs hooked at his waist. I will never get enough of this. If he is addicted then I am a willing enabler.

It's also the first time we forget protection. A fact I don't remember until the early hours of the morning; those nasty creeping darknesses where fears first find their feet.

Six

Of Passion and Fate

In the morning? It's as though nothing has changed.

I'm me.

He's him.

Even the magnets have remembered themselves and sit perched neatly in their usual place on the stainless steel fridge door. He's standing in the kitchen drinking a coffee, his expression implacable. I don't even know he's heard me come in.

"You have uni early?" So I guess he has.

I nod, ghosts of last night making my skin flush.

"Yeah."

He's wearing a charcoal suit today, no tie and the shirt is unbuttoned a little at the neck. I want to rip it off him. I look away. The view beyond his window is of a grey, gloomy sky. The lights of Harrods are just visible a little way down Brompton Road. "I'll give you a lift."

"No." Damn it. I have got to get better at answering softly. "That's fine."

He's tempted to argue but apparently decides to save his objection. "Did I hurt you last night?"

His fear. His desperate fear. I want to scrub it away. "Of course not." I walk quickly into the kitchen, and lift up onto the bench beside him. I put my arms out and he walks into them. I hold him close to my body, between my legs, my heart speaking directly to his. "You won't hurt me."

It's too much. He's not built for emotion. He steps backwards a little abruptly and straightens his suit. "I didn't use protection."

"I'm on the pill."

He nods. "Good." As though that's the end of it. "I'm safe."

"Me too." Such a business-like discussion.

"I would prefer not use condoms anymore."

I bite down on my lip. It's another step for us, a different kind of intimacy and trust.

"Think about it," he dismisses the subject, kissing me on the top of my head. "Are you ready?"

"Oh." I think longingly of the coffee he's drinking but nod. "I'll grab my bag."

We're in the elevator and I'm bracing myself for the inevitable parting of the ways—the low point of my time with him when he reaches down and takes my hand. He squeezes it. I don't know what it means but it makes me happy.

"I searched up your tattoo. Monachopsis," he murmurs, his eyes meeting mine.

"Oh." I bite down on my lip. "It's not even a real word. It's just a thing I saw online and it...resonated with me."

"An enduring sense of being displaced."

My cheeks flush with a persistent yet subtle sense of warmth.

"When did you get it?"

I clear my throat. "A while ago."

"As in a month? A year?"

My fingers run across the inked markings. "I was sixteen. Just."

"A picture is forming. A maudlin, angsty teenager?"

My lips flatten. "Something like that."

He lifts my hand to his lips and kisses me gently. "You are not out of place."

The words make me feel happy. So happy that, twenty minutes later when I emerge solo at Russell Square, I email him a copy of my university timetable. And in the subject? *Thank you.*

I don't know why I wrote it, but I am feeling thankful to him every minute of every day. My time with him, though destined to run its course, is transforming my life. Ours will not be an enduring love story, but the effects of my love for him will prove enduring.

It is a love story ignited by passion and fate; need and wild abandon.

I've got my coffee and am settling into a lecture which proves to be a rather dry affair compared to Carlton's when I feel my phone buzz. It's a text message.

"You won't stay over on Tuesdays and Thursdays from now on."

I drink my coffee, smiling at his stupidly dictatorial tone. "Why not?"

"Your course load."

"I can manage."

"It's not negotiable."

"You're bossy." I send the text with a scowl and try to focus on the finer points of the obligations rendered by international law treaties.

"Agreed. On the other nights you're all mine and I will make sure you remember that."

Heat coils through me. I'm desperate for him again.

His addiction is my addiction. Will it ever fade? Will I ever recover? The day yawns ahead of me, impossibly long.

Something occurs to me before, I think, it has him. "Today's Thursday."

He doesn't reply for a long time. I get caught up in the lecture, note-taking hurriedly to revise later. When I check my phone near the end of class, I see two texts from him.

"Then it's going to be a long two days."

God. Every fibre of my body screeches in agony at the very idea.

"Be at my place straight after your Friday evening class. I'll meet you."

Would there be any point arguing with him?

I'm working out what I can say to wiggle out of his imposed exile when I run into Carlton. He's looking a little dishevelled, his hair escaping the bun it's usually tamed into.

"Don't ask." He grimaces and I can't help smiling.

"That's an invitation if ever I heard one." I'm in a hurry and brush past him but he grabs my arm just as I'm almost out of reach.

"Coffee later?"

I nod.

"When?"

"Um, I don't know."

"Do you have plans this afternoon?"

"I did," I grumble, and shake my head.

"But you're free now?"

"Apparently."

Carlton laughs. "Don't sound so thrilled about it."

"Sorry." I laugh. "I've got a full day."

"Great. Me too. Meet me at the steps after your last class?"

I nod. "Sure. See you."

I'm flat out. Thursdays are epic with back-to-back lectures, study groups, and tutes, and I barely get time to grab the books I want from the library in the basement. It's gone a quarter past the hour when I emerge onto the steps and Autumn's rapid takeover means the sky is already broody. My arms are wrapped around six thick hardcover textbooks.

"Here. Let me." Carlton surprises me by coming out from the shadows. I jump because I hadn't seen him and then I laugh because I don't scare easily.

He takes the books from me with a smile.

"Thanks. I'm starting to wish I had a body building background."

He grins. "I hate to break it to you but I don't think you have the brawn for it."

It's awkward. A comment on my physique blurs the lines a little too sharply.

"What do you feel like?"

"Coffee?"

He shakes his head. "I'm starving. There's good dim sum around the corner."

"Why ask me if you've already made up your mind?" I say with a pretence of irritation.

"You don't want dim sum?"

"I happen to love dim sum, but that's not the point."

"Great." He is one hundred percent rakish charm. He begins to move down the stairs and I'm right beside him. We chat easily the whole way to the restaurant and I enjoy it. It's nice talking to a guy who doesn't set my pulse ablaze with a single look. With Carlton I can actually talk without wondering when I'm going to get to feel his hands on my body.

The restaurant's busy but Carlton manages to snag us a spot at the bench near the bar. He orders a beer and asks if I want wine. "Sure. A glass of Riesling, thanks."

The drinks appear quickly and I leave the ordering to him. "Whatever you suggest will be fine."

He has good taste and a huge appetite. "I had six brothers and a sister. If you didn't eat fast in my family, you didn't eat."

"That's a huge family." I'm surprised. Out of nowhere, I think of my brother and I am suffocating in the painful memories. His little face, his chubby arms, his laugh and the way his lower lip would jut when he was upset. I'm burning. I am an only child now. I can't think of him. He is gone. They all are. I recover sufficiently to limp conversation past my grief. "I can't imagine how noisy that must have been."

"Noisy doesn't come close." He doesn't appear to realise that I'm sitting opposite him on the edge of a despondency back hole. "We had noise complaints from our neighbours and that was on a quiet weekend."

I have dealt with this for a long time. My smile is fake but I nail it. "You're kidding."

"Nope."

"Wow. Your parents must be complete masochists."

"Not quite. They're catholic. Married young, and always wanted a heap of kids."

"Oh. I'm sorry. That's really rude of me."

He shakes his head, a grin on his lips. "Not at all. Are you kidding? I can't imagine having one kid, let alone eight."

"Really? You're what? Forty?"

He laughs. "Around that."

"Okay, so you're not married? And you don't have kids?"

He shifts a little in his seat. "Try the prawn."

I lift one and hover it near my lips. "Wife? Some kind of Bertha Rochester locked in an attic somewhere?"

"You caught me. I'm just waiting for her to throw herself off a flaming rooftop and then I'll be free to find my Jane."

Any man who knows Bronte wins major points with me. I wonder if

Alex reads? Alex. I smile as I imagine him and I become calmer by the minute. He is the antidote to my grief; the only force powerful enough in my life to blot out the vile memories that dominate my nightmares. Is he missing me? He would still be at his office. I don't know anything about the place except it's a whole building in Canary Wharf that must have cost a literal fortune to build.

"As I recall, Rochester didn't wait for Bertha's demise to surrender to Jane's charms."

"More fool him."

"So?" I bring my attention squarely back to Carlton. "You've never been married?"

He holds two fingers in the air.

"Twice?"

"Yeah. No children, two wives. Both ex. Thankfully."

"Why?"

"Why'd we divorce?"

I nod because my mouth is full of delicious prawn dim sum.

"The first one: Caroline, I met when I was young. Still in college. Not much older than you. We married impulsively and came to regret it almost as fast. We were a thousand kinds of wrong for each other—a complete disaster. When I took on Clayton's case, the pressure cracked us. She hated it. She thought I'd wasted my college career and that the stink from my reckless decision would similarly affect her career. We filed for divorce before the tide turned and it became clear I was going to win."

"Poor Caroline."

"She's happy. We're still friends. She actually married my cousin."

"Really?"

"Yeah. She got to keep her last name. It was all very convenient."

I arch a brow. "And the second Mrs Carlton?"

"Ah. A far more tragic story."

"Do I need more wine?"

He nods. "Definitely." He orders another round of drinks and I briefly worry about how much I'm enjoying myself before reminding myself sharply that I am in fact a free agent, that it's my life and I can spend my free time however I want. "Benita Tores. A beautiful woman. Dark and petite, like you. In fact, you remind me a bit of her."

A little warning trembles inside of me.

"Except you're not a scheming, cruel bitch, I think."

"Ouch."

"I fell for her hard and it wasn't really mutual. She was a waitress at a restaurant I used to take clients to. I guess the allure of my...lifestyle left more of an impression than I did."

"I find that impossible to believe."

"Really? Why?"

Warning bell getting louder: bleeeep!

"When I first met you, I thought you were really good-looking." Put the wine down. Step away from the wine.

"And now?"

Shit. Back out. "It doesn't matter." I'm mumbling. I send him an apologetic glance. What can I say? I'm seeing someone else? But is that what I'm doing? "What happened with you and Benita?"

"She cheated on me. A lot, I gather."

I wince. "That hurts."

"Yeah. A lot." He runs his hands down the front of his jeans.

"When?"

"A year ago." His eyes lock to mine. "It's why I agreed to this guest lecturer position. I needed to get away. My company's big now; I have enough partners. I took a leave of absence and got on a plane as soon as I could."

"You're married in California which means ..."

"Fifty percent split, straight down the middle."

"Ouch."

"She's actually not after that, though. She's going to settle for a fraction in order to get it over with quickly and avoid the press. It's still more than she thought she'd ever see in her lifetime. She'll get five million bucks and I get a broken heart and the realisation that I am definitely better to avoid women with dark hair and mysterious, haunted smiles."

My heart turns over in my chest. "I'm sorry that I remind you of her."

"I'm not. There was a hell of a lot of goodness in her. But a woman who's grown up like she did learns to look after themselves first and foremost."

A thousand objections shunt to the front of my mind but I can't utter any of them without risking betraying something of my own experiences. "I don't know," I say finally, choosing my words with great care. "I think you can run as far from your childhood as you want."

"Yeah? Is that what you're doing?"

"My parents are ultra-conservatives who live in a mansion on the Thames. What do you think?"

"Perhaps you're right." Silence falls between us; he regards me appraisingly. "So, that's my sad story. Which is not so sad, because here I sit opposite a beautiful, smart, fascinating young woman eating some of the best dim sum of my life."

I lift another piece of food and taste it but guilt is spreading through me. I know for sure now that Alex wouldn't want me to be here with Carlton. He was jealous of a simple conversation with Tom last night and Tom is vile and I barely know him. Whereas Carlton is someone I actually really like. Someone who, before I met Alex, I might have been seriously interested in. Would have been? I *had* been! Alex wouldn't want me to be sharing dinner with him, and yet here I sit, enjoying myself more than I should.

I hate that I care but I really do. For a moment I imagine the shoe on the other foot: I see him out having a casual dinner with a woman he, at one time, found attractive and I know I would be burned with misery.

"I didn't realise the time," I say once I've finished my mouthful. "I have a heap of work to catch up on."

"It's six thirty," he points out.

"I'm sorry."

"At least pack some of this up to take home for later."

"Nonsense. You'll get through it." I reach into my handbag and pull out a twenty but he shakes his head.

"Don't be silly. It's on me."

"I can't let you…"

"It's twenty pounds less my ex-wives will have claim to." His wink is sweet and I feel truly sorry that I'm bailing so abruptly.

"I'll see you soon," I promise, bundling up my books and moving quickly out of the restaurant. The fresh air hits me like recrimination, right across the face.

And I know then how much I love Alex.

I am so desperate not to lose him that I wish I could take back a perfectly harmless dinner with a university colleague.

He can *never* know. My love for him must be locked away into the same boxes I keep my other secrets.

She leaves the date and ducks her head, weaving amongst the tables. I scrape my chair back, throwing money onto the counter for my meal and push out into the cold night. I match her gait, remaining a few steps behind.

And I follow her, all the way to her little apartment with the dead flowers in the trash bag out front.

I walk quickly through the dark, cold streets of London, my head bent. There are plenty of people around and I'm glad for their background company. And there's a small part of me that's glad to be back in my own home. I step inside the place— there's no smell now—and a smile spreads over my face. For this tiny, unassuming studio flat used to be my bolt-hole. I can hear my neighbours downstairs and take the usual degree of reassurance from their antics. If I peek out of my window I'll look straight into their courtyard and they'll likely invite me over again.

Only, I want to do my homework and go to bed so that I can wake up in tomorrow: an Alex day. And when I see him, I'll talk to him about this ludicrous rule.

My phone buzzes when I'm part-way through typing my notes from the day's lectures.

"Are you asleep?"

I grin as I reply. "It's only eleven."

I can feel his annoyance in his text message. "You're supposed to be resting. You might as well be here."

I groan and bang my elbow into my pillow. "I would be if I had it my way."

"What are you doing?"

I take a photo of my books. They surround me. My toes can just be seen poking out from between their pages.

"I approve."

I grin. "And what about you?"

Impatience tears through me until my phone lights up with a picture. The view. From his bedroom. Not the one we share. The one that is only his.

Food for thought. I study it with interest.

"In bed?" I type back.

"Just."

I sigh. "I wish I was there."

There's such a long pause that I think he's not going to write back, and I'm fuming at how Alex that is as I brush my teeth and shower for bed. I've just slipped under the sheets when my phone buzzes again.

"Tomorrow can't come soon enough."

I don't want to go to sleep. I hover my finger over the keyboard, thinking about what I want to say. What I *can* say that will keep him on the phone to me. "I like your bedroom."

I can see the little dots that show he's typing. I wait, staring at the screen, barely breathing.

"What do you like about it?"

I wrinkle my nose. "Perhaps it's the power the forbidden wields?"

"What's your room like?"

I grin, and to emphasise my amusement send back the little laughing face emoji.

"Why is that funny?"

I take a panorama shot of my studio flat, one that perfectly catches the tiny kitchenette, armchair and my bed. In the corner, there's an enormous stack of my schoolbooks that I use as a makeshift coffee table. My teacup is still there from earlier tonight.

I send the photo and wait for his response. When it comes, it's rather disappointing.

"I'll see you tomorrow. Dream of me."

That's it.

I flick the phone to flight mode (my mum has taught me well: I fear cancer and cancer-causing devices as much as the next person) and shut my eyes.

And just as I've been instructed, I dream of him.

SEVEN
THERE IS NO ESCAPING WHAT WE ARE

"I just can't see how I can make it work." Meera is pulling a face and I try to keep up. It's Friday and I am so desperate to see Alex that my body is almost staging a silent protest and inching towards the door of the upscale wine bar in which we are perched.

He won't be home yet. It is all I can think of to console myself. It's too early; he'll be working. Besides, I've been a shit friend to Meera and she deserves me to sit and talk to her. Beneath the table, my fingers drum against the ridge of my knee.

The wine bar is our favourite. It's between my flat and hers, which sits above the bakery she's owned and run for the last few years.

Have I told you about that yet? Not properly, just those divine cupcakes. I am so focussed on Alex and my own life that I haven't even bragged about Meera, and that's not right, because the truth is, I am so proud of her.

Since she opened Bumblebee Bakery, it has become somewhat of a local institution. There are queues out the door every morning with people lining the streets to get their fix of Meera's delicious treats.

And I get them whenever I want. It's a best friend privilege. "It's only a week," I point out.

She shakes her head. "I don't think I can trust Rafael for that long," she refers to her *sous chef*. "I mean, he's good, but ... my reputation is built on *my* cooking." She pushes a hand into her chest and there is a melodious jangling of the ten or so bangles she has up her arm. "I don't know how I can walk away from that."

I nod, sipping my merlot thoughtfully. "Your brother's getting married, and soon, and the wedding is in Mumbai. What are you going to do? Miss it?"

"I can't miss it." She is softly spoken, and so beautiful that I see several men looking our way. She doesn't realise it though. "My mother would ostracise me and Rajesh would be devastated."

That goes without saying.

"It's, what, a ten hour flight?"

"Nine," she murmurs, correcting me.

"So you could go for a weekend. Book a night flight there and back."

Her laugh rings with desperation. "The wedding is four nights, mini-mum, it's a whole thing."

"Rajesh would understand. No one is prouder of you than him. Except for me, of course."

"Yeah, Rajesh would understand. It's not him, it's The Family." We are quiet, both imagining what The Family entails. Not just her parents, but her aunts and uncles, cousins, grandparents, the close friends who are considered to be aunts by affection rather than biology. At Meera's last birthday there were at least one hundred and fifty guests and they were almost all family.

"So make them understand! Your bakery has been voted one of the top five food destinations in London. You're practically famous. Surely they'll understand."

She rolls her eyes and imitates her father's voice perfectly. "Family is family."

I know this and yet I don't. Family is a subject I don't speak of to Meera, for I am alone really. My family has died. And she is surrounded in so much love that she pushes against it whenever she can.

"Well, then. You have a problem."

Her laugh makes me laugh. "Great, thanks, Sash. You're a big help."

"Have you got your outfits?"

She nods. "But that's the other thing! Indian weddings aren't just about the wedding. I've been busy every night for the last fortnight. There's family visiting, dinners to go to, parties. Devi has selected six saris for me and each one has involved shopping sessions and tailoring. I'm exhausted and I haven't even hit Mumbai yet."

"It sounds like it's going to be incredible. I'd love to see it." It's not what she wants to hear because she really is stretched too thin, I can tell. But she jumps at the slightest possibility.

"Oh, you should!" She reaches across and puts a hand on my wrist. "It would be so great for you to be there."

"I can't invite myself to your brother's wedding," I point out.

"Are you kidding? Your invitation is totally implied. You are like a sister to me. You're ..."

"Family?" I giggle, because her ever-expanding list of who she considers family has been a joke between us for a long time. But I shake my head seriously after a second. "You're a sister to me, too," and I mean it. "But I can't. The timing's wrong. I have so much on at uni."

I do, but that's not why every single cell in my body is screaming in agony at the thought of going away.

I can't leave Alex. That's what it boils down to. Even for a week.

"Believe me, I know how you feel." She reclines in her chair and eyes me thoughtfully. "I was thinking about you yesterday."

"Yeah?"

"I've been so distracted lately. Work is crazy, business is crazy. This damned wedding is killing any moment I have to myself. I haven't called you in ages. But then I realised you haven't called me either."

I feel colour blooming in my cheeks as a drop of food dye might spread through a pool of still water. It is slow but precocious. I imagine my face is red all over. "I'm sorry," I mumble, reaching for my wine again.

But Meera is grinning. "So? Are you going to tell me about it?"

"About what?"

"Where you have been and what's going on? I mean, I know my excuse. But what's yours?"

My breath hitches in my throat. I am caught. I am so used to questioning what I can say to people, even Meera, that disclosing something as normal as a relationship makes me panic. I shake my head, searching for words.

He will be home soon. A matter of hours. I miss him in a way that makes me feel almost as though I am drowning.

"What is it? Let me live vicariously through you."

I bite down on my lip. "It's not serious," I start slowly, finishing my wine then leaning forward, hands in my lap. Her dark eyes swim with curiosity. I have known Meera a long time and her expressions are easy for me to interpret.

She is ten steps ahead of me, probably planning my wedding cake. I open my mouth, prepared to hose down her fantasies but she speaks first.

"You have a boyfriend!" It's a squeal. An actual squeal.

"Bloody hell, Meera," I mutter, looking around. Sure enough, some of the heads that had been turned our way earlier are looking once more. "Do you want to announce it to the bar?"

"I'm sorry!" She isn't, clearly, because she is speaking loudly again. She thumps her hand on the table for good measure and her bangles are background vocalists, ringing with their own little song of joy. "Oh my God. I just can't believe it. You have a boyfriend?"

I feel like I've sprouted green scales and horns. "Jeez, thanks for the vote of confidence. I'm glad you consider me so dateable."

Meera grins and stands, moving around the small table to sit beside me. "I didn't mean that, of course," she laughs, her hands on mine, her face almost literally glittering with her obvious delight and interest. "But you don't date."

"I do too. I've dated," I snap. What's the point? Meera knows all my secrets. Well, all of those that I am willing and able to share. "I don't know if this counts, anyway," I say softly. "I mean, we're seeing each other but neither of us wants a big, heavy relationship. There's definitely no future in it."

She purses her lips. They're a bright red, and her hair, glossy black, bounces around her shoulders as she tilts her heads and tries to decipher what I mean by that.

"I mean we're fucking."

Even now, after all these years of being best friends, she recoils a little from my curse. Meera doesn't swear. Occasionally she adds emphasis to her statements with a little 'bloody hell' or 'for goodness sake' but an actual curse? Never.

"Just...sex?" She queries, her neat eyebrows attempting to form a line across her forehead. "I don't understand. How does that work? What does that mean?"

For some reason, her confusion makes me miserable. What had I expected? Euphoria over the declaration that I have a hot fuck buddy?

"It means you can cancel the subscription to Brides Weekly," I attempt to tease.

She shakes her head. "You don't do casual." She's right. I don't. Not even with friendships.

"People change," I mumble.

"You don't." She sits back a little way, tapping her finger against her cheek as her eyes skim my flesh. "You love him. You're in love."

"Meera!" I respond, looking around with guilt, as though he might be there to hear it, to see us talking.

"What?"

My blush darkens. "Nothing." I look down at the table.

"You are though, right?"

"I ..." am saved by the bell. A waiter arrives.

"Anything else, ladies?"

"No." I answer too quickly and cover it with a bright smile. "Thank you." I turn to Meera. "I have to get going."

"To see him?" She enquires with undisguised interest.

I busy myself with putting my phone and purse into my handbag. "Something like that."

She stands, apparently taking the hint. In fact, as we emerge into the cool evening, London bustles around us and Meera seems to have moved on. We walk several blocks without her asking about Alex. She tells me about her work, and the beginning of an idea she has to open another bakery in the City. I tell her she should absolutely do it. Meera is a genius and anyone who's tasted her perfect pastries would agree.

"I have some treats for you," she says as we approach our usual separation point. The mid-way between her place and mine. "Do you have time to grab them?"

I nod. I don't want to go, but I'm being silly. Alex probably won't be back for hours even now. And I haven't seen Meera in a long time. And treats are at stake.

"Sure." We turn the corner just as a bus accelerates through a stop sign. I look up at it, wary, hearing the rapid acceleration and in that moment when my attention has taken a temporary ride on the seventy-nine cross-town I am slammed into. Hard. It hurts like you wouldn't believe and all those martial arts lessons Rick took me to as a teenager come right back to me.

I tense, and the world is silent. I am seeking my assailant, preparing my defence.

The last thing I expect to see is Carlton staring back at me. He is dishevelled—even more so than usual. His trendy man-bun has slipped so now it's low on his head and he's rubbing his shoulder.

"Jesus, Sasha!" He exclaims loudly. "For someone so tiny you pack a damned punch."

"Carlton?" I am hurt too but nothing that I can't bear. "What are you doing here?"

Beside me, I am aware of Meera studying the pair of us. I flick a glance at her and see the smile playing about her lips. She thinks it's the guy I'm seeing. That annoys me even more.

"Catching up with a friend. Visiting from the States," he says. He's a little out of breath.

"Have you been running?" He's wearing jeans and a jacket. Nothing exercisey about that.

"Just to get my bus," he explains. I think he's not meeting my eye but then he looks and me and grins and I realise that I'm being paranoid. That happens sometimes. I have spent so much of my life looking over my shoulder that I do it even when I don't need to.

Settling my inner Karate-kid back into her *dojo* for now, I reach for Meera, putting a hand on her wrist. "This is my uni professor," I explain. "Dr Carlton. And this is Meera Gupta."

He is politeness itself but he doesn't look at Meera as he does me. He sends her a quick, perfunctory smile. "Great to meet you."

She nods, herself impatient. "Likewise."

The warmth between them is off the charts.

"We've just caught up for a drink," I explain unnecessarily; he hasn't asked, and it's not his business.

"And now we have to go," I tack on. Is he being strange? Or is it me?

"Me too. I'll see you soon?"

"Given that you're my lecturer, there'd be something seriously wrong if not."

He laughs and he's normal again. I'm weirdly relieved. I don't want my emotions to have any echo with his. I already have far too much of that going on.

"Right, right." He turns to Meera. "Nice to meet you, er..."

"Meera," I remind him, a bit peeved now that he's being so standoffish with my friend.

He nods and moves away, waving a hand in the air as he walks off.

"Please tell me that's not the guy."

"That's not the guy," I say with a wry smile. "But he's usually not that weird."

"Really? I find that kind of hard to believe. Though he's got a cute butt," she says, watching him walk away.

I laugh and can't help but look over my shoulder. He does, she's right.

We're walking again, passing buildings that I know so well I could draw them in my sleep, and then we're at the little green door to Bumblee Bakery. It's locked and Meera has to push a big brass key into the mechanism. It opens with a groan and I am hit by a fragrant assault of sugar and vanilla as I step into the shop.

"God, you're good," I mutter, moving to a display case of confectionaries that are more works-of-art than edible delights. Except I know each and every one will taste just as amazing as it looks.

"I know." She grins over her shoulder. "Come on. It's upstairs."

"What is it?" I follow behind her curiously, up the narrow flight of winding stairs that leads to her apartment. She pauses at the door, a look of irritation on her face. "Bloody Rafe," she says crossly. "He's always forgetting to lock my flat."

"Oh? And why's he in your flat?" I ask, dumbfounded.

She rolls her eyes. "He's staying on my couch while he looks for a place. Believe me, he's not my type."

"Your parents would be apoplectic," I mutter, imagining her folks' reaction to their daughter sharing her apartment with a guy.

"Which is why I obviously haven't mentioned it. It's just for a few weeks." She pushes the door shut behind us. "Or not a moment longer if he keeps forgetting to use his key."

"It's not such a big deal, is it? I mean, the shop is locked."

"Yeah, but without this door being locked any one of my nosy customers could come up thinking I've got more donuts and vanilla slice hiding here." She grins. "Or, cupcakes." She pulls a big white box from the kitchen bench and hands it to me. I open the lid, peering inside and smiling when I see my very favourites—three salted caramel and dark chocolate ganache cupcakes lined up like willing soldiers prepared to enter my appetite fray.

"You're too good to me."

"I know," she laughs. "Another wine? Tea?"

I really shouldn't. I want to see Alex. But I haven't hung out with Meera in so long that I hear myself say, "A quick tea. I'll make it."

I'm standing by the kettle, waiting for it to boil, when I hear another sound of annoyance.

"I swear, he's driving me crazy. I can't work with the guy *and* live with him. He's such a pig."

"What is it?" I ask, wondering if my friend doth protest just a little too much. I pull two mugs out from her cupboard and place them on the bench before moving towards her.

"He's knocked my desk and all these papers have fallen off. It will take me all night to get them back in order." I follow her gaze, seeing the mess.

"Maybe he didn't realise," I say dubiously. For how could he have missed it?

"My arse," she says with a roll of her eyes, reaching down and picking up the books. She slams them onto her desk angrily and then groans. "And where's that picture of us that's usually here?"

I know the one she means. It was a gift for her twenty-first birthday. It's from forever ago—when we were teenagers. "What, do you think he's got a thing for gangly, pimply, badly-dressed teenagers?" I murmur. Even I think she's taking it a bit far.

"No," she rolls her eyes and reaches for another bundle of papers, scanning the floor. "The clumsy jerk probably dropped it and broke it and thought I wouldn't notice. He's such an oaf."

"But he's an oaf who can cook, and he likes working with you," I remind her sagely, moving back to the teacups and putting a bag in each.

"Yeah, but no way is he going to stand in my shoes for a whole week. I'm going to have to hire someone else."

I am finding it increasingly difficult to concentrate. My mind is already with Alex. His apartment beckons and I will respond, just as soon as I can.

That was close. A few more minutes and they would have found me in her flat. I thought they'd take longer over a glass of wine and so I was slower than I should have been.

It doesn't matter.

I have what I need.

It is a proof that I suppose is unnecessary. But in this picture, I know beyond a shadow of a doubt that this is the woman I seek. Almost a decade ago, she was yet to outgrow the resemblance.

It is her.

I know it.

She doesn't understand it yet but our fates and futures have linked— the past has joined us for life; there is no escaping what we are. The only question now is when?

Alex arrives less than an hour after me. I am studying, my attention drifting to the cupcakes, wanting to eat another, but knowing two really should be my limit in a day. I have just given into temptation and moved towards them when the door opens and he enters the flat.

My stomach churns but not with hunger now. There is a moment—a small slice of time—before he sees me and I watch him unobserved.

He places a bag by the door and kicks off his shoes. Every movement of his resonates with his strength. He walks deeper into the apartment, towards the dining table with interest. He flicks the pages of one of my text books and reads some, then looks up. Immediately his eyes pin mine. That is how it is with us. I draw him, just as he does me.

"Hi." I smile. If I seem guilty it's because my hand is hovering over the third and final cupcake, and I had meant to save one for him.

"Hi, yourself." He doesn't move. He is my pull; I am his wave. I crush the distance in between us, seeking him on autopilot.

It's been too long.

"I don't like your stupid rule," I say against his mouth. His tongue clashes with mine. His hands are at the back of my head; his fingers tangle through my hair, pulling it from the plait I had zipped it into while studying.

"What rule?" He lifts me up and sits me on the edge of the table. I am compliant in every way. I will be his anywhere, anytime. I cannot fight this; I do not want to. He moves a chair so that I can rest my foot on it and he stands between my legs, his hands dropping to my bottom and pushing me forward, so that we are intimately connected despite our clothes.

I groan and arch backwards, tilting my head and silently begging him to join with me. His breathing is the only sound in the apartment. It rasps through space and each sound makes my stomach lift and fall in time with his. I hear his belt and I am so, so glad I can't find words to express it. The rustle of clothes is next; his pants drop to the floor. I curse the fact I'm wearing jeans. It's going to take too long to take them off. But his fingers are at the button, pushing it deftly, and I am lifting my arse and wriggling while his hands glide the denim down my legs. He is quick and I am eager.

I smile, my eyes locked to his. I hope he knows how much this means to me. That sex isn't just sex with him. Every time we join together I feel it as a pledge. A deepening of our bond.

It's absurd. I know it's not the same for him. That doesn't make it less so for me.

"I don't like it either," he admits darkly, pulling at my legs, his fingers digging into the space behind my knees as he pulls me forward to meet him. I'm perched on the edge of the table and he thrusts into me with a groan. It is animalistic and my answering cry is no less so. I wrap my legs around his waist but he reaches for them and places them back on the chairs, keeping me wide and lessening my control and grip on him.

He is so far inside of me and I need this so badly. I rock backwards, lying on the table. My head hits something hard; it's one of my textbooks.

I nudge it with my cheek and then don't think of it again. He pulls me closer, and my eyes chase his. I am walking through fire.

This need is out of control. I have not seen him all day and for a night before that, and we do not speak. We need only this. This insatiable joining, this coming together, that speaks of physical lust and uncontrollable symbiosis.

Symbiotic.

Yes.

That's what I feel for him.

"Do you know what you do to me?" He demands, and he is almost angry. I understand. The darkness of what we feel doesn't make sense. It has blindsided us both but I am willing to let it.

"What you do to me," I answer through broken breaths.

His movements are demanding. I meet each one. I lift my butt, and he grips his hands beneath me and I am there, embracing my orgasm even as the force of it terrifies me. He watches me, and he waits for me to cry out and then he moves again, this time I watch him and when he begins to fall apart I feel tears wet my eyes.

Monachopsis doesn't apply here.

EIGHT
Dark Places and Muffled Screams

So far as I'm concerned, Saturdays are for sleeping in. It's my guiltiest, happiest pleasure to lie beneath the sheets, half-dozing, aware that I'm doing something somehow illicit.

My mother has no such feeling. She was fastidious about mornings when I was a child. I arrived at their home as a timid, shell-shocked ten year old. I had been ripped out of my own life, as though a vital organ had been cut from my still-breathing frame, and then I had been given a new life. A new identity. A new hope? I didn't think so then.

I wanted to die.

I wanted to curl up beside my mother's body (my real mother) as the blood gushed from it, as her tortured, rasping breaths were expelled to the point of diminishment, and I wanted to seal my fate to hers. I was ten years old and the idea of reaching eleven was anathema to me.

I look back and wonder how Ally knew that sympathy would shrink me further from this existence? How did she understand so intrinsically that forcing me to keep waking up, to keep eating, to keep taking part in this life, was the only way for me to move forward? Had I been allowed to wallow and slump, I never would have climbed out of the grief.

It was so pervasive.

My real mother always smelled like flowers; roses, lilies, and her favourite—lavender. We had them in every room of the house, and when the lavender dried, she would stuff the wizened little pieces into bags and use them to ward off moths. I cannot smell that fragrance now without experiencing a clenching in my gut that almost rips me in half. Flowers are a recurrent theme in the first two acts of my life—the first and the second, and now, the third, where I exist as my own fledgling person, finding a path that is not formed by grief nor gratitude, though I still feel enormous amounts of both.

Ally saved me; of that I have no doubt. It was a year before I allowed her to hug me, though my body was weak from lack of maternal affection. But loyalty to my birth mother was fierce and I would not betray her by bonding with a replacement mother. I wouldn't. Yet I did. Day by day, nightmare by nightmare, Ally was beside me. And eventually I got used to her. I looked for her when I was sad and I missed her when she was away.

It has been many years since I accepted that I can love Ally without betraying my birth mum. And when I indulge the side of me that used to love Disney movies and Happy Endings, I imagine that Ally and my mother would have been friends. That maybe a part of my mum would be happy I had found my way to people who were such good parents, though biology apparently didn't agree as they had never been able to achieve a child of their own making.

When my phone begins to vibrate on the side-table next to me at the ungodly time of seven o'clock, I know it can only be her. And yet for all these reasons, I don't care. I would answer my phone for Ally at midnight and not begrudge her this for she loved me out of choice and with all of herself, and I return that to her willingly.

A quick glance at Alex shows he's fast asleep. I swipe the phone to stop it vibrating and push out of bed. My body doesn't thank me. Then again, my body's been pleasured to the point of torture recently and it's issuing silent complaints with every step I take.

I turn to look at him and smile. He's shifted a little, one arm now thrown above his head. I ache to kiss him.

"Hello?" I'm whispering. I don't want to wake him up but where the hell is a robe? It's freezing in his oversized penthouse apartment.

"Sasha?" Like all mothers, she has a gift. When she is pissed, she can communicate it with the weight of her sigh. The way she says my name is def-con one. I'm instantly alert. "What is going on?"

I freeze (and not the cold type, though that's imminent). "What? What do you mean?" I wrack my brain. What have I done? Was I meant to call her back the other night? Have I forgotten dad's birthday?

"You're in the papers." It's a hiss. She's not angry; I hear her fear in a visceral way.

"Not in the obituary section, I hope." It's a lame, oblique joke. Since mum turned fifty, she reads the obituaries in the paper every morning, tracking down anyone she might know, even tangentially—the aunt of a neighbour or the mother of a school friend—so that she can send a sympathy card, flowers or schedule a funeral attendance. She is unfailingly polite and has a scale for her grief. Acquaintances get a card, old friends flowers, and people that were very special to her or me get a personal appearance.

"It's a photograph." Her lips are smacked together, I can tell from the tightness in her words.

"What?" I send one more look at Alex. He's stirring. I reach for the throw at the foot of the bed and wrap it around me toga style then seek privacy in the lounge. "Which paper? What are you talking about?"

"The London Sentinel."

I wrinkle my nose at her reference to the tabloid staple. "Why in the world are you reading The London Sentinel?"

"Don't be absurd. Of course I wasn't. Betty Douglas texted me."

I run my toe against the kitchen grout, bringing to mind the face of Betty Douglas. "She's such a gas-bagging ninny."

"Yes, well, that's beside the point. Who is this man and why the hell are you getting your photo in a national weekend paper?"

"What man? What photo?" I'm groggy in a hungover kind of way, but not from too much wine. Sex is my poison and my whole body is striving to digest *him*.

"*Alex LaMar and friend S-a-c-h-a L-o-u-i-s* (Who are these 'journalists' and where did they get their degrees?) *seen leaving London hotspot The Grave.*"

I lower my voice. I can't let him hear me. For over five weeks I've had the closest thing in my life to a proper relationship and I have been so careful! I haven't slipped even once. My secrets are so safe. I will not fail now. "How good is the photo?"

"Good enough to obviously be *you*."

"Mum, listen to me. This is not a big deal." But my heart is racing. I tell myself it's just because of the lectures I've listened to again and again while growing up. They were a part of the tough-love I was met with. The mask of my new identity was built around me speech by speech, and the fear that was instilled in my soul was done brilliantly—always with love, but utterly and completely. I push that fear as far from me as I am able and try to speak calmly. It is mum that needs comfort now and I must work out how to give that to her. "At some time or another this was bound to happen."

There is a heavy silence; it pulsates with words she is choosing not to speak. "But are you actually...involved...with this man?"

"It's not like that." I squeeze my eyes shut. "It's very casual."

"Casual?" She draws in breath as she speaks, making it sound as though I've said, *"We're planning to rob a bank together."*

Actually, I suspect she'd prefer that to the truth, which is that I've got a kinky, dark sexual dependency on someone totally unsuitable. Definitely dark. Definitely kinky.

"Yes, mother. Casual."

"Alex LaMar is famous."

"He's not famous," I laugh at the very idea. Alex—my Alex.

"Your father was astounded. He's had texts from several of his golf friends."

I bite down on my lip. "Why is everyone reading The London Sentinel suddenly?"

"It only takes one busybody." She sighs heavily. "You know that. You know how word spreads. Sasha, this is dangerous."

"It's okay," I sound calm even when my pulse is rushing like water in a drain. "I've just met him and it's not serious. It won't happen again."

"Because you know better than to get involved with a man like that."

She's about to have kittens. "Of course I do."

"You're out of PPU now. There's no relocation if you're outed. There's no Hail Mary if somehow your secret is made public."

"That's not going to happen."

"You have to make sure of it." Oh, God. My mum never cries but her words are infused with desperate, silent tears now. I hear them and a part of me dies. I think of the flowers in my apartment out of nowhere—the way I let something so beautiful turn into shit in the laziest of ways. Guilt is my shadow, and it only worsens when mum pushes on. "Our worst fear has always been something happening to you. Or something happening that meant you were taken from us. We can't keep you safe now so you have to do it for us. Please, darling, please. I beg you to make the right decisions. You must stay safe."

"I am." I blink away tears, lifting my gaze from the floor and my chipped toenail-polish and my eyes clash unexpectedly with his. He's standing in the door frame to the bedroom, staring at me with an oddly impenetrable expression on that ridged face of his.

"Will you come and see us this weekend?"

His eyes are trying to read me. Is he succeeding? I can't say. He's so clever at knowing what I feel though that I suspect he is and I turn my back on him without realising what I'm doing. Is it the first step of blocking him out of my life?

"Soon, I promise. Mum? I have to go."

"Sasha?"

"Yeah?"

She is silent for a long time. I stare at the fridge magnets and remember how Alex moved inside of me, how we knocked the magnets away in a state of fevered sexual possession.

"Do you think they've forgotten about you? Have you forgotten how brutal they are? What they would do if they found you? Is there another soul on earth who knows more than you how violent and ruthless they are? How determined to finish this? Do you doubt they're still looking for you?"

"Stop it." I'm sick in my stomach. The memories I keep deeply locked in the darkened recesses of my brain are sending tendrils into my present.

"I can't bear to upset you. I love you, darling, and I have seen you grow into a woman so wildly beyond what I could ever have hoped. You have faced this death and this loss and you have fought. You are a fighter. But you will always be fighting them, and this. It is a battle that will never end. Yet you're acting as though nothing is at stake."

Her words shred me; she's right. Alex has allowed me to feel as though I am through that. I want him with such an intensity that I have forgotten other people want something so much more than I can imagine. They want me dead, just like my parents and brother are dead. I hate it when people complain that life isn't fair, because of course it isn't. Yet in that moment I rail against the injustice of not being able to *simply be*. "Don't you want me to live a good life?"

"I want you to live a good and *long* life! And in order to do that you must be discreet. Surreptitious. Your life is your own, but you must keep it private."

I shake my head. What can I say? She is so right. Everything she says is a truth I know and have simply been ignoring. I have grown careless even as I congratulate myself on how well I've guarded my secret from him. That isn't enough. "It won't happen again." The words are cold; my determination comes from the same part of me that woke up and faced each day even knowing that I would never see my mother again.

"I love you, blackbird." The childhood nickname makes tears spill from my eyes. "Please come home so I can make you safe."

My voice cracks. "Soon. And I am. Try not to worry."

"Far easier said than done, my love."

"I know." Alex is behind me now. I hear his footsteps and I feel his curiosity like a bolt of lightning. "I love you so much. And dad."

I hang up the phone and drop my head. I stare at the floor and it doesn't make the heaviness in my chest go away but God, I wish something would.

"I thought you were joking."

I look up at him curiously. "About what?"

"Your curfew. Boys. Was that really your mother checking up on you?"

I have to look away. I don't know what to say. I don't want to lie to him anymore. The past is barrelling towards me and he's the best person in the world to speak to. But also the worst.

"She's protective," I hedge, knowing it's hardly an answer. I'm racking my brains, trying to remember what he's heard. What I need to cover. "Apparently there's a photo of us from the other night."

"I see."

"Yeah." I shrug, attempting to make light of it. I can't believe how easily I am able to sound calm when my insides are being spun like a badly built house caught in a tornado. "I don't know if she's more upset at the possible damage to my reputation, or the fact the paper spelt my name incorrectly."

He doesn't acknowledge the joke. He is focussed on me and seeing beyond the mask. I know he is. I pull away instinctively, stitching layers over the lies.

"Why is she so protective?"

I hear my mum again, telling me not to frown. My birth mum, the one whose blood spills through all of my memories and all of my days. I stop frowning because avoiding wrinkles seems like the least I can do for her now. "Other than the fact she's my mum?"

He nods thoughtfully.

"I don't know. That's just her."

There's so much more going on and he obviously gets that. He's too astute not to. But thank God he doesn't choose to pursue it in that moment. "Are you hungry?"

"I'm strangely starving." And I am. My tummy is in hunger knots.

"Not strange." He plants a hand on either side of me. "You were very active last night."

I remember. I remember everything. And these memories are pleasure and relief; a balm from this new heartbreak. So much better than the other old memories; those memories of dark places and muffled screams. My mother's eyes as she begged me to stay in the wardrobe, safe from harm even as my brother could be heard dying just rooms away. "I missed you." Shit. The conversation with mum has left me panicky. I need to get a grip. "Well, your body at least," I compensate—badly.

His expression is droll. "Of course."

"So? Breakfast? Do you have eggs?"

He drags a hand through his hair; it's adorably self-deprecating. "I don't think so."

"Is that code for 'no'?"

"Pretty much."

I think longingly of the cupcakes Meera baked me but they are already gone; eaten quickly and enjoyed gratefully. I would love one now and I think the sugar would be good for me. Perhaps it would make me come back to earth.

"Well, I don't really cook anyway, so …"

He laughs. I don't realise until then how completely I need to hear it.

"We'll eat out." But the second I suggest it I feel afraid. Afraid of photographers and, let's face it, isn't everyone guilty of that? What are the chances a picture won't end up on twitter or Facebook with Alex tagged into it? He's a public personality; going out with him and hoping for anonymity is insane. Some people are too big to be boxed away, even at breakfast. "Or we can order in," I substitute quickly.

He's still staring at me, trying to understand and yet I can't think of the right way to remove his doubts and suspicions. When in doubt, stick close to the truth. I can't remember who told me that. That's right, one of the advisors who first entered me into Protected Persons. Anyway, way back when I was first 'put under', I was given a lot of advice about making the lying easier. I grab that kernel now. "Am I being weird?"

He doesn't answer. He's staring at me. It's easy to picture him in a corporate setting. He's fiercely analytical and bone-meltingly intimidating.

"It's just hearing my mum upset; I don't like it." I'm mumbling! I need to take a moment. I am more at risk than I have ever been of losing control.

"She doesn't approve of you having a social life?"

"Something like that." My smile is lopsided but inside I'm quivering.

He's not sold. Not even remotely. He's caught the hint of mystery and Alex LaMar is not a man to leave a stone unturned. I should leave; end it. I can't though. How could I? I have lost so much already and choosing to lose Alex is something I am not prepared to do. I realise as I make this choice that I am accepting I may die. I would die for him. I would die for what we have. What the hell happened to keeping it light?

He is watching me; seeing every emotion flit across my face, I am sure of it. "I'll go get us something to eat. Why don't you have a shower? Or go back to bed?"

I worry that I'm being dismissed but he kisses me hard and fast, wrapping his hands around my wrists. "Don't go anywhere."

My nod is just a jerk of my head; an involuntary acquiescence.

As soon as he's gone tears glide down my cheeks. Mum didn't mean to upset me, she was just worried. She had often talked to me about the dangers I would face, but she was always so careful not to scare me. Her words were chosen almost as if from a script. She would hold my hand and remind me of what I had, what I had to lose, and how I could make sure I wouldn't. A week before I turned eighteen was the most serious discussion, and the closest she'd come to actually scaring me. I'd been due to go out with Meera. For the first time, we were heading into London solo and she was obviously concerned. The PPU, and the officers within it, had been a sort of silent guardian angel for me but their term of watch was due to end at the same time I came of age. I know she chose, at that point, to scare me. It was a tactic. She wanted to be sure I behaved.

And I have behaved.

Alex is my first slip.

I'm only wearing a blanket toga. I drop it to the floor and step into the shower. It's half the size of my studio apartment, easily, with a large circular shower head that comes from the ceiling. It took me a while to get used to the idea of a shower raining on me, not to mention actual water pressure in central London (all my shower gives me is an extremely bad-tempered, reluctant drip), but now I love it. I stand there as the water washes away my tears and certainty.

As the water falls, I let the memories swirl. I feel That Night wrap around me as though it's now, here, in this apartment, and not half a country away and thirteen years in the past.

"Bianca!" It's Andrew's voice. I'm never going to forget the way my little brother screamed for me. His screams hit me even as I stood in the closet, hiding, shaking, silent, just wanting it to be over.

He screamed my name over and over and the only thing worse than hearing the horror in his sweet little warble was the silence that followed the popping of the gun.

I waited until the cars screeched away and then ran to his room. I knew mum and dad were dead. I'd watched a blade get dragged across their throats and all the life seep from their bodies.

But Andrew? Still I held hope.

There was none.

I feel sick. Nausea is biting me. I crouch down in the shower because I know I won't make it to the toilet and I purge. I cry loudly and I vomit and still all I can hear is Andrew's voice. "Fuck!" I shout, slamming my hand against the bottom of the shower.

Fuck that stupid photo. Fuck the photographers who took it. Fuck everyone except Alex.

I squeeze my eyes together and collapse against the wall. The water falls, washing away my tears, my hope and now my vomit. I am numb. Purged of emotion. I sit there for a long time, staring at the water as it pools in the bottom of the shower washing away all the evidence of my traumatic memories. I don't know how long I sit there, flooding my mind, but eventually, a voice breaks through.

"You're going to drown, little fish."

My eyes sting. I just hope they're not rimmed in red. I force a smile to my face; the effort costs me. "You're back."

"Coffee. Breakfast burgers. Hash browns. Yoghurt. Some disgusting looking thing with chia seeds and açai powder." He shrugs. "You all good?"

"Yeah. I'll be right out."

"Here." He reaches for one of the huge bath sheets. "Allow me."

Can I do this? Can I fake it that I'm fine?

Surprisingly, when I switch the water off and open the glass shower door, my gaze lands straight on him and I do feel better.

He's wet.

"Is it raining?"

"Almost as much as it has been in here." He's teasing in that droll, sarcastic way of his but I struggle to smile.

The towel is soft. He wraps it around me and spins me in his arms, a frown etched deep across his face. He had been about to walk away but he thinks the better of it and starts towelling me down, rubbing my skin gently until the last of the water drops are gone.

Then, he lifts my naked body against his chest. It's not sexual. He knows something isn't right with me. He carries me to his bedroom. Not the room we've been sharing, but the one that is solely his. It is a sign of my mood that I don't feel any pleasure in this incursion into his private territory.

He places me on his bed, sitting on the edge, while he pulls a shirt from a drawer. It's black and enormous. He slides it over my head and threads my arms then returns to his bureau to fetch some boxer shorts. They swim on me but there's a string. I pull it tight around my waist.

"I must look ridiculous." I catch a glimpse of myself in the mirror and it confirms that suspicion. A pale, terrified child is looking back at me.

"You don't."

I arch a brow, trying to recapture my spirit of impishness. But my inner-imp is rocking in the corner, wanting the world to go away.

"Come. Eat."

He's watching like a hawk. While I walk to the breakfast table and as I sit down, and while I pick up my coffee and sip it, my hands curled around the take-away cup contemplatively. The thing is, I really don't know what I'm doing.

The night I met Alex, I knew it was a bad idea to get involved with him. But I wanted him so badly and he made it so hard to say 'no' to what he was offering. He even gave me the perfect assurance: nothing serious. That's what I needed—what I still need. Because I'm not ready to talk about my past yet and isn't that what serious relationships lead to? Confessions and conversations? I'm not ready to walk away from him but there is an inevitable risk. And yet haven't I just accepted all of those risks if it means I can be with him?

He has a high profile. If I go anywhere with him, I risk exposure.

And do I even care?

For my mum, yes. Of course I do. Hearing her cry has knocked me sideways. But I've been running for a really long time and I think I might just be a bit sick of it now.

"Why is she like it?"

"Huh?" I don't know what he's talking about it.

"Your mother."

"Like what?"

He raises a brow thoughtfully. "So protective."

See? This is exactly what I didn't want. "Aren't all mums?" I cringe as I remember his own poor mother's fate. "I'm sorry."

He shakes his head impatiently. He's not going to be put off. "But you're twenty-three, not thirteen."

I shrug, aiming for nonchalance. "That's how she's always been."

He appears to be mulling this over but I know Alex better than that. Sure enough, a moment later, he fixes me with eyes that see too much. "But why?"

"Why are you so bossy? Why do I have brown hair? Why is the sky blue and the earth round? That's Ally Lewis."

He compresses his lips. God, they're beautiful lips though. I stare at the little cleft in his chin, covered by stubble. "Fine. Let's try this another way. If this is truly just what she's like, then why did it upset you so much?"

My stomach churns. "I'm not upset."

His laugh is bullshit. It's more of a grunt—a recognition of cynicism. "You're a wreck."

Fuck.

What can I say? How do I answer that? "Any chance we can not talk about this?"

His eyes narrow. He doesn't want me to shut him down. And I know I can't; that my request may temper his curiosity but it certainly won't extinguish it.

"Fine." He pushes back in his chair, his eyes still studying me. I feel like a bug in a microscope; an insect in a spider's web. The silence crackles around us. When I put my coffee back on the table the sound of the cardboard against glass seems to echo through the palatial apartment.

NINE
I'M HIS, FOR A SMILE

It is a week after my mother has called in tears, begging me not to get photographed with Alex again. A week after he saw my turmoil and told me we could let it go. I have had to remember that other people have drama in their lives. I am not alone.

He addresses me calmly as I read the morning papers, coffee steaming between us, breakfast uneaten. He speaks as though there is no agenda in his words. "I have a thing tonight."

"A thing?" He's so casual. I frown. He hasn't mentioned it before. I hate the thought of not seeing him though, and on a weekend, when we have agreed, without speaking, to be each other's exclusively. "Oh, okay. I can do something else."

He doesn't answer. Doubts slip under my skin. Monachopsis.

"That's not what I meant. I want you to come with me."

He's too flipping crafty for his own good. I immediately know what he's doing, trying to back me into a conversational corner, forcing me to confide in him when I don't really want to. He hasn't forgotten about the phone call. He's waiting for me to bring it up.

I don't want him to know from the beginning that my answer is a 'no', so I hedge around it, sipping my coffee and trying to appear nonchalant. "What 'thing' is it?"

"A party."

"Another party? Jeez, for a corporate type you sure have an active social life."

His lips lift a little to acknowledge my attempt at humour, but I know he's not amused. My voice has gone a bit screechy. "It's the launch of an app that I funded. It will be in bad taste for me not to at least show my face."

"Do you care if something is in bad taste?"

"Yes. The developer is also a friend of mine. He's counting on me."

Now my interest is piqued. A friend of Alex's? I'd love to know who he chooses to surround himself with socially. But I hear my mother's warning from the week before and I'm shaking my head. "You go. I'll wait here."

He nods, as though he's going to drop it. "The party will be at The Astrid in Mayfair. I usually enter through the garage to avoid being photographed. In case that makes a difference."

I can feel my cheeks burning up. He knows. He knows that I'm avoiding being photographed and he's going to want to know why. Has he been planning this all week?

"So?" I smile serenely, playing my part to perfection.

"So maybe you'll reconsider and join me."

I drop my eyes to the table. "Why?"

He makes a noise of frustration and stands up. I follow him with my eyes. He walks towards his bedroom. No answer? Curious, I stand and follow behind him. When I reach him, he's stripped his shirt off and is wearing only a pair of low-slung, far-too-sexy jeans.

"I asked you a question."

"Yeah. I know." He's frustrated! I have lived in fear of a time when he would look at me with that coldness and annoyance and here it is. I brace for impact.

"So?"

"I want you to come with me tonight because I like being with you. I like spending time with you. I enjoy your company. But you only seem to believe that when we're having sex." His hands reach for me and I walk quickly, my mind digesting what he's just said. His kiss is wrapping around me as his hands push to undress me. "I like you," he breathes the words into my mouth. "Come with me tonight."

I know I shouldn't. He's pulling me to the bed with him and everything is better again. Just as it always is. I will do what he wants; go where he wants. And I will not be afraid.

Here, in bed, in his arms, our bodies moving in unison, I forget the rest of the world and I think maybe it forgets me, and the vendettas I owe.

She is dressed up, and so is he. My certainty that it is her sits on me with a weight I hadn't expected. I have waited for this moment a long time and now that I have her in my sights, I am overpowered with the emotion of it.

It is her. Bianca DiSotto: the sole survivor. The girl who should have died with the rest of her family. The girl who saw too much and made sure powerful people spent the rest of their lives in prison.

Does she realise how close her past is? Does she think about it often?

Judging by the smile on her face, I think not. I am a long way from her mind – but not for long.

I don't think I'll ever see more diamonds for as long as I live. I'm talking about diamonds that are as big as my thumbnails, strung around beautiful, elegant necks. Women with perfect hair, perfect faces, amazing make up and facial contouring, couture gowns, sky-high heels and an air of glamour that eludes me utterly. The men are no less spectacular. Actually, that's a lie. Some of them are beautiful, all of them are filthy rich.

But my man—and that's how I think of him, now (we have crossed a frontier since I realised I would face death just to be with him; how could I not think of him as mine?)—is both. He is by far the most handsome in the room, and I know he's worth a packet. But his charms are not uniquely known to me. Apparently he is a figure of serious interest to any unattached (and apparently in some cases attached) women (and some men) in the room.

The place itself? Oh, it's perfect, of course. A sumptuous ball-room overlooking Hyde Park that has been transformed for the night into a sort of Midsummer Nights Dream winter wonderland. There are fairy lights strung across the ceiling in a higgledy piggledy criss cross, and candelabras are spaced periodically around the edges of the room, laden with gold candles that are dripping fragrant wax over the polished floor. The curtains, sumptuous gold, are also flecked with fairy lights, and they're drawn to reveal the passing evening traffic. And, perhaps, to give a glimpse of within to those forever blocked out.

I stand at the edge of the action, watching it, admiring it, and yes, resenting it a little. So much wealth, so much privilege. I imagine all the people in this room getting together and deciding to do one singularly worthy task. What could they achieve?

"There you are." His eyes are appraising me. He's still wondering. Our conversation from last week is back at the forefront of my mind. It hangs between us like a particularly sticky spider web. I'm being drawn towards it yet I know it is a trap; his quest for knowledge will end us. If he keeps pushing, I will push back. I cannot let him discover the truth of who I am; everything else, he has.

"Here I am." I smile brightly. My breath catches a little, as always, when he's near. I wonder if I would feel that in a year's time, were he to still be in my life (he won't be, so I can waste energy imagining).

He hands me a champagne flute. Its stem is impossibly fine and elegant. If I squeeze it, I think I could snap it clear in half.

"Are you enjoying yourself?"

I grin. "Sure. What's not to like?"

"Plenty."

It makes me laugh. I nudge him with my shoulder. "So why are we here?"

"I told you."

"I would have thought your friend would choose a more…I don't know—urban—location? Somewhere a little more with its finger on the pulse of your average app user."

"You don't think these people use apps?"

"Other than money counting ones, you mean?"

His smile flips my tummy upside down. "You're a cynic."

"I'm a realist." The champagne is excellent; I feel it bubble down to my toes. "What's the app, anyway?"

A woman walks past with a truly awesome hairstyle. Creamy pink and spiked around her very pretty face, she wears matching pink diamond earrings and a skimpy yet somehow elegant gold dress. Her eyes practically eat Alex up as she passes. Me? I don't think she so much as notices I'm there.

"Someone you know?"

His smile is dismissive. "Somewhat."

I don't like that answer one bit. It shows in my voice when I respond, "How somewhat?"

He angles his head to me, his expression mildly amused. "Does it matter?"

"I'm interested."

"In?"

My shrug is a study in unconcern. I pin him with my eyes, locking his face to mine. "You."

It's a simple confession but it surprises us both. I sip my champagne, turning my attention to the rest of the room. But his silence is reverberating through me. My pulse fires. I have the sense, familiar to me now, that I'm in way too deep.

"Alex." A man's voice provides pleasant relief. I plaster a smile on my face; it's dismissive. I turn to see a guy, maybe fifty or so years old and wearing a dark blue suit and pale grey shirt, cutting through the crowd towards him. Alex's eyes hold mine unwaveringly.

"I thought it was you." The man is insistent. It's bordering on rude that Alex hasn't acknowledged him. I feel sorry for the guy, but more so for me—a bug in his microscope, unable to escape.

"Excuse me," I smile blandly at both of them, laying the ground work to walk away. Alex's fingers catch me; lacing our fingers together, squeezing my hand.

His eyes skim my face, warming me from the inside out—for a moment he creates a bubble that is just him and me—before he turns to the man. "Richard. How are you?"

"Not bad. And you?"

"Fine. Richard, this is Sasha Lewis. Sasha, Richard and I worked together a few years back."

"Hardly," Richard laughs in a bellowing way that I fear draws more attention than I'm comfortable with. "I tried to keep up while Alex ran literal rings around our group."

Alex's smile is flicked from his face, perfectly polite but I see his impatience. He doesn't want Richard's praise; he doesn't welcome it and he accepts it very, very unwillingly.

His fingers are too hot around mine. I feel panicked and I can't say why. Is it being here with him? With these people, in his world, where Alex is essentially a God? Is it because it reminds me how temporary this is, how out of place I am with him? I squeeze his hand back. "Nice to meet you. If you'll excuse me, I was just on my way to the bar."

Alex sends me a look of curiosity as he unfurls his grip. I rub my hand as I walk away, eyes skimming the crowd. I'm not looking for a bar though. I'm looking for a place to cool my heels and calm down, to regain my equilibrium.

There's a band. They're playing beautiful jazz songs, and the vocalist has an amazing sound. I pause a little, closer to them, to listen to the Harry Connick Jr cover.

"Sash?"

I know who it is before my eyes catch the direction of my name.

"Carlton?" I'm both surprised and thrilled to see him. He's a lifeline, a touchstone to normality. "What are you doing here?"

"I was about to say the same thing to you." He hugs me. It's strange, but it's not. We haven't hugged yet. Then again, I guess this is a new social setting and it's a not-unknown convention. He smells nice. Like soap and library books.

"I'm here with a friend." A complete obfuscation; isn't that what I'm good at, though? I justify the introduction—it's how Alex described me to his associates, why shouldn't I use it too?

Carlton makes an exaggerated show of surveying the crowds around us, as if looking for the friend I've just mentioned and then shrugs in a gesture of bemusement.

"He's talking to someone."

"I see."

"And you? I didn't picture you as the elegant after-five party type."

His laugh is thick and deep. "Believe me. I'm not." He points to his hair, tamed into its usual man-bun. "I was tempted to get my hair straightened but I think that pushes me into dangerously unmasculine territory."

"The flowing blonde locks don't do that on their own?"

His grin is compelling. He leans closer. "They're the tip of a very masculine iceberg."

I laugh but inside I'm feeling that guilty burst again. He's flirting with me—I can no longer pretend it's anything but.

"So why are you here?" I sip my champagne to break the flow of our conversation.

"The university had a few tickets and I was at a loose end."

"No dim sum tonight?"

"When there's free canapés? No way, babe."

"Babe?" I wrinkle my nose. "Please, don't." But my serious tone is belied by the quivering of my lips.

"Don't tell me I'm the first guy to call you Babe?"

"The first one I haven't punched," I respond sarcastically.

"Okay, okay. At the risk of getting my nose flattened, what do you prefer? Sugar? Honey? Darlin'?"

I make a sound that I fear may best be described as chortling. "Definitely none of the above. You're edging frighteningly close to pervy old man territory."

"Old man, huh?"

"Well, old*er*," I'm quick to clarify.

His fingers wrap around the stem of my glass. As he takes it from me, I'm reminded forcefully of how handsome he is. Especially tonight, surrounded by suits, and he's wearing a simple pair of beige pants and a blue shirt, unbuttoned at the neck. No tie.

"Dance?"

"Um..." I toss a glance over my shoulder. Pink Hair has done another pass and this time, Alex's taken the bait. He's talking to Richard but Pinky's there too. And more importantly, he's not looking my way. "Sure. Just one."

He puts his hands around my waist and I have no choice but to interlock my fingers behind his neck. I keep my body tense though, not relaxing into him as I would with Alex. This is not intimate, we are simply dancing together.

"Are you having a good time?"

My shrug is noncommittal. "We just got here a glass of champagne ago."

The music swirls around us. "You were in a rush the other day," I say, simply to fill the gap in conversation.

"Yeah, sorry about that." He grins at me and I know for sure that he's flirting. "Maybe that's going to be our special handshake."

I am curious and it shows in my face.

"You know, rushed goodbyes? Me the other day. And you running out on our dinner?"

"I didn't run off," I contradict, my cheeks pink.

"Sure you did. You hurled a twenty at me and steamed out the door."

I laugh because it's such a good description of exactly what I did. "I didn't mean to."

"So my divorce talk didn't scare you off?"

My hair is down, falling in a long curtain of dark ebony around my face. It flicks my cheeks as I shake my head. Realising what I've inadvertently agreed to I rush to clarify, "Scared me off being your friend? Of course not. Why would it?"

"Subtle as a brick," he teases, rubbing his hand up my back. "You can just say you're not interested."

I swallow; my throat is impossibly, desert dry. "Romantically?"

"Yeah." He grins. It's lovely. "I think I've been rejected before."

I roll my eyes with amusement. "Don't be ridiculous."

"What's ridiculous about it?" He's looking at me seriously now and I'm a little concerned he really wants to have this conversation.

"I'm seeing someone." I blurt the words out like a shield. "I didn't know you thought we had anything more going on or I would have said so sooner." I drop my eyes. "Sorry."

"Don't be." His hand is still running up and down my back, slowly, but in a soothing way that makes me think maybe he's forgotten he's doing it. "We've already covered my history of falling for the wrong woman."

"Don't fall for me," I beg. I'm not dancing anymore. This is too serious.

"Too late." He wraps his hands more tightly around my waist. I need to get out of this situation. How can I do that? What can I say? I like this guy! He's nowhere near the same ballpark as what I feel for Alex, but I like him enough that I don't want to offend him with the abrupt rejections that are springing to the forefront of my mind.

"Who is he?"

I can't quite meet Carlton's eyes. I don't want to tell him. I don't want to tell anyone about Alex and me. I'm all tangled up. "Just someone I met a while ago."

"And? What stage are you at?"

"Stage?" I purse my lips. "What do you mean?"

"You aren't familiar with the six stages of relationships?"

I groan. "Why do I feel like I'm going to regret this?"

His expression is curious.

"Okay, okay. Enlighten me."

"Gladly." His grin is heavy with mischief. "Stage one. Eyes lock across a crowded classroom. Er, room."

"My eyes are rolling in their sockets, Carl."

"Carl? I've been downgraded?"

"Yeah. You betcha. It's payback for 'babe'. Go on."

He's not dancing either now. We're just two people in the middle of the room, hugging. The second I realise that I pull away, reaching for my champagne perched on the nearby table as a pretext for the separation. "So stage one. Eyes meet. Infatuation ensues."

"To clarify, is infatuation still stage one?"

"It's more of a bridging stage. Sort of a stage one point five."

"Right." I shake my head and take another sip.

"Stage two is pursuit. The moment you realise you really want to be with someone and you make that obvious."

"Which leads to?"

"Stage three. Bliss. Those heady few weeks where everything is perfect and you exist in a state of sensual euphoria and mental stimulation."

I clear my throat. "Then?"

"Reality bites. Stage four. The real world makes itself known. Jobs. Families. Friends. Stress. Pressure."

"Yikes. Scary stuff. The real world."

"Hey! Don't mock it, babe."

"Don't call me that," I plead laughingly.

"Stage four is crucial. For a lot of people, in a choose your own adventure book, stage four spells disaster. Stage five is where you find that out. Can you weather reality? Do you even want to with this person? Is it worth it?"

"And stage six?"

"The inevitable separation. Whether through death, disease or dislike. All roads lead to ..."

"...Divorce?"

He laughs. "Pretty much."

"In your experience at least."

"Hey, I gave you death as one of the reasons. That could be at the end of a supremely happy sixty-year marriage."

I tilt my head, "That's true."

"So what stage are you and this guy?"

I frown, thinking it through. "I guess three."

He scrunches his face in an exaggerated gesture of hurt. "Sexual euphoria? Bliss?"

My cheeks flush. "I didn't mean that! I just meant...we're...Oh, shut up." I slap him lightly on the arm and he laughs softly.

"So you and I are in stage two. I'm only one behind. There's hope for me yet."

"Give me a break!" I am entreating him but I can't stop smiling. I can't explain properly but there's just something about Carlton that brings a huge smile to my face. We have a spark, a chemistry, but it's the *friend* kind, the happy-making kind. Not the burning my skin intensity I share with Alex.

"How about we get you another champagne and you can keep telling me why I have no hope."

"There are a lot of reasons," I promise, suddenly serious. "But the biggest one is that I'm really not...I really don't...you don't know who I am. I would just break your heart. Again. I'd be some woman you'd end up telling a student about in five years' time."

His eyes, so blue like the ocean, are unpicking the locks of my brain. When he speaks, his voice is husky. "If that's your main reason then I can hit it out of the park. My heart is immune to breaking."

How did we get here? I shake my head and step away a little bit. "I'm with someone. A guy I... a guy I want to be with." As I say it, I know it's true. It's not what Alex and I agreed to, it's not our future, but oh, I wish it were. I wish it could be.

And then, Alex appears, as if conjured by my words.

"Someone you know, Sasha?" A perfectly urbane question but I hear the frayed edges. I sense the tightened coil of this man, the surprise at seeing me so close to someone else and instantly want to reassure him.

"Oh, hey." I wish my heart would stop hammering into my ribs. "Alex, yes. This is Carlton. Dr Carlton. He's one of my professors at uni."

They're staring at each other, the macho sizing up so obvious I want to make a pithy comment about it—but don't. I put a hand on Alex's arm. "Carlton, this is Alex."

"Stage three?" He asks with a wink, and I nod.

"Meaning?" Tension radiates from him. I wonder if Carlton sees it, or if it's only that I'm so attuned to him.

"A personal joke," Carlton is making it so much worse and I'm pretty sure he knows.

"It's a relationship theory," I correct, taking the sting out of that comment. But Alex isn't biting and I start to suspect he's genuinely bothered by Carlton and me. Again, I have very little experience with men, dating, expectations but Alex must know he is the centre of my universe— there's no room for jealousy when you light all the dark places of a person's soul, right?

"Can I see you a moment?" I smile at Alex, he returns just a flicker in response.

"Yes. A good idea." His voice is barely above a growl.

"Excuse us," I murmur to Carlton, reaching down and entwining my fingers in Alex's. I pull him away gently but once we reach the edge of the crowd we switch roles. He's pulling me, leading me back to the bank of elevators we used when we arrived.

"You're going too fast," I snap, wrenching my hand free. He doesn't look back, but he does slow down.

When we reach the elevator, he jerks his finger into the call button and stares straight ahead.

I don't bother to pretend I don't know why he's mad. "He's just a friend."

He turns to face me slowly. "I don't think that's true." His eyes are not angry, they are cold, assessing, hurt. God, the first two I can deal with, the latter is painful. I don't want to hurt Alex, ever.

I seek clarity; I need him to voice whatever he's feeling so I can tackle it directly. "What exactly are you accusing me of?"

The elevator pings open. A couple is in there. Alex and I join them, neither speaking.

The elevator shifts downwards and the doors opens seconds later, releasing the older pair, but still we are silent until it descends to the parking garage. It appears deserted.

"Can we talk..."

"I want to talk about it," he mutters. "Just not yet."

He reaches into his pocket and his car bleeps.

"You want to leave?"

He doesn't answer until we reach the Range Rover. He opens a door, stares back at me.

I stop walking. "No. I will not be treated like a naughty child. We'll talk here."

A muscle hammers in his jaw as he stares across at me, not speaking. Because he doesn't know what to say?

"Why are you so angry?"

"Come on, Sash. Don't I have a right to be a little pissed?"

"Not from where I'm standing. You took me to a party, and I saw someone I know, someone I like. I hung out with him while you were busy. Is that seriously such a big deal?"

He's cold now. His expression gives nothing away. I am sure he's feeling this as deeply as I am yet to look at him, you might think he were giving a stranger directions. He's slipped into his business-like persona.

"Are you coming home with me or would you prefer to stay?"

"Obviously I'm coming with you," I snap. "But you need to listen to me. He's just a friend. Someone I know through uni. He means nothing to me beyond that."

"That guy's hands were on you as though he wanted to make love to you." There is torment in the accusation, a crack in his cool, controlled facade.

My throat is thick because I know Alex is right. I can't deny it. Carlton was flirting with me, and he was honest about his feelings too. I move to Alex quickly, put a hand on his arm. "That's not how I feel," I tell him seriously. "You know that, right?"

"But he does want you."

I batter my lids closed; I don't want his eyes reading mine so easily. "How he feels is irrelevant."

"Do you have any idea how it felt to see you two dancing together, Sash?" But I cannot answer, because he kisses me quickly after speaking. His tongue is demanding in my mouth and his body heavy as he pushes me back against the car. He uses his knee to separate my legs and he lifts my arms high above my head so that I'm a prisoner of his kiss.

There is a spirit of defiance tumbling through my surrender. I pull away, force his eyes to meet mine, my hand bunched in the front of his shirt. "I was dancing with a friend. That's all."

He nods slowly, drags a hand through his hair. "I hated it."

"Sure. I hated seeing you talking to that woman in there too, but I'm not going all neanderthal about it. We're both going to have to be mature adults and accept that we have lives outside of our relationship."

His lips clamp together; he doesn't like it. "We were talking, not dancing."

"So I'm not allowed to dance with other men? You don't trust me?"

"No. That's not what I mean."

"Isn't it?"

"You can do what you want. I just—," he shakes his head.

I have to concede that I would feel the same way, if I'd found him arm in arm with a beautiful woman. Nonetheless, I need to stand my ground, because Alex is so strong, and he is so completely a part of me that I need to maintain some boundaries, for my own sake. "You can't drag me out of parties because I'm dancing with someone else. I'm yours, I'm completely yours, but you don't own me."

He stares at me for several long seconds and I hold my breath, needing him to get this point, needing to agree. And he does, quickly. "I know." His lips take mine. Gently now, I feel his own surrender to this, to needing me, to being mine as much as I am his. I lift my arms, wrapping them around his neck. My gown shifts, slipping. Alex presses his forehead to mine. "I wasn't prepared. To see you with him, to feel the way I did." He hesitates, scans my eyes, moves closer. "I'm sorry."

My dress is slipping down, revealing my breasts: I move to pull my hand so that I might fix it but he doesn't release me. Instead, he runs his gravelly, stubbled jaw lower, kissing my neck and décolletage then nuzzling my dress lower and taking a nipple into his mouth.

I swear loudly and he laughs.

"Please, would you get in the car?"

I'm not going to hesitate this time. I quickly slip in the still-open door and he follows immediately, shutting us in the relative privacy of the car before resuming the kiss. "There's something here, Sash. Something I can't explain." He shakes his head and his cluelessness takes my breath away because we're navigating something new, for both of us.

In the privacy of the car, I reach for his pants and unzip them, eyes locked to his. "We don't need to explain it. I'm yours. And you are mine. It's just how it is."

My dress is tight. Too tight to push up and ignore. It rips as he pulls it. I don't care. He keeps ripping, right down the side, until it's open and I'm free; naked except for a flimsy thong. He holds my hips and pulls me to sit on his lap, his dick hard, his breath raspy. He pushes my thong aside and lowers me over his shaft. I press my hands into the ceiling and roll myself over his length. He swears; the curse is oddly erotic.

His fingers are back to my hips, digging in as he lifts me and pulls me, moving me as he needs to feel me, pleasing me in all the ways I have become obsessed with. He thrusts hard too, timing each movement with when he pulls me down, so that he's so deep I can feel him straining muscles I hadn't even known I possessed.

And when I'm on the edge of sanity, he brings his mouth to my breasts, and bites down on a nipple. Not hard, and not with his teeth. His lips clamp around it though, and my breasts are so sensitive that shock sears me. I tip over the edge, trying to take him with me but he's too strong.

I realise later that he's trying to own me after all, and in order to own me, he wants to make me come as often as possible. He doesn't understand that I'm his for a smile.

TEN
PHASE FOUR

"He looked familiar to me."

I'm naked beneath Alex's jacket, beside him in the car as he drives us to his home. London passes in a blur. I'm tired. My eyelids are heavy.

"Who did?"

"The man with his hands all over you. Who is he?"

"Carlton?"

"Why do I know of him?" He insists, reaching across and running his fingers over my exposed legs. Goosebumps lift my skin, pleasure and promise mingle inside me.

"He's well-known I guess. Certainly in legal circles." I shift a little so that I can see his features better. "Alex?"

He turns to face me briefly.

"Do you remember what you said to me, the night we met?"

He frowns.

"You said you don't do serious."

"Yes."

"This is serious."

He compresses his lips. We're close to his apartment now. "Don't do it, Sash."

"Don't do what?"

"Don't ask questions that neither of us knows how to answer."

Frustration pulls at my gut. I am the mistress of evasion, of secret-keeping, yet his non-answer is irritating as all hell. "Calm down. It's not like I want to marry you, jeez."

It's so unexpected that he bursts out laughing. I'm not in a humorous mood though. "No, I mean it. You aren't the only one who wants to keep this casual and light." I drop my eyes. It's like looking at the sun. "But it isn't that. It's not remotely light. Nor is it casual. I'm practically living with you. We both know this will end, but for the moment, where we're at? It's serious. So I'm asking if this intensity is normal for you?"

He shakes his head, a tight smile on his lips. "I should have run a mile from you that night."

"That's not an answer."

"No, it isn't."

He isn't going to offer me an assurance. He's going to offer me nothing.

It infuriates me. "Damn it, Alex. Talk to me. I deserve that."

The silence in the car is static. He pulls to a stop at traffic lights, turns to face me.

"You said you don't want to marry me." His voice is so thick and gravelly. I've never heard it like that. "I would marry you though, Sasha. If that was what I had to do to keep you in my life. I can't imagine not having you, in my bed, on my arm, with me."

"What...I...what are you saying?" I swear to you, my heart is about to spill onto the fine leather upholstery. I definitely did not see this coming.

"I need you. I want you. I want you to live with me properly. You are in my blood; you are my life force. But only if you want it."

I can't quite connect the dots. It doesn't make sense. "You don't believe in love."

"I'm not offering love." He's so quick to tear down my dreams! Just like that. They're in tatters between us. I'm confused and it shows on my face. He strokes me gently. "I don't want love. I want you, this."

"But nothing more?"

"No. There is nothing more than this."

It's a ghost of what I want though, and yet I nod. I'm being stoic. A word I heard often back then, when It first happened. The investigators called me stoic; so too the prosecutors. "But you don't want me to fall in love with someone like Carlton?" It's petty. It's juvenile. But damn it, my heart is aching.

"No."

I'm tired. My head is resting against the seat, my eyes are closed, but our conversation is swirling through my mind. "Why me?"

He laughs, a twisted sound without humour. "Why me? Why not him?"

"That's..."

"No. Don't hedge the question like you always do. You want me. You combust in my arms. You would walk this street naked if I asked it of you. Why do you feel that for me?"

He begins to drive once more as the light turns green.

Because I love you. I swallow the words, knowing how unwelcome they would be. "Because I'm an idiot."

He nods slowly. "I think we both are."

He turns into his own garage, pulls the car to a stop, turns to face me, his expression earnest. "I don't want to lose you."

It's an admission I thought he'd never give and though it's so far from the words I want to hear, I'll take these. I will take them and wrap them up close to my heart.

"We're just sex." God. It's true. And it kills me to say it. "Just sex. And you've had plenty of that with plenty of women. You can't tell me why I'm different. You can't tell me why you want me instead of anyone who came before me. You could go and pay for sex. Or find a one-night stand. You don't need me."

"I need you. Just you," he denies fiercely, his eyes sparking angry heat off mine. "Shit, Sasha! What else can I say to get through to you?"

I shake my head. "It's too complicated."

"Then let's simplify it. No more going out. Just us. My apartment. No pressure. When we're there, it works."

"Fine." But I'm angry. So angry. What he's offering isn't real life. It's not sustainable and it foreshadows the end of what we are in a way I do not want to contemplate. "I had dinner with Carlton the other night."

He jerks his head as though I've pushed his chest, hard. He steps out of the car, comes around to my door, opens it for me.

I exit the car carefully—wearing only a silk thong and his jacket, it's no mean feat.

"Did you hear me?" I ask him, my voice reverberating through the empty garage.

"I heard you." He sighs heavily. "I just want us to get inside, okay?" And despite everything, he smiles, reaches over, tucks my hair behind my ear, and something in my heart shifts.

We ride the elevator in silence. When we step into his apartment he shuts the door swiftly and clicks the lock into place. His chest moves rapidly, each breath drawn from his body with effort. "When did you have dinner with him?"

My cheeks burn red. "The night you bossed me into staying away."

He nods, giving nothing away, but he doesn't have to move a muscle on his face for me to see his eyes change, for me to understand that I've hurt and surprised him. "You were supposed to be studying."

I narrow my eyes. "My uni timetable is my business, not yours. So's my life, come to think of it."

When turns from me, I have only his back to stare at and it's rigid as anything. "And yet you tell me I can trust you?"

"Yes. Dinner is dinner. It's not like we checked into a hotel room." I want to say more but I know I'm doing the verbal equivalent of sticking a knife in his side. "I'm telling you this so you know you can trust me. I'm not keeping anything from you."

Though he sounds calm when he speaks, and he turns to face me, eyes probing me. "You tell me honestly you don't feel anything for him?"

"I used to think he was kind of cute." I have surprised him. He didn't expect this confession. "And then I met you, and my whole world tipped off its axis." I move closer to him. "I keep telling you, he's just a friend."

Alex's eyes probe mine. "I don't suppose it'd make a difference if I suggested he become a friend you never see?"

Indignation fires in me. "I won't agree to ditch him because you're jealous."

His eyes spark. "Fair enough." And he's cold again. Ice cold. It's as though he's pulling his feelings under control as one might draw an anchor from the middle of a stormy sea. Bit by bit he boxes away the swirling emotions until there is a businesslike pragmatism in his words. "I don't want you to leave; I don't want to lose you. But things are changing between us, clearly. We need to face that head on."

I do my best to imitate his no-nonsense approach. "What do you suggest?"

He looks relieved by my acquiescence. "No more staying at your flat. I'd prefer you to come here when you're not at uni or work."

"What you're really saying is that I can't see him at all if I want to be with you?"

"No." He crosses to me, his expression unreadable. "You can see him whenever you want. I get it. It's your life. All I ask is that you tell me about it. Like you said; no secrets."

I nod my acceptance immediately. I love him. I will give him my soul. But I can't let him know that.

"Sasha?"

I'm tired. It's been a big night. "Yes?"

He scoops down and picks me up, carrying me towards the ensuite bathroom. "I have never cared about anything as much as I do having you in my life. This is new to me. Be patient, okay?"

———

In the week since that conversation, I have come to accept that we've crested out of phase three and are bumpily approaching phase four.

Reality is hitting us. And I think that maybe it does bite.

But there is nowhere I want to be more than by his side. With this man. He drives fast and yet I don't feel endangered. I feel safe. As his car swings around a bend in the road he turns to face me and his smile sets me free.

"You're an adrenalin junkie."

I laugh. "Really? Me? Why would you say that?"

He lifts a brow and turns back to the road before pressing down hard on the accelerator. As the car speeds up my tummy twists and I grin. "Point proven. Slow down."

He does so immediately, softening the trajectory of the car until it is humming nicely along the country roads on the outskirts of Ballymore.

"Do you get back to see your parents often?"

"Not as often as they wish."

He gives me a considering look. He's so on to me. Those little deflective comments are losing traction with him. But what can I do about it? Relax. Trudy was my favourite advisor, though I rarely took her advice on board. After all, she encouraged a terrifying degree of relaxation. "You are safe now," she'd said. "Those men who did those things live far away. You are unrecognisable from the girl you were." She'd reached for my naturally fair hair and run her fingers through its darkened ends. "You have a new name; a new identity. This is your life. You should feel free to live it to its fullest extent."

This was kind of her to say, and the advice might have eventually carried weight with me if she hadn't been shot six months later, protecting another little girl just like me.

"When did you last come home?"

I contemplate telling him that 'home' is in London. Worse, that it's where he is. But I know what he's asking. "A few months ago."

His jaw clenches with impatience at the unconsciously vague reply.

"It was my birthday," I hasten to add, giving him more breadcrumbs to show him that I'm playing along. "They threw a party."

He visibly relaxes. "Sounds nice."

I nod.

"It must have been a beautiful place to grow up." He's turning into the village and lovely little stone buildings topple over one another forming an uneven row.

"It was." I blank the first ten years of my life. "I was happy here."

He studies me. "Did you go to school in town?"

"Yeah." The glance I give him is thoughtful. "My parents thought about sending me to boarding school but decided to keep me close."

"I get the impression you were quite a handful."

"Actually, it was the opposite," I murmur. "I was meek as a mouse back then."

"I doubt that," he drawls. The GPS gives him a disembodied instruction to turn right.

"Why?" I curl my legs beneath me on the seat, turning to face him.

"I don't think you have a meek bone in your body." He slows the car and leans over to kiss the tip of my nose. "And it is a body I know very, very well."

"Better than anyone," I whisper, blinking my eyes shut. "Thank you for driving me today."

"Thank you for letting me."

I consider that. It's an odd sentence for many reasons. Mostly because Alex LaMar is not a man to be allowed or disallowed to do anything. But also because it's one of those unexpectedly sweet comments that fills me with a gooey warmth. I think about his day: what's ahead of him once he leaves Ballymore. "I ..." I shake my head.

"What is it?"

"It's stupid. Never mind."

"I doubt it."

"I was going to say I could come with you. But my mum would flip if I didn't stick around."

He's quiet and it's strange that I know his types of quiet. The Quiets where he's thinking about work; the Quiets where he's cross about something and is trying to push his annoyance down inside of him; the Quiets where he is planning and shaping ideas to fit together. And this is, apparently, one of the latter.

"Why don't you?"

I shake my head; my hair flicks across my eyes, catching in my lashes. "I told you, my mum..."

"What if we go to Bath and then come here afterwards?"

"You mean drop me off afterwards?"

His eyes flicker to mine. "No. I mean stay here afterwards. For dinner. A sleepover." His smile sends sexy little butterflies flickering in my gut.

It's on the tip of my tongue to issue a denial. What would my mum say? But the idea has merit. I think I'm far more curious about his mum than I am worried about my own. "I'll think about it. Let me... see how they are."

He nods. "The decision's up to you."

"Thank you."

Maybe reality doesn't bite after all.

They're waiting out the front of the house when his car sweeps in the drive. Dad's arm is around mum's waist and their faces wear smiles of determination. The worry is palpable. I ache to comfort them.

Alex kills the engine and I step out almost instantly, temporarily forgetting anything but my parents. I walk quickly across the gravelled drive. I no longer notice the grandness of their estate; the red brick Edwardian mansion on the brink of the Thames. "Hey," I force a bright smile, wrapping mum up in a huge hug before dad barrels us both into his arms.

"Hiya, kiddo." God, it's bad if dad's voice is shaking like that. "How are you, blackbird?"

Damn that nickname! My eyes sting with tears. "I'm fine, you guys. It was just a photo. And see? Nothing came of it." Their eyes meet over my heads and I realise how great their burden is. How constant their worry must be. Is this the legacy I have to offer?

I feel Alex behind me before he so much as speaks. I break the patented Lewis family cuddle party and step back towards him. I notice for the first time two bags in his hands. They're brown calico.

"Mum, dad, this is Alex LaMar."

"From the paper." It's just an observation but we all hear the accusation laced through the words.

"Guilty as charged." His smile is disarming. It disarms me, anyway.

"This is my mother Ally, and my father Rick."

"Pleased to meet you both." He holds a bag out for Rick and then one for Ally. Curious, I step closer. There's a bottle of aged scotch in my dad's and for my mum he has a beautiful Molton Brown gardeners' hand care kit. How the hell does he know my dad loves scotch and my mother to garden?

It's uncanny.

"How thoughtful," Ally smiles at him. She's still on the fence but she's being polite. "Please. Come in."

"I'll put a coffee on."

"That'd be great." I reach down and link my fingers through Alex's. Yes, this phase four thing isn't bad. In fact, everything feels so right that I have to work really hard to remember that we both know this is just a temporary thing. I mean, it is. It has to be. Doesn't it? Why did we agree on that? *This isn't a prelude to love, Sasha. I'm not looking for Happily Ever After. I'm not offering romance. If you want those things then you should go now, before we begin.*

He'd said that the night we met and he showed me he still meant it only a week ago when he told me he'd marry me to keep me in his life, even when he didn't love me.

"You have a lovely home."

"Thank you," mum responds with that frosty grievance in her tone. It makes me smile. I squeeze his hand.

"I'll show you around, if you'd like." My dad is obviously more willing to go with this occurrence. The first man I've brought home.

"Actually, dad," I interrupt. "There's been a change of plans." I can feel my mother stiffen ahead of us.

"Alex's mum is... in Bath. He was going to drop me off and head over to her but ..."

"I asked Sasha if she'd like to accompany me."

"I see." My mother's disappointment is a knife to my heart.

"If it isn't too much of an imposition, we'd like to come back and join you for dinner tonight," Alex takes over. You know, it's been at least ten hours since I've remembered that he's this incredibly formidable, dynamic tycoon. He's becoming, simply, mine. Alex. But his comment is issued in the tone of a directive. "We can, of course, pick up food to save putting you out."

Ally spins around, her big blue eyes skating over us. Does he realise how physically different I am to my parents? They're both tall and coltishly slender, lean and long, whereas I am tiny and curvaceous, with hair that has been dyed dark brown, green eyes and a nose that ski jumps upward just like my real mum's used to.

"I wouldn't hear of it." And now she's smiling, looking from me to Alex with genuine surprise. Apparently the vista of a man who might encourage me to dine at my parents' home erases a multitude of high-profile sins.

"Wonderful." Dad claps his hand together. "Coffee before you go?"

"Yes, please." I speak over anything Alex might have been about to say.

I am salivating at the thought of one of my dad's French Press coffees and I will brave any hurried disapproval from the man at my side for the promise of it. But he's smiling.

Yeah. This Phase Four business is going to be just fine...

He's quiet.

So quiet.

And this is a new Quiet. One I don't recognise. But only the most insensitive idiot in the world wouldn't know.

We sat with her for an hour. He spoke to her. He even introduced me. But she didn't do more than flicker her eyelids.

It was confronting and awful for me; how must it be for him?

We are near the village when I feel compelled to break the long, sad silence. "I'm so sorry."

"Why? It's hardly your fault," he says softly.

"No, I know…" I swallow. "Shall we just go back to London?"

"Why?" He takes his eyes off the road for a moment to study me.

"Surely socialising with my parents in the last thing you feel like doing?"

He expels a breath. "That's the first time you've seen someone like that, isn't it?"

I nod.

"I see her often. I'm used to it. It's not easy, but it no longer cuts through me like it once did."

"I didn't expect her to be so…"

"No." He interrupts to save me from having to finish the sentence. "I know."

"Can anything be done?"

"No." His smile is grim. "She's comfortable. Well-cared for. She has one of the best consultants in the world. But there's no brain activity and hasn't been for a long time."

I want to kiss him. I want to take away that pain and grief in the only way I feel capable of. And yet I want to do more. To give him more.

"Is it... because of..."

"The beatings?" Again he supplies the conclusion to my question. I nod hurriedly.

"Undoubtedly. She suffered repeated brain injuries. Like a football player or boxer, only worse. There was no protection for her."

"God. You must hate him."

He laughs, a short, sharp sound in the confines of the luxurious car. "Yeah." He remembers the way to my parents' house as if he's been there several times, not just once.

"Does he ever try to see you?"

"No."

Okay, I get it. Conversation closed. I shift direction, moving to safer ground.

"That was thoughtful of you to bring my parents gifts."

He doesn't say anything to that either, but it is my silence that is speaking volumes.

"Ask the question," he prompts after a weighted moment.

"How do you know I have one?"

"Because I know you." A simple, beautiful statement that tickles a smile across my mouth.

"Fine." I bite down on my lip, trying to choose my words. "How many...how often..." I squeeze my eyes shut. It's hard to say what I'm thinking.

"Go on," he prompts, turning again. He pulls up outside a row of shops, sliding the car easily into a small space.

He cuts the engine and gives me the full force of his attention.

"You know what I want to ask."

"I think I have an idea." It's a mocking, teasing response to a question that's ripping me up a bit inside.

I force myself to meet his eyes unflinchingly. "Meeting the parents...I mean...How many women like me have you...been with?"

"None."

I shake my head, dismissing the answer that surely serves as a platitude and little beyond.

"You are unique."

"Thank you." I brush aside the compliment. "But we are all unique."

"Not in many ways. I have a type, Sasha, and you are definitely not it."

"Aren't I?" My heart accelerates painfully in my chest.

"No. You are beautiful and smart and yes, that's my type. But you are different in every other way to my usual partner."

"Partner?" I look away from his intensely probing eyes. The word groups me with them and I don't like that.

"Lover?" He substitutes, sensing my distaste at the word and not understanding its reasoning.

"How many lovers?"

"Will a number change something vital between us?"

I shake my head. "I'm just curious."

"I'm aware of that." He reaches down and puts his hand on my leg. I crave the contact but I want more.

"So?"

"Enough," he bites out eventually. "To know how special you are."

I try not to let the compliment in.

"Are you always so charming with parents?"

He laughs. "I guess I'm just a charming kind of guy."

He isn't. I mean, he is, when he's not being bombastic, arrogant, mocking and determined.

"Do you have a preference? For wine?"

"Wine?" The swift conversation change makes my head spin.

He nods behind me and I realise we're stopped right outside an off-licence. "Oh. No. I don't care."

"Wait here." He kisses me sharply on the lips. It's started to rain so I don't argue. I watch as he strides into the store then sigh. He can't have slept with that many women. Surely. A dozen? Two dozen? A hundred?

He's in his early thirties. He probably lost his virginity young. I guess there've been several every year.

Several a year? This guy has an irrepressible libido. He's probably partaken in wild orgies and hooked up with a dozen women a night. God. How long before he bores of me?

He returns with a brown paper bag, twisted at the neck of the bottle. He passes it to me once he's taken his seat.

"How about you?" He pulls the car into traffic.

I lift the bottle from the bag. It's not a label I recognise so I slip it away again immediately. It's a nice gesture, regardless of the wine he chose. Though, as with all things Alex LaMar, I know it will be expensive and excellent.

"Your boyfriends."

"Oh." I shake my head. "I've never really…I mean…"

"Yes?" He prompts with unhidden curiosity when I fade away.

"I don't really have boyfriends."

"No?"

"That surprises you?"

"Yes, frankly." It's a simple agreement but I can hear the cogs of his brain turning behind it.

"Why?"

"You're too nice not to have left a string of sweet, innocent young men in your wake."

I laugh at the description. "Is that how you see yourself?"

"No. I'm the Big Bad Wolf who's tempted Cinderella away from Princes Charming."

"That's a mixed metaphor." He is a wolf, though and I would let him blow my house down again and again for the lure of being with him.

"So sue me." He slows down outside my parents' driveway. He waits for me to continue and I don't feel inclined to lie.

"My mum and dad never really approved of boyfriends. I mean, they didn't say as much but I had a strict curfew and I guess they just provided enough objections and resistance to make that already awkward teenage phase impossible. I could never have had a boy over in high school; I wouldn't have been allowed to even go to the movies without my mum."

He runs a hand over his stubbled chin. "That's a very oppressive way to grow up. Why were they so strict?" Straight to the heart of it.

"They just were."

He files the information for later-analysis. "So then? You're fourth year at university. Surely there have been…"

"Yeah." I nod, my cheeks bright red. "Obviously. I mean, I wasn't a virgin when we met. I've dated."

He nods, his eyes scanning mine. "No."

"But it's not like…" He's smiling at me and I roll my eyes, pushing his chest. "You are unbelievable."

His laugh sends darts of desire spinning down my spine.

"You're enjoying this."

"The idea of you and other men? Definitely not."

I'm blushing to the root of my hair. "What if I said there were only two men."

"Two?" It's as though his jaw has literally dropped to the bottom of the car. "Two?"

"What's wrong with that?"

"It just beggars belief," he says finally, rubbing his jaw again and focussing his gaze straight ahead before turning back to face me. "Two? Really two?"

"No. Two hundred." I roll my eyes. "Of course two."

"Who were they?"

I don't even consider not answering. "Andrew was my first."

"Boyfriend?"

I shrug. "Kind of. I mean, we went on a few dates. It wasn't serious either. He was on exchange from Australia for a semester."

"What is it with you and overseas men?"

The oblique reference to Carlton makes me nervous. We haven't spoken about him since that night.

"And the second?"

"I'm looking at him."

"Jesus." He closes his eyes for a minute, then blinks straight at me. "You're serious?"

"I'm sorry if that makes me weird or something. Like, I've been on dates, you know, here and there. Dinner, a movie, a club, but usually after one date I'm done. I can tell pretty quickly if someone's, I don't know, interesting enough to spend time with." The more I say, the quieter he becomes, so eventually, I can't even look at him. I pretend fascination with the centre console. "Where did parking breaks go? What was wrong with that big old handle in the middle of the car? How does that tiny button do the same thing now?"

He shakes his head. "You're telling me that besides me you've slept with just one other guy."

"Can you just drive? You're making me feel like some kind of pathetic loser."

"That's so far from what I'm feeling, Sasha."

"I just... I don't..." I furrow my brow, frustrated by the secrets I must keep. "It's hard for me to get close to people," I say finally. "You could say I have trust issues. Going out with someone brings with it the inevitable swapping of life stories and I don't want to do that." I meet his gaze unflinchingly now. "You were different. You told me from that first night that we wouldn't be about that. You're the first person to offer me sex with no strings. I liked that. I loved it."

Silence fills the car; awareness swirls around us. "And now?" He murmurs, dark in mood.

"Nothing's changed," I shrug to hide my prickly confusion.

"Hasn't it?" Confusion grows.

I move the conversation on—I am self-conscious and I want him to experience the same. "Come on. Tell me about you. Are we in the tens? The hundreds? The thousands? Just how many women have you done... what we do...with?"

"None." He leans forward and presses his head to mine. "You make everything new."

My heart turns over. He begins to drive again, turning the car into my parents' home. It's beautiful in the day, but at night, with the lights glowing golden and the Thames sparkling behind it, it is a picturesque property indeed.

"I'm strangely looking forward to tonight," I say when he comes to open my door.

"I am too." His arm around my shoulders feels like the most natural thing in the world. "I've never had this kind of happy family scenario."

He's looking up at the home thoughtfully. "I mean, they sound stricter than jailers but they love you. It must have been nice to grow up with that kind of security."

Oh, how I would love to answer that question truthfully. "Yeah." I nod slowly. "Kind of."

Rick pulls the door inwards before we ring the bell and I imagine him watching for us, as he used to for me after school.

"Hi dad." I kiss his cheek and try not to notice the way his skin has aged.

Alex holds a hand out and dad shakes it. "How was your mother, Alex?"

"Much the same as always," Alex's answer gives little away.

"It's not a bad drive to Bath now. The roads have been widened out nicely."

"True." Alex hands the bag to my dad. He lifts the wine from the paper, just as I did.

"You're quite the connoisseur," he says with obvious appreciation. I take a closer look at the label; it still means nothing. "Unlike my daughter."

"Hey. I like champagne," I defend.

"Yeah, or bucks' fizz," dad laughs. "But that's okay. At least we never had to worry about you drinking too much and getting yourself in with the wrong crowd."

"Sure didn't," I agree, sending Alex my best butter-wouldn't-melt smile.

"Meera and Sasha were always good girls."

"Meera?"

"You haven't met her?" Dad asks, leading the way through the house. "I'm surprised. The two girls are generally inseparable."

"She's flat out at the bakery," I murmur. "But we caught up a week or so ago."

"When's the wedding?" It impresses me that dad has even remembered there *is* a wedding.

At my look of surprise, he grins. "I ran into Aja at the club. She was in a bit of a state about the menu."

My smile is natural. "In a couple of weeks. It's going to be quite the production."

"So I gather."

Dad moves towards the bar and Alex is watching me in that intense way he has that makes me wonder if he's decoding me fragment by fragment. "Your best friend is getting married?"

I shake my head. "No, Rajesh. Her brother."

"Darling!" Mum's smile is aimed solely at me as she walks into the lounge area. Until she enters, I don't pay the décor any attention. I can see now that she's had a busy afternoon. The table in the centre of the Arts and Craft period room is covered in a crisp white cloth. Four places have been set and an arrangement of roses sits in the centre. Classical music filters from the kitchen.

Dad uncorks the wine and passes it under his nose appreciatively. "Will you have a martini while that breathes?"

"Great, thanks," I speak for both of us, though I don't know if Alex drinks Martinis.

Mum places a tray of canapés on the top of the bar. There's prunes wrapped in bacon and miniature quiche—two of my favourites and the realisation she's made them especially brings me a wave of nostalgia. She comes to stand near me; her expression is strained. "Where did you two meet?"

"At a party Meera dragged me to."

"Ah!" Alex is remembering that night; he must have seen Meera with me. "So she's who I have to thank."

"Another party?" Mum smiles but I know there is disapproval there.

"It was low-key," I say, though it's not entirely the truth. Alex catches my eye with interest. The concern over my social life seems strange to him, obviously.

"In any event," Dad jostles our conversation away from the palpable tension. "It's been too long. I've had a whole new hedge planted in since you were last here, you know."

I hide my smile. Dad and his garden; mum and her roses. "You can show us after dinner."

Us. It slips out but it seems to swirl through the room. My mum is tense but she has had years of experience entertaining and she gestures towards the tray of nibbles. "Please, help yourselves."

"Another reason I love having you visit, Sash. Your mum doesn't cook like this for me, you know."

"You're capable of preparing a meal for yourself from time to time," Ally interrupts with a firm smile. Now when she looks in my direction her eyes flick to Alex as well. They linger on him and I sense her speculation. He is very handsome and in person his charisma is actually a tangible force. "He thinks because I have book club on a Tuesday night and leave him a marmite sandwich in the fridge he's eligible for The Most Neglected Husband award."

Their bickering is too sweet. I catch Alex's eye and we share a smile but realisation follows swiftly for me and I look away. This is not our future. Happy, affectionate teasing. Sharing laughs and grumbles in a big family home. Not even this—dinner with my parents. More than likely, this is a one-off.

"How is book club, mum?"

"Oh, you know, the usual. I think we're doing Pride & Prejudice for the eighth time."

"Don't pretend you're not thrilled," Dad interjects.

Mum reaches over and takes a just-poured martini. "Tax. For that comment."

He shrugs. "More where that came from."

"Martini or sass?"

"Can a man be sassy?" Dad ponders, lifting up the martini shaker and tossing it expertly from one hand to the other. I turn to say something to Alex and see his expression of total bemusement. It has been a long time since I've looked at Ally and Rick as an outsider but I remember that sense of sinking into a pleasantly warm bath. They were unlike anything I'd ever seen. Not once in all the time I lived here did I hear them fight the way my other parents did.

"I think technically it's roguish," Alex chimes in, his own smile setting my heart trembling.

"There. I prefer that infinitely. I like the idea of being a rogue. Sassy makes me sound like a fishwife."

I squawk. "For God's sake, dad, don't say anything more or you'll be eating dinner in the kennel."

Mum nods approvingly. "Too right. Just until you remember which side your bread is buttered on."

"Always yours, my love."

I take a martini on autopilot and sip it appreciatively. Dad adds a twist of orange with the olive; they're incredible. But potent.

"Now, you'll stay the night?" Mum asks, turning back to me.

My cheeks flush pink. Why does the fact my parents probably suspect I'm sleeping with this guy make me feel like I've broken all the rules? I'm a twenty-three-year-old woman, and I'm head over heels in love with him. It's not like I've taken up a second job as a call girl. "That'd be great, thanks."

Mum turns away but not before I see the tears in her eyes. None of her blood runs through my body but I understand her completely. This is a big moment for her. Meeting the first guy I've been serious about. She's probably hearing wedding bells, just like Meera. Is it wrong of me to have brought him here? To give them false hope? I will never settle down with a man, and even if I were to do so, it couldn't be Alex.

"Well." Dad is barely able to wipe the smile off his face. "Why don't you show Alex around, Sash?"

I reach for Alex's hand. It's hard to believe that, when I first met him, I found him impossibly intimidating.

I give him the basic tour of downstairs. It's a pretty spectacular house, with enormous windows that overlook the gardens sloping to the river. Ally has impeccable taste and she's furnished the house beautifully—a fact I didn't fully appreciate until seeing it as Alex must. We walk up the stairs and turn into the wide corridor.

"That's quite the display."

I follow his gaze to the wall that's lined with black and white photographs of me dressed in my ballet tutus. Each picture has been box-framed with the ballet shoes that correspond with that year's concert. Nine in total, though of course there should be seven more—from the years I studied with my other parents.

"I think they held high hopes I'd be *prima ballerina* material."

"And it wasn't for you?"

I wrinkle my nose as I shake my head.

"I can see you as a ballerina."

"Because I'm...vertically challenged?"

"And flexible," he winks gravely.

"I think that's gymnastics," I say with mock seriousness, earning an equally sober nod.

"So why'd you quit?"

"I didn't quit. I went to university."

He moves closer to one the younger pictures of me and I hold my breath. His eyes linger on my face and the first dart of worry shivers through me. Concern perforates me. I've learned to be wary of anyone who pays an undue amount of attention to me, especially a younger version of my current self.

"You were a cute kid."

Does he mean that? Can I take it at face value? Or is there a deeper, more concerning basis for the observation?

"Do you miss it?"

"Being cute?" I'm making light but my mind is going in every direction.

"Ballet," he laughs huskily. His eyes meet mine.

My breath is a little rushed. I shake my head and tuck my hair behind my ears as I step closer to the photo. "A little, I guess." My finger is shaking as I lift it to the picture frame. I wipe the glass, though it's dust-free.

"Have you always been such an overachiever?"

I begin to move further down the corridor. "You can talk. What, were you like eight before you'd earned your first million?"

"Twenty," he corrects without ego.

"How is that possible?"

His eyes seem to be boring lasers into mine. "I was determined not to be like him. Like them."

A shiver runs the length of my spine at his intensity.

"Poverty enslaved my childhood. I look back at those years through the grime of not being able to afford anything. There was no happiness and a lot of hunger." My heart is cracking for the boy he must have been. I stop walking and he does the same.

"I think you're amazing." I lift my hands to his face but he shies away from the comfort.

"You think I'm amazing because I recognised a skill I possessed and I turned it into a profitable exercise?"

"That simplifies things." I refuse to be pushed away. "I'm sure there was a lot of hard work involved."

"Yes." He makes the admittance as though he's angry at it. "I worked hard. Tirelessly."

"But it's determination too," I point out. "You could have accepted the cards you were dealt. Instead you changed the deck."

"Much like you," he murmurs cryptically and again my pulse fires on overdrive.

"What's that supposed to mean?"

He takes a step away from me and another until we're walking again. But I'm completely distracted. "Your life has been the complete opposite to mine." He points around the mansion, indicating the view of the moonlight river through a window before us. "Your parents dote on you, their only child. They have money. You were adored to a fault. And yet you've moved into an apartment the size of my bedroom. You've deliberately turned your back on the comforts of your life; isn't that also changing the deck?"

I swallow, relieved at his meaning. "I was given everything I could want." My cheeks flame. How can I explain to him? Ally and Rick thought they'd never have children. When they had the opportunity to adopt me, it completed their family. "Except independence. I have that now."

"Do you?" He wraps his arms around my waist, bringing me close to him. I ache to kiss him, but with us, kissing inevitably leads to more and I can imagine mum plating up our dinner downstairs. I don't think she's planning a side serving of sex with whatever elegant meal she's prepared.

"Well, more so."

"So, Miss Lewis. Do I get a peek in your bedroom or would that break the rules of the house?"

"Almost certainly," I grin. "But I won't tell if you won't."

He kisses me quickly as though he too feels the confines on our usual behaviour, before breaking the embrace. "Which way?"

I nod to my left. We walk hand in hand until we reach my door. I pause on the threshold.

"What? Is it covered in pink and fairies?" He teases, wiggling his brows at me.

"Hardly." I push the door inwards, a sense of curiosity bouncing between us. "I haven't been in here in ages. Months."

It's basically like any other room of the house. Elegantly furnished, with very few traces that distinguish it from the guest rooms. There's a pin board above the desk and most of the paper on there is mine from high school and first year uni, when I would come back every few weeks. There are photos, too, and he moves closer to them.

"Meera?" He points to a picture of us at graduation, her arm around me, our smiles broad.

"Yeah." I can't help but smile. "We were such dorks."

"Beautiful dorks," he observes softly.

"I was always so jealous of her. Isn't she stunning?"

He nods. "I suppose so." As though he hasn't noticed that she could be a supermodel. "Who's this?"

Andrew. Oh, shit. I had forgotten about that. It is a small token; a single picture of my life before that I was allowed to keep hold of. "He's just a little kid I used to babysit."

"Yeah?" He studies the picture more closely and I wonder if he's finding it easy to pick out the similarities between his youthful face and the girl in the ballet outfit downstairs. "Why do you have this picture of him?"

I turn away; it's hard for me to lie to him, remember? And every time I do, I feel a sense of anger at the boundaries of our relationship. "He's dead. I didn't feel right taking the picture down once he...when he..." I shake my head.

"How old was he?"

"In that picture?" I can't help but smile. "He was almost five. And so proud of the fact." Damn it, my voice cracks in a betraying way.

"I meant when he died."

"Oh." Goosebumps have covered my body. "It was a few months later."

"What happened?"

I spin around, and I know my face is pale because of the instant jerk of worry I see on his handsome features.

"Do you mind if we don't…"

"I'm sorry." The apology is automatic and obviously sincere. "I was allowing my curiosity to make me insensitive."

"You're always a little insensitive," I respond with a wan smile, but it's a silly joke in a moment of true pain.

"It's tragically young to die."

I nod. "Yep."

"So," he spins around my room. "This is it? No life-size pictures of Brad Pitt? Or were you more of a Leonardo DiCaprio girl?"

"Please. Try Justin Bieber."

"Oh, don't!" He clasps his hands to his chest in an exaggerated sign of pain. "And here I thought you had good taste in men."

"Dinner's ready, blackbird," my mum pokes her head around the door, and smiles at the sight of me in the middle of my old room. She waits in the corridor and as we emerge, quietly watchful. Her eyes move past us to the pinboard; her lip tightens as she sees the photo of Andrew. I understand her worry.

Alex is unaware of her tension. "Blackbird?"

"Oh, yes, well, Sashie's got such dark colouring compared to her father and me." The line is practiced but I hear the nuanced subterfuge; what isn't revealed in the statement. There are many differences between us, and all of them easily explained by our lack of biological link.

He nods, accepting it, and reaches a hand for my hair. It tangles in the ends and I smile, craning my head closer to him until he puts an arm around me and I am tucked to his side.

My mum has not spared any effort for dinner. There's roast duck, gratinated potatoes, Brussel sprouts with almonds, red cabbage and orange sauce. My absolute favourite.

"Jeez, you're really pulling out the big guns, huh?"

Alex holds the seat for me, and his manners don't go unnoticed by Rick. He watches with obvious approval as Alex joins us, taking the seat to my right.

"So, Alex. Tell us about yourself. What we don't know from the papers, I mean."

The night goes surprisingly well. I'm relaxed and enjoying myself, surrounded by three of my favourite people, when disaster almost strikes.

"And how's that American teacher you were so excited about, Sash?" Dad's chin is resting on interlaced fingers beneath his face. He can have no idea that he's stirring up a hornets' nest.

"Dr Carlton," Mum supplies unhelpfully. I feel Alex's tension ratchet up as though he's being dialled manually.

"Good," I supply, casting about for a way to shift the conversation to something less dangerous.

"You should have heard her when she found out he was going to be on the faculty. She's idolised him for years."

My cheeks are tomato-stained, I'm sure. I can't meet Alex's eyes. I look at my mum instead, beseeching her silently to change the subject. She's oblivious. "He's quite the hero to you, isn't he?"

"I wouldn't say that," I mumble, shaking my head.

"It's better than looking up to any number of pop culture idiots," Dad soothes. "So? Does the man live up to the promise?"

"And then some," Alex interjects, his smile perfectly pleasant. Only I detect the undercurrent of something darker.

"This was a delicious dinner, mum," I move the conversation along and my parents seem to accept the change in subject.

The night resumes and yet I am waiting. Waiting to be alone with Alex to see how he reacts. When finally I've helped mum clear the table and wash the dishes, Alex and dad are ensconced in conversation in dad's study. The fire is blazing, each holds a balloon glass of port. I stand in the doorway feeling oddly excluded.

Their talk seems to revolve around business, which makes perfect sense.

"Ah! Blackbird. Time to turn in?"

I nod. "For me, at least. It's been a big day."

Alex stands, unbidden. He extends a hand towards Rick. "Goodnight, sir."

"Please, call me Rick."

Alex nods before crossing to my side. I feel as though a jolt of electricity is live-wiring between us.

"Night, dad." I blow a kiss but he stands and wraps his arm around me, pressing his cheek to the top of my head.

"Thanks for coming home."

I smile at his sweetness before we leave the room.

"I'm sorry about that," I say, as soon as we are alone. The guest rooms are downstairs. I take us down the corridor instead of towards the stairs.

"For what?" But he knows. The cold reserve in his voice can only be explained by the conversation we had about Carlton.

"You know. My parents. Dr Carlton."

His sigh is impatient. "We've dealt with this issue."

It confuses me. "But you're annoyed."

"Yes." His eyes, carefully shielded from showing me what he doesn't want me to see, travel to mine. "But we have dealt with that too."

"I can't...I mean..."

"I know." He's trying. I think he's really trying to make peace with my relationship with Carlton. It means so much to me. "He's in your life. He'll probably be in your life long after I'm out of it. That's for me to deal with."

The stark reality of that comment tortures me all night. I lie in bed imagining him in the room beneath mine, and I wonder what he meant. I don't want him out of my life. Not now. Not ever. But he's right...this will end, and my focus will shift back. Won't it?

TWELVE
DEMARCATING PROGRESS AND GROWING ATTACHMENTS

The roses are beautiful, but I reach for two bunches of tulips instead—purple and white. They remind me of tall, wiry women with flamboyant hair. I pay for them, declining the offer of a bag with a shake of my head.

It is a decision I regret almost instantly when my phone begins to ring and I cannot easily reach for it. I turn down a side street and rest the bunches on a window ledge before fishing my iPhone from my back pocket. I see my mother's face and swipe the call to answer.

Sometimes I wonder if she senses my presence. Does she realise I'm here? She mustn't, for she has turned away from the safety of a main road and entered a side street. She is distracted by the phone and she is all alone. Is this the moment for which I have prepared?

"Hey!" I'm out of breath. It's cold and I wish I'd thought to bring my gloves. "Are you there?"

"Darling." Mum sounds more relaxed in the weeks since we went home. Perhaps meeting Alex was all she needed by way of reassurance.

That I am safe. But am I? There are times I look at Alex and feel so over-whelmingly terrified of what I feel for him, of what he's come to be in my life, I don't know how I'll go on without him when the time comes. "I had coffee with Aja today and she asked if we want to go to Rajesh's wedding! Isn't that delightful?"

I wrinkle my nose, imagining by now that this wedding will take up the whole of Mumbai if Aja and Meera keep issuing invites at the last minute. "Yes, quite." I turn around, pinning my back to the stone build-ing. Someone has pissed against the wall opposite, and fairly recently. It is stained dark in an arched shape and there is an odour.

"Are you going?"

"It's next weekend, I can't."

"But think how beautiful it would be. Aja says they're going to set four thousand Marigolds floating down some river, and watch them go out to sea. Can you imagine? The water will be yellow."

"Well, why don't you and dad go?" I pick up the bunches of tulips, tucking the phone under my ear.

She is going to move. This is it. I cannot delay any longer.

I run my foot back and forth over the paved ground. "But it would be so fun to do together. A spontaneous family holiday. I'm sure Alex would be welcome." The last sentence is tacked on almost against her will and I frown. She imagines us to be a normal couple. That we are at a point of taking holidays together.

"He definitely wouldn't be able to get away from work."

"So come without him."

I shake my head. "Honestly, mum, Meera did ask me but it's just not a good time. Uni is pretty full on at the moment."

She lets that sentence hang. I wait for her to say something and at the same time, I lift my head, looking out towards the street. A black cab zips past, honking his horn at a pedestrian who has crossed the street against the lights. A guy in a hoodie, walking this way. I hope he's okay.

· · ·

Fucking cab. She has seen me. I pause, pretending interest in my phone.

"Where are you? It's so loud I can hardly hear myself think."

I smile. "In Knightsbridge and it's peak hour."

"Why are you in Knightsbridge?"

"I'm on my way to Alex's."

A pause as she digests this, shooting a quick glance at my wrist watch. I'm late. I tuck the tulips across my chest, carrying them like a baby and move out of the alley way. The guy who was almost flattened by the taxi is just beside me. I send a smile of commiseration in his general direction before turning right and sweeping towards our meeting spot.

She's moving quickly and I hurry to keep up. But I am finding it difficult to breathe. Out of nowhere I am questioning this. Can I do what I must? Can I do this to her? The Sole Survivor has found a new life; should I just let old dogs lie?

"It was nice to meet him," she says thoughtfully. There are layers in the statement.

"I think he enjoyed it too."

"You're welcome to bring him whenever you come to see us," she continues in the same, slow way. She worries that if I don't feel he's welcome I will come even less often than I already do. She doesn't want to lose me.

"Thanks." I run my finger over the plastic wrap of the flowers. How can I assure her that I'm not going anywhere?

I am so close I can hear her end of the conversation. Who is she speaking to? Is it him? The man she lives with?

"Meera's here, mum."

"Oh! You didn't say you were meeting her."

I grin at my best friend and hand one of the bunches of tulips to her. She takes it and passes a coffee cup to me. Our trade is complete. Flowers for coffee; has there ever been a better swap?

"We're going to look at a possible shop for her."

"A new shop?"

"Yeah. Watch out, there'll be Bumblebee Bakeries all over the country before long."

Meera pulls a hopeful face, crossing two of the fingers that hold her coffee cup.

"What a clever girl," mum says with pride. "I'll let you go. Give her my love."

"Will do. Bye mum." I disconnect the call. My fingers are ice. Alex's apartment is only a block away and his key is somewhere in my bag. The key he gave me the day after I danced with Carlton.

I am trying not to read into this—into these milestone moments that, in a normal relationship, would demarcate progress and growing attachment. He wants me at his apartment whenever I'm not at university and I want to be there with him. Having a key makes sense, that's all. But I am unsure of what expectations govern its use. I think, for a moment, about inviting Meera up to see it. Not because I want to show off his apartment but because I want to bring her into this part of my life. I want her to be a part of it.

Somehow that will make it more real.

"Come on. Show me the site of the soon-to-be hottest new eatery in London." I am a magician and am able to hold my flowers and coffee in one hand, enabling me to sip and link an arm through Meera's. Her warmth breathes life into me.

"No way," she shakes her head, hair flouncing as she looks at me for a long minute. "Not before you explain yourself, madam."

"Sure. What for?"

"You've taken this guy to meet your parents? Ally and Rick have actually got to cast an eye over your mystery man before your best friend?" She is joking, pretending to be annoyed, but I think beneath that she truly is a little offended. "Am I not like a sister to you?"

"How did you even know? Have you got spies all over the place?" Though of course I can guess.

"Virtually." She wiggles her eyebrows at me. "My mother. Your mother. You know they talk."

"More than us at the moment," I say almost apologetically. "It just sort of happened."

"And? Did they like him? Did he like them?"

I think of Alex and his impossible-to-read reactions. My shoulders lift as if carried by the breeze. I sip my coffee, searching for the words. "Mum has said he's welcome to come back again, so that's something."

Meera's laugh is sweet. She understands Ally's paranoias even without knowing what is at the root of them. Her friendship is one I will always, always be grateful for.

"So tell me about the new shop. Will you be based there more than in Marble Arch?"

She shakes her head. "No, no, no. We'll get to that. But seriously, you took this guy home to meet your parents?"

And I am grinning now in an uncontainable way, because I want to talk about Alex whenever I can. It is a novelty for me to have something in my life that I can actually share.

But how can I possibly explain to Meera what it is that binds us? That we are not simply in love, that it's more a question of coexisting.

"I feel like," I search for the words. She is waiting for me to say something romantic and profound. "He can make me come just by looking at me."

She bursts out laughing, a snort escaping with her amusement. "Seriously?"

"It's more than that, though," I add gently. And then, because honesty is such a relief, "I feel...I'm scared I've forgotten how to live without him."

Some time later, Meera has sucked every bit of factual information out of me that she possibly can. I am embarrassed to realise that I know very little of the hard and fast facts she seeks. But it doesn't matter.

"I can't explain it," I say quietly, as we stop walking on the corner of a busy intersection. "I don't know the boring stuff, but I know him. And I love him, Meera. I love him with everything I am."

She raises her brows and finishes her coffee, then stares at me thoughtfully. "Then you'd better introduce me to him, hmm?"

I don't plan to, but after we've inspected her could-be premises (which are amazing) we are on a high. I message Alex:

What time will you be back at your apartment?

The little dots appear to show that he is typing and his response is almost immediate. *Not late. Why?*

I think about it, watching as Meera weaves through a Tesco express, a bottle of wine in one hand and a big bag of crisps in the other.

I thought I'd catch up with Meera. I'll be out a while, so don't rush back.

Dots appear and then disappear. He is thinking and that makes me smile.

Finally, *Do you want to go to my place for a while? We could have dinner together.* And then, in a separate bubble, *I'd like to meet her.*

Fuck. It's another step, another something new, and my heart kicks up a notch.

Okay. Great. It sounds calm, off-handed, but that's the opposite of how I feel.

Meera emerges, waving the Prosecco in the air. "Let's celebrate."

"You don't want to wait until you sign the lease?"

She shakes her head. "Life's too short to wait."

Don't I know it? I clutch both bunches of tulips and she our makeshift picnic. "Alex is …" I blush as I try to tell her my exciting news without seeming like I'm completely losing the plot. "Alex suggested we go back to his place. He'll join us for dinner."

Meera grins. "You mean I get to meet your secret lover *and* decide to expand my business all in one day? Talk about excitement."

I've come to Alex's often enough to see it now just as 'his place', but when Meera enters, I am reminded of how I felt the first time I stepped across the threshold into this ridiculously luxe penthouse, with floor to ceiling windows and an interior that's all greys and muted creams, with dull gold highlights, such as the chandelier that hangs overhead. Not only that, everything is *big*, which is the opposite of most living spaces in London, that have to be squeezed into old buildings and just made to work. His apartment has double height ceilings—made possible because he bought two stories of the building and amalgamated them to create this sanctuary. The bedrooms are enormous and his study is state of the art with some of the best views in the house. Naturally, Meera appreciates his kitchen most of all, with the range of top of the line appliances including a double width, french door fridge.

I place the flowers in a vase still in their paper, and add Farrah's to it to keep their stalks happy, then pop the bottle.

The champagne is still ice cold. Ensconced in Alex's living room, we drink it slowly at first, savouring the dry coldness of it, celebrating Meera's developments.

"What have you decided to do about the wedding?"

She pulls a face. "I'll go for the whole time. I've been able to get on a flight with mum, tomorrow."

"And the shop?"

"Rafael is determined he can handle it."

"Great. I'm sure he'll be up to it. I'll go in every day if you want me to check on things."

She smiles. "And buy a salted caramel cupcake?"

I take another sip of Prosecco. "Look, it's a tough job, but for you, Meera, I'll do it."

"Oh," she snaps her hand against her thigh. "Remember when you were over the other day?"

"And he'd sent your desk into wild disarray?"

She purses her lips. "He swears it wasn't him. How weird is that?"

Out of nowhere, a shiver runs down the length of my spine, and back up for good measure. "Really? So what do you think happened?" My voice is measured, though a little higher in pitch than is normal. This has nothing to do with me. Bad things happen—weird things happen—all the time. The picture probably did just break or get misplaced.

"Who knows? A nosy customer?"

My heart is so loud I can hear it in my ears. Thud, thud, thud. Walls come out of nowhere; they're squashing me. "Are you going to call the police?"

Meera looks bemused. "No, it's not worth it. There's any number of things that could have happened. I've been so busy lately, I may have shifted the picture myself and forgotten."

I nod, but it doesn't seem likely. There is something strange happening inside of me. Is this what a stroke feels like?

I am barely able to concentrate through the rest of the bottle. I drink faster than I should, and I feel it go to my head. Worries are fraying at my mind. All I can think is, 'is this because of me?' It is a long bow to draw, but those that killed my family are not good people. They are determined and they are malicious. Have I put Meera at risk by being her friend? Is it possible they've found me?

I'm being ridiculous egocentric, I know, but such is the worry that has been with me for so long. I've spent a lifetime looking over my shoulder, waiting for some sign that I've been found: what if this is it?

But surely Meera's right and it's just a bizarre string of coincidences. A nosy customer, the frame got knocked, they took it away because they felt guilty? Or maybe Rafael felt bad and was lying?

I am in the bathroom when Alex returns. I hear them speaking and move quickly. I step out into the living room and he is so beautiful and Meera is so beautiful that for a moment I am struck by what a stunning couple they would make. It's a red herring. Because he's mine, and I am his, and this is the first time I've had someone I love that I am introducing Meera to.

His eyes meet mine and there is no longer anyone else in the room. My breath burns in my throat as he walks towards me. His suit is perfect on his frame; his eyes show amusement.

"Hi."

All my worries ebb away. Alex is here. I am safe. This is reality. The rest is just a hangover from childhood fears.

"Hi yourself." He presses a chaste kiss to my mouth that leaves me hungering for more then reaches down for my hand.

"Well, ladies? Would you like to stay in or eat out?"

"Eat in," I say, glad that they're meeting but not wanting to prolong this night. Or rather, wanting to fast forward to when I am alone with him again.

"My thoughts exactly. Meera?" I am pleased with his consideration of her.

"Sure." Meera is watching us like a hawk and I blush a little.

"Why don't you have a seat and I'll bring you a cocktail?"

I arch a brow and wonder if I should tell him that I'm already three sheets to the wind. Meera has accepted for us though. I follow behind her until we are on the sofa. She sits beside me so that she can whisper more easily. "Oh, my, God."

My smile is echoed through my body. "Yeah?"

"Ummm, he is seriously divine."

"Tell me about it." He appears with a martini for each of us. I note he has nothing for himself, but takes the seat opposite.

"I understand you've been friends a long time?"

Meera is a straight-shooter. With me, at least. I see all sides of her, and I know she is always herself. But in front of Alex, she becomes the version of herself that I have only seen on a few occasions. She's shy and it makes her incredibly quiet and polite. "Yes, we've known one another since Sash moved into the area."

"When was that?" He prompts.

I sip the martini, happy to ride this wave and enjoy the moment.

"How old were you, darling?" Meera presses a finger to her cheek. "Ten?"

I nod.

"We live a street over. My parents went to welcome Rick and Ally to the neighbourhood—,"

"Meera's parents are the community welcome van," I interject. "They are honestly the nicest people you'll ever meet."

"They're pretty sweet," Meera agrees. "Anyway, Sash was reading up a tree. Do you remember?" She turns to smile at me. "And she was such a bitch."

I burst out laughing, almost choking on my martini. "I was not."

"Yeah, you were. You used to sulk up a storm." Meera grinned over the rim of her glass. "But I'm nothing if not persistent."

"Well, that's true." I try to remember that summer when we met but it is an age ago, and I have spent so long trying to forget. My mind cannot penetrate the memories that have formed, brick by brick, a wall around that time in my life. Naturally, I didn't want a new friend, or a new family. I didn't even really want to be alive, if being alive meant living with the memories of that night, of living without my mother and father and brother. Rebuffing Meera's friendship overtures wasn't conscious but it was natural.

Alex stands and I watch him, my stomach clenching achingly as he moves powerfully towards the kitchen. I'm confused but a moment later he is opening a door. Four people appear, all dressed in white shirts and black pants.

"Dinner," he explains, returning to us.

Meera doesn't bat an eyelid. She is enjoying reliving memories of that first summer—the long, warm days that marked the start of our friendship. I am watching the cyclone in the kitchen. A table is laid with a fresh white cloth, flowers are placed and wonderful, foodie smells abound.

When Meera excuses herself to use the bathroom, I stare at him, agog. "I thought you meant you'd bring takeaway?"

"This is takeaway."

"From the Ritz?" I murmur in disbelief.

"The Astrid. Why?"

My jaw drops. I feel like a cartoon. I want to reach for it and push it back into place. "You didn't need to do this. We like greasy Thai food."

"I think you'll like this more."

"Yeah, I'll bet we will." I furrow my brow. "But honestly, it's too much. You understand I generally live on a shoestring?"

He nods, and stands, prowling towards me (it's the only word for it). His hands reach for mine and I stand without realising I'm doing it. Closer to his face, my breath is now rushed. I want to take him to bed. I want to kiss him all over.

"Tell me about your shoestring," he invites, his hands latched behind my back.

"What about it?"

"Your parents are obviously extremely comfortable." He moves back to a sofa but pulls me with him, so that I'm sitting on his lap. "They don't support you?"

I eye him cautiously but his proximity is intoxicating. Between his touch and the alcohol I've consumed I am floating high above the grey clouds of London. "You think it's their job to support me?"

That interests him. "You don't?"

"Are we going to bounce the same questions back and forth all night?"

He grins. "I can think of better ways to pass the time with you."

"Yeah, me too," I mumble. My eyes lift to the door; there's no sign of Meera.

"So?" He prompts.

I am pretty sure it's my question and that he's tricked me into answering it, but I answer. "I love my parents. And you're right. They're generous as fu—," an afternoon with Meera has left me realising how frequently I push the 'F' word into service. I switch at the last minute. "As hell."

He nods encouragingly, a cryptic smile on his features as he realises that I've censored myself.

"But I don't want them to waste their money on me."

He nods thoughtfully. "Do you think it's a waste?"

I frown. "I don't need it, so yes."

"So you don't use their support at all?"

I shake my head. I am actually really proud of the fact that I haven't touched a penny of my allowance. "I've saved everything they've given me over the last four years. When I graduate I plan to write them a cheque."

I expect him to smile but instead he stares at me as though...as though...I don't know what it is. If I didn't know better I would say he was looking at me as though he loved me with every bone in his body.

"Why?"

I tilt my head. And while I'm thinking he leans forward and kisses my nose. It is unexpectedly sweet. I am a little drunk anyway but this makes thought impossible.

"They obviously want to support you."

"Yeah, but that's silly. I mean, how many people my age have parents who are happy to pay their way?"

"So this is generational solidarity?" He hazards.

"That makes it sound a bit more grandiose than it is."

"I'm trying to get to the bottom of that," he says with mock impatience.

"I know why." Meera is back. She sits opposite us and smiles brightly. "You just have to understand Sash to get it."

"Oh?" He prompts. I understand him so well that I know he doesn't appreciate her comment, even when it's off-handed. The implication that perhaps he doesn't know me best in the world sits awkwardly around him.

"Ally and Rick smothered Sash. She had everything she could ever want in life except the ability to go out on her own and do her own thing. It's a hard-fought freedom and she doesn't want to taint it."

"Ding! Ding! Ding! A hundred quid to the beauty in the front row." Oh no. I realise I'm actually drunk because I think I'm hilarious when no one else laughs. And there's still a whole dinner to get through.

I put my martini down and resolve to swap to water.

The food is exquisite, yet all I can think of is him. I watch as they talk and I wonder about how this would work if we were an actual, bonafide couple. Would we see Meera regularly? Would they become friends?

Hours pass in the blink of an eye, but eventually, Meera yawns. "I have to go."

I make small sounds of demur. They are token and we all know it. She winks at me. "I'll call you tomorrow." She skirts around the table and pulls her collection of tulips from the vase I nestled them into earlier in the night.

"Talk then." I follow her to the door. "Well?" I whisper, though I think I'm still drunk and it comes out as a hoarse shout.

"I'll call you tomorrow." Then, glancing over my shoulder, "Night, Alex. Thanks again for dinner."

He nods his response and Meera smiles at me.

"Text me when you get home," I remind her—a ritual of ours, formed from a promise we made our mothers when we moved to London.

For a slight woman, she can really handle her alcohol. I watch her swan away from the apartment as though she is stone cold sober. Whereas I, on the other hand, am completely silly.

"I have a question for you." I hiccough a bit. He watches me as I sashay in what I hope to be a sexy fashion across the room.

"Yeah?"

"Uh huh." I hold my arms out, my wrists touching. "Remember how you used your belt to tie me up that time."

His laugh is throaty. "I remember everything about that."

I grin. "I really liked it."

He arches a brow but doesn't move. I slip my arms around his neck, straddling him, sitting on his lap. "Yeah?"

I nod.

One of his hands snakes up and his fingers surround a wrist. "You're tired." He employs a euphemism for drunk and I'm touched.

"Not too tired." I smile at him. My eyes are blinking in what he might construe as an attempt at seduction but is, in fact, sheer exhaustion. "Is it something you like to do?"

He is still and then he sighs. "Yes." He stands up, dislodging me easily, then scooping me up against his chest. "And you need to sleep."

I protest most of the way to the bedroom, but by the time he crosses the threshold, I'm asleep.

Thirteen
The whisperings of the Past

I deserve the hangover that stalks me the next day. It is cranky and grizzly, just like me. I nurse it through several attempts at meals until the afternoon when finally it and I succumb to a bowl of cereal.

My hangover eventually parts ways with me and I shower to celebrate. I foam my flesh, covering it in the citrus soap Alex has on hand, washing away the memories of the night before. They are not bad memories, yet I wish to cleanse them; to purge them.

I can't say why. Something is chafing at the edge of my mind.

I dress up. My clothes are beautiful and I've been neglecting them. I choose a black Donna Karan dress with long sleeves. It is made from wool and falls to my knees. It was another gift from Ally—my budget doesn't extend to designer.

I rub moisturiser all over my just-shaved legs and I curl my hair so that it sits around my face with disarray. I have applied make up, too. The bare minimum to make me look like I'm attempting to be fashionable. It is something I used to do often that I have recently neglected, and dressing with the intention of surprising Alex pleases me.

I have many ideas for how best to achieve that. Yet when he arrives, I am so engrossed in an article in the newspaper that I don't even hear him.

The first I know, he is standing over me, smiling at me with wonder, sexual heat and confusion.

"Are you going somewhere?"

I close the paper; my cheeks flush. "Yes. Or rather we are."

"Oh?" His hands are reaching for my hips and I suck in a deep breath the minute he makes contact. I briefly question the wisdom of my suggestion.

"I was thinking we should go out tonight."

He doesn't skip a beat. "Go out? Doesn't that break the rules?"

Does that mean he doesn't want to? Or is he employing the same bag of self-preservation tricks that I usually have on hand? "Somewhere low-profile. There's a sushi place nearby."

He looks less than convinced; I don't know if it's because I've suggested going out, or because he doesn't want sushi.

"Or we can go somewhere else. What do you feel like?"

And the look he gives me is pure sexual anticipation. "What do you think?"

My tummy squeezes and my knees grow weak; I fear they may buckle any moment.

"Alex—," I lift a hand and clutch his lapel. "I want to go out. With you." *Like a normal couple.*

"We'll go out," he promises, his mouth seeking mine.

My hands push at his buttons. It is inevitable now; we will be together. "Where?" I'm not asking about a dinner destination and he knows it.

"Anywhere you want."

"Your room." It's a challenge I hadn't known I wanted to make.

He doesn't balk. He kisses me, half-pushing, half-leading me to the bedroom we always share.

"No, *your* room," I clarify.

He changes direction after the smallest pause, understanding instantly what I need from him.

"Why don't we sleep here?" I can hardly speak for the urgency of our kiss. Our hands bump as we race to undress one another.

"I don't want to sleep."

"I didn't mean now. I mean, in general. Why don't we sleep here?"

The words are punctuated by our rushed breaths.

"Because." His hands push my shoulders so that I fall backwards to the bed. "Have you really only been with one other guy?"

It is a question out of left-field but I answer it directly. I nod, my eyes seeking his.

"Fuck." He kisses me so hard and I want him with all of me.

"I just never…"

"Don't. Don't even dare apologise."

"I wasn't going to."

His lips trace lower, kissing the sensitive flesh of my neck. "You're so sexual."

"Only with you."

"I want to show you…I want you to feel everything that you can. I want to pleasure you, Sash, so that you never forget me."

Forget me. The implication of facing life without him at some point wounds me deeply but his kiss and his touch push away anything but sensual heat. "You do pleasure me."

He shakes his head and pulls at my shirt fiercely, popping the buttons. "Not enough." He takes a nipple in his mouth and I'm on the brink of collapse when I push at his chest, lifting him off me.

"Wait." My cheeks are flushed; I can feel the heat of his arousal. And I'm embarrassed and I'm shy but I say the words that are swimming through my brain. "Stop."

Instantly he lifts higher, giving me breathing space. "What is it?"

"I want to…I want to pleasure you."

"At the risk of serving as your mimic, you do pleasure me."

"Not enough," I tease, and I push up to sitting and then stand.

He follows suit out of curiosity and I unbutton his pants, sliding them down his legs. They're strong legs, well-muscled and tanned. He wears a simple pair of black underpants.

When I kneel before him, he stiffens. "Sasha, I don't think…"

"Yes?" I flick his underwear down his legs and bring my mouth within a millimetre of his shaft.

"Don't…"

"I've never done this before." Kneeling on the floor, my knees pressing into the carpet, I push his thighs until he connects with the wall behind him. I am right there, my mouth never more than an inch from his dick. "I want to make you feel like I do."

"You don't know what you're saying."

"Teach me," I whisper. "Tell me what you like."

"Fuck. Please stop," He groans. "You need to stop being so perfect. You're everything I want and I can't do it. Just...stop."

"I'll make you a deal." I tilt my head to look up at him.

"Yeah?"

"Give me thirty seconds. If you're not enjoying it then I'll stop straight away. Okay?"

His nod is like a tortured concession and I don't let a beat of time pass. I open my mouth wide and take him deep into my throat, slicking him with my moist warmth and letting my muscles wrap around him. But I have no idea what I'm doing. I tease his tip with my tongue but still it feels counterintuitive. Until his fingers tangle in my hair, and he pulls at my head, moving me back and forward along his length, so that I'm taking him deep into my mouth and then releasing him.

The way he's moving my head is driving my wild; I feel my own core heat to molten lava stage and I dig my nails into his legs. He's so deep in my mouth I feel my throat muscles close up a little and he senses it. He pulls out, waiting for me to give him the okay. I want more.

"I want you to own me," I say simply. And God, it's true. I want him everywhere, any way, I just want to have him in me. It's the most basic of needs and honestly, I'm ashamed of it, but I would do whatever he wanted of me.

His fingers are rough on my head; he knows I like it. He's deep in my mouth, his back against the wall but his hips can't help thrusting. God, he's making love to my mouth. It's overwhelming but I desperately don't want it to stop.

I taste the hint of his essence and I wonder how far this will go, how far I'm willing for it to go, when he pulls out and presses himself back against the wall, his face tortured as he stares over my head.

I bring my mouth closer but his hands are still in my hair and he's holding me back. "Sasha—," I have never heard my name like that. It's an animalistic cry.

"I want to," I promise, not really knowing what I'm saying.

"Not now." He closes his eyes and his breathing is tortured. I can only guess that he is close to releasing himself and the idea of doing so into my virginal mouth worries him. If I'm honest, it worries me too. I like having him, tasting him, but I'm not sure about going all the way.

"Fuck me then," I beg, standing up and leaning over, bracing myself on the bed and presenting my arse to him. I want him to take me; I'm aching to feel him.

He groans as he enters me, as though it's against his will and willpower. But I don't care. I'm so, so, so fucking aroused. Taking him in my mouth has set every fibre of my body on fire.

He moves hard inside of me and I cry out as he finally comes; I feel him explode and follow after, my body vibrating with emotion as I coax that pleasure from him.

I'm covered in a fine sheen of perspiration. I drop my head against my forearm and laugh into the dark room. "I've changed my mind. Let's go back to plan A. Let's never go out."

"Fine by me." His fingers move over my lower back, needling, massaging, delighting.

"I will never understand how you have stayed so sheltered sexually."

He's still inside of me. I don't want to break our connection yet I long to face him. He knows, as he always does, what I am thinking before I have express it. He pulls out and cradles me to him in a single manoeuvre, so that we fall to the bed as one.

He holds me against his chest; I hear his raging heart and it echoes my own.

"I told you, it wouldn't have been easy for me..."

"Sure, in high school." He waves aside the assertion. "But in the last few years? There's got to have been more than one man who's been of interest to you."

"Nope." I am tired. I am satiated. And my eyes are heavy.

Silence hangs over us. It is soothing and settling. I am almost asleep when he shifts a little beneath me.

"Are you hungry?"

"Not really."

"What if I told you we could order in anything you want?"

"Except sushi," I murmur sleepily.

His laugh turns my tummy. I wrap my arm over his chest, hugging him. I don't want this moment to end.

"I'll surprise you." He eases out from beneath me and places a lightweight blanket across my legs. "Sleep, beautiful. I'll wake you when it's time to eat."

And he kisses my forehead so gently that I smile, perched as I am on the brink of sleep and wakefulness.

My dream is fragmented.

My parents (the real ones), oozing blood. Only it's not red and goopy as it was in real life. It's golden and it sparkles a little. When I reach down to shake my mother awake, my hand bursts with starlight. And her eyes flicker open, meeting mine reassuringly.

"It's okay, Bianca. Everything's okay."

In my dream, I breathe out an enormous sigh of contentment and relief. My father sits up and rubs his hand over my hair. It is only later that I see it too is covered in golden blood.

"Where's Andy?"

"Playing on the swings."

I move to their window—the enormous bay that overlooks the play equipment in our heavily fortified backyard. It's no longer daytime. The sky is dark grey with a bleak sun pushing through it, and it's eerily silent. It reminds me, in my dream, a little of the opening scene of Terminator Two. You know the one? The post-apocalyptic playground with the screeching, spinning equipment.

I focus on the swings that are moving slowly in sync with one another. Andrew isn't there at first. But after a moment my eyes adjust and I see him. A tiny little skeleton with that red baseball cap he always wears. He's just a collection of bones, but when he turns his face to look at me I see his eyes in the sockets. And they're loaded with accusation.

"You didn't help me."

I scream, but the glass is too thick and the window won't budge. "I wanted to!" I shout, tears running down my cheeks at the futility of it all. "I wanted to!"

"You didn't help me."

I wake, and he is watching me. Not Andrew. Not my poor, dead brother.

Alex.

I sit bolt upright, self-conscious, and lift my hands to my face. My cheeks are boiling hot and my face is wet. "I had a nightmare," I mumble, by way of explanation.

"A bad one apparently."

He's dressed again, in a pair of casual jeans and a black shirt.

"Was I asleep long?"

He shakes his head. "Only half an hour or so. What was it about?"

"I don't remember," I lie.

He knows I'm covering but lets it go. "Dinner's ready."

I had little appetite before I slept. Now? My stomach is twisting painfully. "Great. I'll be right out."

He walks across the room and sits on the edge of the bed. It depresses a little with his weight. "What is it, Sash? What are these nightmares you have?"

I know then that it's not my first time; that he's witnessed this before.

"I've always had crazy dreams," I dismiss. "What are we eating?"

His eyes probe mine, watching, holding. "You wanted sushi, right?"

He stands up and holds out a hand for me. I take it, feeling more connected to the Here and Now when we touch. "Give me a minute to get dressed."

"Is that really necessary?"

I offer a small smile but it doesn't resonate in my spirit and the way he kisses me gently on my forehead tells me that he knows—I need to be alone to centre myself, to push aside the dream and its last tangential grip on me. I dress quickly, into a pair of yoga pants and t-shirt. No underwear.

When I enter the dining room I see he's ordered a small feast from a high-end sushi place on Kings Road. Two trays show several choices of sushi and there are a couple of glasses of white wine at either setting.

He gestures towards one spot. The moment I sit down, I hear the strains of my phone.

"That could be mum." I offer an apologetic smile. "Do you mind?"

"Of course not," he says, his manner impossible to decipher. He takes his own seat and lifts his wine contemplatively, watching as I move from the room. I trace the sound of the ringing to the foyer, where I hastily deposited my handbag near the front door at some point in the last two days. I think when I came in with Meera the night before.

Speak of the devil, it is Meera's face that blinks up at me from my iPhone screen. "Hi," I answer breathlessly, guilt assailing me.

"Hey."

"Where are you?" I flick a glance at my watch. She was due to fly out early that morning. "Have you landed?"

"Just got through customs. Waiting for my bag. Look," she pauses while an announcement is made over the loud speaker. "It's going to be crazy and I'm not going to get much time to call. Wedding's are a serious business, remember."

I smile, imagining how beautiful it will be. I know Meera is excited, too, for all she pretends it's inconvenient. "Make sure you send me pictures, okay?"

"I will. Sash, about Alex..."

I brace for it. She is my best friend and I want her to like him. I need her to like him because if she doesn't, I will have to find a way to juggle them in my life. "Yeah?"

"He seems...nice," she pauses and I laugh.

Nice is not the first word I would use to describe Alex.

"But?"

"I just don't know about the two of you. I don't know if he's *right* for you." She is my best friend. She knows me; she understands me. She will protect me even now as I am so madly in love that I really don't want to hear what she's saying. That is her job and it is a sacred one. I would do the same for her.

I sit down on the step and it's then that I see it. The white paper. It's a simple act of curiosity, isn't it? To pick up a piece of paper and flick it over? How many times have you done that? Whether in your own home or at a cinema; it's human nature to wonder.

I reach for it on autopilot, listening to Meera as I unfold its centre.

Sasha, we need to speak. Meet me after your last class tomorrow. Don't mention this to another soul. It's about Bianca.

My fingers are trembling and my eyes water. Adrenalin fills my mouth with its tell-tale metallic taint.

"Sash? Did you hear me?"

I feel like I might vomit. Did my dream do this? Did it somehow conjure up the spectre of my past, bringing it into reality anew?

"No." I shake my head, my temperature racing from over-heated to freezing cold. "I...Meera, I have to call you back."

"Oh, come on. I don't want this to turn into a thing. Don't be mad."

"I'm not mad, I promise." It's hot. And I'm cold. And my legs hurt, like all the blood has left them, or maybe there's too much blood pooling in them, I don't know.

Perhaps there is something in my voice that calls to him; or maybe he just *feels* that I am distressed. He steps inside the foyer at that moment, a glass of wine in one hand and his other thrust casually into his pocket.

"Nothing." The paper drops from my hand and I scramble to catch it. Though he doesn't move, his eyes follow the gesture and I know then that my secret will no longer be safe.

Panic surges through me; adrenalin spikes. I reach for the note, clasping it in my fist.

"Sash? Honey? What is it?" Meera's voice is worried, but almost drowned out by background airport noise.

I shake my head. "I....It's nothing. I...Look, we'll talk when you get back. Love to the family."

I disconnect the call and have no clue what to do next. I am immobilised by confusion and worry.

"Sasha?" He strides towards me and kneels at my feet. It's inappropriate given what I've just read, yet I am reminded of how I knelt before him only a short while earlier. And my mood then had been so sensually buoyant compared to this state of utter dismay. I had felt unbreakable; defiant.

"I'm fine," I lie unconvincingly. "We should eat." As if I could. I shake my head and stare at my phone. Should I call my mother? Ally? Or would it give her a heart attack?

"What are you holding?"

I contemplate, for only a moment, not handing it over. But his expression brooks no argument and in truth I want to lean on him. To show him, in the hope that he might fix this.

He scans the note and frowns. "This doesn't mean anything to me." His eyes lift to my pale, pale face. "But obviously it does to you. Explain."

I swallow and shake my head. "I can't." My voice cracks and I realise that, like it, I am close to breaking point.

"Explain," he prompts again, taking the space beside me on the carpeted entrance step.

"You don't understand. I really, honestly can't."

"Who is Bianca?"

Tears glisten in my eyes. I can't properly put into words what a strange occurrence it is to have this man, the man I have fallen head over heels in love with, use the name that my real parents gave me. A name I have long since relegated to my firmly inaccessible past.

My breath is coming in fits and spurts.

"Who is Bianca?"

More deep breathing. "I need to go."

I stand up but he follows and places himself between me and the door. "No. What you need to do is tell me what the hell is going on."

"It's not something I can tell," I snap, angry and terrified in equal measure. Where can I go? Not to Ally and Rick. If someone has found me then I cannot lead them to my parents. Oh, God. Unless that's how they found me. And Meera! I think of the picture and a new fear moves through me. Thank God she's far away. Surely in India she is safe from this madness? The thought of having put her in any kind of danger makes me want to vomit.

"I need to call mum." I have left my phone on the floor and when I scoop down to pick it up my fingers are skittish. I can hardly find her number, because it's so difficult to coordinate movement.

He takes the phone from me easily.

"Alex." It's a warning and a plea.

"I'll help you," he says softly. "I'll help you."

I shake my head. I'm trembling all over.

"Who is Bianca? What does this note mean?"

"They've found me." My eyes are enormous in my face as I stare at him.

"Who has found you?"

"I don't know what to do."

"For God's sake, Sasha. Stop mumbling and give me something concrete to work with."

I flinch at his demand. I am scared and I am worried and it dawns on me that the note was here, at Alex's house. "They know I'm seeing you. That photo in the papers. The photo at Meera's. I'm being hunted."

He nods. "You're Bianca."

I brush aside the statement. I'm not interested in helping him understand. I'm talking aloud, but for my benefit alone. I need to make sense of this turn of events. "They know I'm here and they know about you."

Alex is big. And is strong. But so was my birth father and they killed him so easily.

"You're not safe."

His expression is impossible to comprehend; I have not seen this reaction in him before.

"I don't give a shit about my safety. What's going on? What do you need?"

"I need to get out of here."

"Fine. I'll take you..."

"No." I shake my head urgently. "I don't think you should come." I am walking in circles and talking in them too. "I think it's better for you if I go. I mean, I don't think they'd hurt you if...I don't know. I don't know. It's me they want. Not you."

"Stop and listen to me a moment." He grips my shoulders, just hard enough to make me stop mumbling and focus on his beautiful face. "Haven't you worked it out by now?"

I shake my head. "Worked what out?"

"You're not getting rid of me. Whatever trouble you're in, I'm with you." He wraps his arms around me, the embrace instantly empowering me. "If you're worried about something, I want to fix it."

It's not the first time he's said that. I remember then that day in the café, so long ago now, when he'd caught me frowning and promised just that. I shake my head. "You can't fix this. I have to go"

He's exasperated and he interrupts. "How long do you think it's been since I gave a shit about anything other than you? You're not leaving me. And you sure as hell aren't going to walk away from me now, when you obviously need me."

"Alex—,"

"I am with you," he rides over the top of my objection. "Got it?"

Fourteen
Years of Carelessness Coming Home to Roost

There are dark forces at work. I have long since desired that they didn't exist and yet that was a childish wish; one I ought never have given myself over to. I have become lax. I have forgotten to take care and be observant. All of the lessons that at one time cloaked me like a shield are discarded and recent years of carelessness are now coming home to roost.

"Here." Alex wraps a blanket around my shoulders, his eyes wary as he studies my shivering frame. And I can't stop shivering. The shaking is as involuntary as it is uncontrollable.

"Thank you." My teeth chatter. Where is the cold coming from? Perhaps the adrenalin that is spiking through me.

He doesn't answer. He is grim. It is another of his silences that I don't recognise.

"Where are we going?" London is passing quickly. I presume he has conveyed some of the sense of urgency to his driver.

"My office."

"Oh." Despite this sense of panic, I am still myself enough to be curious at this idea. A spectre of a visit to the place in which he spends so much time can't help but poke a hole through my temporary brain fog.

"So you and Bianca are one and the same," he murmurs with a deep, husky voice.

I am too shell-shocked to obfuscate. I nod, my eyes not meeting his.

"Fine. How long have you been Sasha for?"

I don't answer.

"Who wrote this?" He holds up the note; I didn't realise he was still holding it. I frown. He's slipped it into a plastic zip lock bag. When did he do that? I have a fuzzy dark patch in my memory of that night. I remember fragments but so many of them are missing. There is my mother's blood, my brother's cries, and voices that are frightening and foreign. Voices that shout. There are doors being opened and slammed shut again. They are looking for me but I am safe in my hiding spot, so close to where my mother is dying.

My shivers are getting stronger. He realises and wraps his arms around me, holding me tight to his strong, warm chest.

His office is in Canary Wharf. The car glides through London's ancient streets and across its sludgy, fast-moving life-blood river, burying us in a cacophony of high-rises and bright lights. His car park is underground; we are swallowed into the bowels of the earth and I imagine the tube trains scurrying around us, buffeted by the thick, dark concrete walls.

The driver opens the door and I smile at him out of habit. What a pathetic sight I must make though. My hair is still messed from being made love to, my eyes are red-rimmed from crying and my slender frame is shrouded in a big, grey blanket.

I am tired yet simultaneously utterly energised, as though my life depends on rational thought and action.

On the back wall of the car park there is a large metallic sign. It exclaims elegantly: LaMar Corp.

He holds up his phone to the elevator panel and the lights flash green; presumably meaning he has freedom to access any floor he chooses. His finger presses the second to top button and we sail up, up, up, into the sky. To my surprise, once we lift from the basement levels, one side of the elevator is wrapped in thick glass that shows the impressive visage of Canary Wharf by night. What is it about big cities that offer a sense of solidarity and safety even in moments such as this? I feel the excitement of the surrounds and try my hardest to focus on their beauty alone. Not on the note tucked into his pocket and whomever penned it.

The office is dark, but for the faint illumination cast by lamps on the wall. He doesn't bother to switch any other lights on. He grabs my hand and pulls me down the corridor a little way then through an enormous set of timber doors.

"Your office?"

"Yes." He waves towards a sofa. "Sit."

I ignore his commandment and walk instead to the huge windows that show off that impressive view.

The room we are in, where he spends his long days, is enormous—many times the size of my studio flat. The sky sparkles from every direction of the panoramic view. His desk is in the centre, and there is a conference table as well as two leather chesterfield sofas.

An enormous, very flat television hangs on one of the walls.

"I need Renway, Smith and Langham."

This means nothing to me so I turn to query him then see the phone under his chin. His face glows in the faint light thrown from his iMac screen.

Curious, I move closer. I am still shaking but I have become used to it now. The screen is black, filled with green writing. He types quickly, his brow furrowed.

It is the first time I really see him as a tech billionaire. He is so strong and sexy, that in my mind he exists purely in that facet. But behind his desk, in his office at the heart of the empire he has built out of the ruins of a tragic childhood, I see him as the rest of the world must: a true Goliath.

Reassurance surges through me. He is an incredible person. And he's on my side.

A grainy black and white image blinks onto the screen. I recognise his hallway immediately.

"What is this?" I lean closer. The blanket he placed around my shoulders drops and I don't bother to pick it up.

"Security."

"You have footage of your apartment."

"Just the entrance, yes."

I see myself appear on the screen. It's from days earlier. "That's not today."

"No." He lifts his mobile off the desk and presses the screen. "It's not."

"What's on there?" I nod toward his phone.

"Usually a feed to my security cameras."

"Usually? And not now?" This seems particularly ominous.

"Not now," he confirms. I must look even worse than I had previously thought because he lifts his eyes to me and startles a little. "Sit down." Perhaps knowing I'm about to object, he doesn't attempt to direct me towards the bank of couches. He holds his desk chair out for me and purely by virtue of the fact it's at the heart of his command centre I sit into it.

"Why not now?" I ask his back as he strides across the room. I can't help but appreciate how at home he is in this environment. Before seeing him here I would have said that he was a man of the wild, more suited to being outdoors and enjoying rugged pursuits than being surrounded by steel and screens and the crucible of modern life.

Glass chinks together softly and then the sound of pouring liquid fills the room. He returns with a single tumbler, fine and intricately carved, half-filled with a mead-like substance.

"It's whisky." He holds it out for me.

"No, thanks," I grimace at the very idea but he lifts it to my lips.

"You're in shock. This will help."

My eyes lift to his handsome face. I don't drink scotch. I can't say why, but it's never interested me and I find the smell repellent, but I part my mouth slightly and allow the alcohol to pass my lips.

It burns all the way down.

I don't mind it.

I take the glass from him and hold it, taking a little more of its contents before placing it on his desk. "Thank you."

He curves a hand over my shoulder; it's oddly reassuring, even more so because it is something small done out of habit.

The image of the hallway flickers and bright white follows, then black.

"What happened?"

He squeezes my shoulder. "Someone deleted the feed."

"What?" I blink up at him in complete shock. "Why?"

"I can't say just yet. It could be a glitch."

But of course it isn't. He is simply trying to placate me. "Have you ever had a glitch before?"

"No."

"You must have fail-safes in place to stop that."

He nods carefully. "The camera is always active. It's notified when the alarm is set or unset, and records in different intervals. There is a possibility the programming malfunctioned."

"Would you have found out about that?"

He smiles at me, but I see the tension in the lines of his face. "Try not to worry."

"This is because of me," I speak over him. "I'm sure of it."

"Why?" He crouches beside me so that our eyes are almost level. "Who is it that left that note? Why would you possibly have any reason to be afraid?"

I angle my face away from his with obstinate determination and he sighs.

"I want to help you, Sasha, but it's a lot harder for me to do that if you insist on keeping this a secret."

"It's not your job to help me," I promise him softly.

The door opens after a cursory knock. He fixes me with a glowing stare and then stands. "Yes, it damn well is. And you know it."

Three men enter. I don't know which is which but presumably they are the trio he called for only minutes earlier. Langham, Smith and Renway. Said together like that they sound like a cheap law firm; the kind that my real-dad would have called Ambulance chasers, with a hint of derision.

They speak quietly and their conversation doesn't reach my ears, but I detect the tone of reverence and respect that radiates from each man. Several times a pair of eyes flick to me before returning to Alex's face. He is a picture of determination and command. He speaks often, and several times interrupts the other men. His manner is serious and businesslike.

I watch as he pulls the note from his pocket and hands it to the shortest of the men. They all look at me. Eight eyes seeing me not as Sasha, but as Bianca.

She is dead, I want to shout. She died with them!

I begin to tremble again.

With fingers that shake I lift the scotch and allow its balm to pour through me.

"I want answers tonight," I hear him say a little more loudly. They leave quickly. We are alone.

"I want you to tell me the truth now."

Perhaps it is because I've just witnessed three grown men practically bow down to him as Lord and Master, or maybe it is because here in his office we are surrounded by the signs of his power and success, but I am not so sure I can resist his questioning. I shift out of the seat and walk slowly towards the windows.

London twinkles at my feet.

"I haven't told anyone the truth in such a long time. I don't think I know where to begin."

He is silent. Later he tells me that he was afraid I would stop speaking if he interrupted me but at that point in time it never occurred to me that he would ever fear anything.

"I have been Sasha Lewis since I was ten." I swallow, wrapping my arms around my chest. "And who I was before died the day I became her." A shiver runs down my spine. I am thinking of my brother, as I often do. For though I miss my mother and father, and I cry for their deaths, it is my brother and I who were the true innocents, bonded forever by our parents' decisions and the path of danger they laid out for us.

"Maintaining this secret is a part of who I am now."

"Someone knows the truth."

I blink. The irrefutability of that statement is like a brick on my shoulders. "I know that."

"Your friend Meera?" He murmurs from just behind me.

"No. She has no idea. And even if she did..." I shake my head. "Notes left under doors are not her style. She would never do anything to hurt me."

I bite into my lip, thinking, nervous.

"It's strange." My eyes are drawn to a light in the building opposite. It flickers with that familiar determination of fluorescent bulbs, illuminating the room in several little spurts of whiteness before remaining on. A woman moves past the glass; a backpack vacuum cleaner around her middle. She pauses, her gaze resting out the window. Does she see me as I do her? Does she think I am Sasha or Bianca?

"What's strange?" He prompts.

"I have never been tempted to tell anyone the truth until I met you." My lip lifts in an asymmetrical acknowledgement of the irony. "From the outset I knew us to be transient and temporary and yet lying to you has been so difficult."

"So tell me now." His words are edged by steel.

I nod. "I'm trying. It's hard. I feel like by talking about it, I'm unlocking a part of me that I'm glad as hell is closed over. I don't want to open the door."

"Except it's been opened for you."

I nod. He's correct, as usual. Still, it takes me several long moments to gather my strength. When I speak, it's based in fact. Emotion is suppressed from my words—at least, as much as possible. "When I was a little girl, my family was killed." My eyes stay on the cleaner across the way while I speak. "I alone survived. I alone was able to bear witness to their deaths."

He closes his eyes briefly. "You're in witness protection."

"Yes. It's called the Protected Persons Unit, but it's the same thing. And I passed out of the programme when I turned eighteen."

"Where are you from?"

"The North." I wince at his visible frustration. "I'm sorry. It's a habit." I try again. "Manchester."

He nods his approval. "And so you testified against the man who killed your family."

I clear my throat. "Yes. Sort of."

"Sasha, for God's sake..."

"I'm trying," I snap, biting down on my lip. The cleaner has moved to a different window now. "My father worked for the CPS. He was very ambitious." I swallow. "He became hell bent on prosecuting a gang operating in the area."

"They killed him?"

"No, they gave him a party with a bouncing castle. Of course they killed him. These guys were the most brutal gang in the UK. They make the mafia look like fucking babysitters. I mean, the heinous stuff they did

—to children, to women, to business rivals." My smile is twisted. "Anyone with a shred of common sense would have been terrified of these guys."

"And your father wasn't?"

"No. He taunted them. He gave press conferences belittling them, laughing at them. He was determined to destroy them. It became his life's mission. The director of the CPS wanted him to back off, to take a different approach. I remember my parents fighting about it all the time. They would argue and she would beg him to draw back from the case but he refused."

A muscle moves in Alex's cheek. I want to lift up and touch it but I don't. "I presume he felt passionately that the pursuit of justice was worth it."

Alex's eyes hold mine; still he is silent.

My fingers tingle, my chest hurts. "Our dog was killed a week before it happened. His throat was slit, he was left on our doorstep." I shudder, remembering his beautiful, fur-covered, blood-stained body, his loving, loyal eyes still open. "I found him." But it is a grief that hardly registers for me now, for it has been superseded by the slow, brutal death of my parents and brother.

He's listening silently, his eyes glued to my face. He's seeing every nuance of emotion in my features because that's what he does. Just as I knew his silences, he knows my expressions.

"It was the night before the trial was due to open. He had a high-profile informant. Someone who was going to make his case. I didn't know that at the time, but during the trial—the murder trial—that piece of information came out. My parents were killed. My brother was killed. As a warning to the informant, it's presumed, and to anyone else who'd think about prosecuting the gang members."

"And yet you survived?"

"My mother hid me. In hindsight, I think she'd been grooming me for a long time for the possibility of danger. We played an elaborate game of hide and seek; one in which silence was absolutely vital, no matter what. She drilled that into me, time and time again. And so, I saw their throats slit, just like our dog's had been, and I didn't make a sound."

"What about security?"

I nod. "We had security. Not enough though. It's taken me a long time to accept that my father was arrogant to the extreme. He wanted to be the guy who brought these men down, but he pursued it with such single-mindedness that it never truly occurred to him he might not win."

My voice sounds funny. It's coming to us from a long way away. "Even when I heard my brother cry out for help I stayed where I was, watching the blood slowly seeping out of my mother's body, my father's tortured breath as he reached for her. The shock in his emptying eyes. Then there was a gunshot. Bang. Bang. Bang. And then everything was silent." I feel sick. Nausea is rising like a tidal wave in my throat. "I stayed hidden and they looked for me. They even opened the closet door but I was very, very good at hiding, Alex."

I am terrified and I am traumatised; Alex stays silent, waiting for me to continue.

"After they left, I went to Andrew. My brother. He was dead. I called triple nine and then I went back to hide until the police arrived."

"Yet you saw these men well enough to identify them?"

I nod. "I had known two of them for as long as I could remember. They were my parents' friends—police officers. We had them for dinner several times a month. I played with their children." I swallow. Could it be one of their children, Wren or Michael perhaps, who had found me? "Those bastards killed my brother. It is bad enough that they did what they did to my parents. But Andrew? A child?" And now I give in to the tears that are cloying at my throat. "He was the sweetest kid."

"The photo in your room," he murmurs and I nod.

"Yes, that's him."

"I'm sorry for what you endured. Your father could have had no idea that it would come to that. If he did, I'm sure he would have changed course."

My head jerks to his so fast it reminds me of the time I drove Rick's car into a hedge and gave myself whiplash. "Like your dad might regret hitting your mum?" I am angry and scared and it is easy to vent that at him. "You have no place to imbibe his actions with a remorse I know he wouldn't feel."

It surprises him; that much I can tell. "You're right," he nods firmly. "I have no right." A frown smudges his lips. "That was a stupid attempt at making you feel better." He is surprised because he despises platitudes as much as I do.

"You do make me feel better." My own expression is one of acceptance. "But not by pretending that he was anything other than selfish, greedy and utterly responsible for their deaths." I expel an angry breath. "I am studying law because I believe in justice; that is a gift from him. I'm not saying he shouldn't have pursued prosecution but he did it in a way that was lined with danger and he didn't care. He didn't care that he was putting us in harm's way in the pursuit of the result he wanted. The career progression he craved."

"And you think these men—this gang—is after you now? Why?" His brow furrows. "It's so long after the trial."

"Didn't you hear me? These men are pure evil. Not only did my father build a rock-solid case against them—a case that was prosecuted with success after he died, putting several of these guys into prison—but on top of that I lived and took down two of their highest ranked members. These people believe in blood debts and I haven't paid mine."

The statement fills him with disgust and fear. He doesn't want to think of me or my blood being in that kind of danger.

"I believe they will hunt me until I am dead. I forgot, for a long time, that there are people out there who hate me like this. Forgetting was the stupidest thing I've ever done."

I am sick and I am sorry and I know I'm being unreasonable to him, somehow. Dumping everything on him and throwing his father's abuse in his face.

"I didn't mean to snap at you."

"Don't." He lifts a finger to my lips in an age old gesture of silence. Our eyes are locked. "You must be exhausted."

I shake my head. "I'm restless. I'm worried. Ally and Rick..."

He nods. "Why don't you call them?"

My throat is dry; I swallow nervously. "What if they're..."

"Call them." He links his fingers with mine. "I'll be right here."

I know that I have to face this music, even though I am more afraid than I have ever been. I lift the phone from my back pocket and press my mother's face. It begins to ring. And it rings. And my heart is pounding. Where is she? Anxiously, I look at the time. It is late. Perhaps she is asleep.

It goes to voicemail.

"Oh, God. Alex."

He shakes his head. "Try Rick."

I nod but my fingers are clumsy and I accidentally press the wrong name in my phone. He takes it from me and presses Rick's picture instead. I don't attempt to take the phone back so Alex puts it on speaker and holds it just in front of me. It rings. And it rings.

And finally, Rick's groggy voice comes to me a hundred miles away.

"Hello?"

"Thank God." Tears sparkle on my eyelashes. "Oh, thank God you're okay."

"Yeah. Course I am. What's going on, Blackbird?"

I'm shivering again. Relief, intense relief, makes speech difficult.

"Rick? It's Alex."

My father is silent. I think he realises something important is happening and of course he immediately goes to my troubled past.

"Yes, Alex?"

I hear movement on my father's end of the phone line. He's walking through the house.

"Sasha received a note tonight, at my apartment. Someone wants to speak to her. About Bianca."

There is a longer silence, and it prickles with alertness and worry.

"Right." My father is grim. "Sasha? You know what you have to do."

I nod, but my mind is screaming a thousand objections.

"You have to get out. Go to the place we talked about."

Alex is scowling. "Rick, she doesn't need to run away."

"Like hell she doesn't," Rick grunts. "You don't know what these bastards are capable of."

"I do. Sasha's told me. But she's with me, and she's safe here. I have security raking over the footage of my apartment. We will find whoever is responsible for this."

Buoyed by Alex's words I am nodding. "I want to stay in London, dad."

"That's crazy." He's angry, and I hear my mum murmuring in the background. "We have a plan for this. You know how important it is to stick to it."

"We made that plan when I first moved out," I say haltingly. "Before I had anything worth staying around for." My eyes are burning into Alex's. Does he know he is my reason for risking everything?

"You can rebuild. You can even go back one day, when the danger has passed."

"It will never pass," I groan, dragging my hands through my hair. "I will never be really safe and we all know that."

Alex expression shows bloody determination. "Yes, you will be." He turns his attention back to the phone. "I swear on my life, nothing will happen to Sasha while she is with me."

"You're the reason they've found her," Rick groans. "That bloody photo. I knew when I saw it what it would mean."

I squeeze my eyes shut. "Dad, stop." My voice is shaking. "This isn't Alex's fault. They've been in Meera's flat, too. I'm pretty sure, at least. They would always have found me. That's what they do." And it's true. I am right. I think I always knew I was living a little bit on borrowed time.

"Sasha..."

"I know." I interrupt him. "I'm scared too." I bite down on my lip. "But mostly I'm scared for you and mum."

"This place is Fort Knox," he demurs. And it is. As soon as we moved in, the security system was upgraded to rival any prison in the world. The safe-room in the basement has enough provisions to last weeks and runs on separate phone and power supply in the event of a problem in the house. "What's the plan, Alex?"

"I'm not going to let her out of my sight," he says seriously. "And, Rick? I will find these men. They will not come near her, I can promise you that."

Fifteen
We are Darkness and Light; One Cannot Exist Without The Other

I did not think I would sleep and yet I must have, for I wake early. The surroundings aren't familiar at first. I blink and sit up, letting my eyes come into focus.

Alex's office.

I am on one of the Chesterfields, and a soft blanket lays on top of me; there is a cushion where my head was.

It is early—still dark outside. The hours of pre-dawn when danger and darkness seem to tiptoe across the globe are groaning to a close, but slowly. So slowly.

I reach for my phone to check the time.

5.32am.

I am desperate to pee. I stand quietly—I don't know why I'm tip-toeing but the silence of his office is like the still top of a beautiful lake. I do not want to ripple it.

His desk is in disarray. I walk behind it, my eyes scanning the computer screen. It's black.

On the other side of his office there are two doors. I push one inwards and startle. It is an apartment, larger than my studio. There is a bed, armchair, a kitchenette and presumably a bathroom.

I feel as though I am invading a secret sanctuary but still I move inwards. The door clicks shut behind me of its own accord.

He is not here and the bed does not appear to have been slept in.

The bathroom is almost identical to his at home. The same product lines decorate the shelves and the shower—the sight of them plunges me back to a comforting and familiar space, and yet it's out of my reach.

After I have freshened myself up, including splashing water in my face and combing my hair back from my brow, I spray some of his fragrance on my neck and clean my teeth with one of the spare brushes I know I will find in the top drawer (just like his home).

My tummy grumbles and I remember the sushi meal he had organised the night before.

I can't think when I last ate and my stomach is not happy about that.

Even at this hour, in Canary Wharf, a cafe will be open to cater to the diligent bankers who front up insanely early—or the night owls just finishing their trading on international markets.

In hindsight, I wonder why the hell I thought it was a good idea to leave the safety of his monolithic prison but in that moment my only thought was of a *Pain au Chocolat* and piccolo latte. Anything that would drag me, tastebud by tastebud, back to normality.

The hallway is deserted; it is only a short walk to the bank of elevators. Now, in the morning, and with a little distance between me and the catatonic fog that enveloped me last night, I take more notice of the surroundings. The beautiful beige carpet that spreads in every direction, lights that glow golden and artwork on the wall that would be at home in the Tate Modern.

My finger jabs the lift button.

"Sasha." He's right behind me. I jump, startled, naturally. "Where are you going?"

I bite down on my lip, spinning around to face my saviour. He looks terrible. Or as terrible as it's possible for Alex LaMar to get. His face is covered in stubble and his hair is in disarray. His shirt is untucked at the back and he wears no tie. Also, he has no shoes on. It's a tiny detail that makes my heart flip in my chest. The sweetness of his socked feet surprises me.

He doesn't look terrible at all, actually. The dishevelled air suits him. Of course. It is a great injustice that he is so handsome even under stress.

"I need a coffee," I wrench my gaze back to his face. I've said something wrong. He's looking at me with mounting frustration. "And I didn't know where you were…"

"Listen to me." He puts a hand on my back and begins to propel me back down the corridor towards his office. "You can't leave here. Not until we find out what's going on."

"I'm not going to hide," I whisper, shaking my head. I'd said the same thing to Rick last night, basically, but until now, I don't think I fully understood how fully I mean that. I don't want to hide. I'm sick of it. So sick of it. I have been hiding, and I have still been found. What's the point of any of this?

"What?"

But certainty assails me. "I have been hiding my whole life and I am so tired of it. I want to go and get a damn coffee."

He stares at me. Does he see that I'm on the brink of a meltdown? He must because he nods. "Fine. But I'll go with you."

"I've already derailed your whole night…"

His laugh is a short, sharp sound. "Did you think I had any plans for last night that didn't involve you?"

My cheeks are warm. "That's different." I force myself to confront this. "You don't have to do this. To be all protective." I can't meet his eyes. "I'm not your problem."

"I'm not having this conversation again. Come on."

"I don't want a bodyguard."

"So what do you suggest?" He moves towards his desk and slips his shoes on.

"I don't know."

"Do you want to go to class today? To wait and see who comes looking for you?"

The idea sparks in my brain. My eyes show that and he groans.

"I was being sarcastic."

"I know, but…wouldn't that be the easiest way to find out what's going on?"

"Yeah," he rolls his eyes. "Great idea, Sash. I'll be sure to make a note of what an investigative genius you are in your eulogy."

A shiver slips along my spine.

"Sit down." He nods to the sofas. I am torn. I find it hard to butt against him and yet I am so sick of being told what to do. Of being cautious. Recklessness fires my spirit of independence.

"I want a coffee."

His eyes are zipping with fury. He lifts his phone to his ear. "What kind of coffee?"

"Oh." I blink. He is the personification of impatience. "Um, the usual. And I'm hungry." The request comes out as belligerent and childish.

"Would you bring a piccolo latte and some breakfast—pastries, fruit—to my office?" He disconnects the call without so much as a word of thanks.

I sit down on the edge of the sofa. My heart is racing. "What's with the little flat through there?"

"For when I work late," he grunts.

I stand up again, wrapping my arms around my mid-section. "Any luck with the security feed?"

"No." He snaps but it's not me he's annoyed with. "Whoever disabled it knew what they were doing. My system has a shedload of firewalls. It shouldn't have been possible..."

This makes me anxious. "Do you think whoever it is knows I'm here now? In your office with you?"

He nods slowly. "Probably."

"God, Alex..."

"Nobody can get to you here."

"You don't think?" I see my brother's face. *You didn't help me*. Am I destined to join him? Will my death complete the fates of our family?

"You're safe here. Not wandering the streets of Canary Wharf at dawn."

He's right. Of course he's right. "But how long am I going to have to hide out?"

"That doesn't matter. You're going to be safe. Got it?"

"You must hate me." I walk slowly to the windows and stare down. Cars are zipping far below.

"Must I?"

"Of course. This isn't meant to be getting serious, remember? And now you've been dragged in to serve as my unwitting knight in shining armour."

"What did I say to you last night? You are in my blood. Does that sound simple?"

I close my eyes. It is oddly reassuring to know that he is muddled in the same way I am.

His voice is low and deep. "You think that because of some stupid line I said when we first met that I still feel that way? After everything we've shared?" He crosses the room and grabs me by my arms.

He spins me so I am facing him. "Let me tell you why I am fighting you. Because I need you to stay alive. Because the idea of anything happening to you fills me with the kind of rage that I cannot contain. If you walk out of this office and someone hurts you, I will kill that person. I would kill anyone who causes you to tremble like you did last night." He lifts his hands and grips my face on either side. "When I met you, I thought you were just a beautiful woman I wanted to get in my bed as soon as possible. I told you that I didn't want this to get serious. But that's all bullshit. I don't know when I started to love you but I do. I fucking love you. So would you do us both a favour and just...let me help."

I have never been more shocked. From the desperation of my situation to the height of delighted shock, I am smiling so broadly that my face hurts.

"Did you just say you love me?"

He seems as momentarily surprised by the admission as I am. "Yeah." He shrugs off the confusion. "I do. Come on! I don't meet parents. I don't take women to see my mum. I don't spend entire days thinking about a woman's movements, waiting until I can see her again. I am obsessively, unstoppably in love with you."

I am soaring high, high, high up into the heavens. Stars surround me. I lift up on my tiptoes to place a kiss against his lips and everything slots into place. This man is not my knight in shining armour, he is my other half. My perfect complement. We are darkness and light. One cannot exist without the other.

The sound of his phone vibrating cuts through our kiss. He jerks away and lifts it to his ear. His eyes stay pinned to me; the intensity of his watch-fulness is incredibly reassuring. "Got it."

He drops his iPhone to the desk.

"What is it?"

"They've recovered some footage."

"What?" I am still grappling with his declaration of love. It takes me a moment to comprehend what he's saying.

"Yeah." He misunderstands my confusion. "The cameras can be switched off remotely but the footage still logs. It's just buried. We've been working on it all night."

So he looks like he could fight a bear with his hands and win, but he's also a keyboard warrior. "Okay. Let's see it."

He crosses to his computer just as the door opens. I jump. My nerves are shot. One of the men who was in his office last night comes in carrying a brown paper bag and two white coffee cups, one delightfully petite. My tummy grumbles appreciatively but my mind is focussed on whatever information Alex's team has discovered.

"Thank you," I murmur, taking the proffered cup with a tight smile.

"You're welcome." His smile is kind.

Alex flicks his eyes to the man's as he dials up his computer. "Langham's found something."

"We were close," he nods, coming to stand beside Alex.

"Sasha, this is Graeme Smith. He's my Head of Operations here in the UK."

"And you have him fetching me coffee," I say with a shake of my head and a look of frustration at Alex. But he loves me, so I can't be too annoyed. I smile at Andy instead. "I'm sorry to put you out."

He seems momentarily surprised by the comment. "It's no trouble."

Alex smiles but it's more of a grimace. "Graeme is one of my oldest friends. I trust him implicitly."

That's interesting. I spare a passing glance at the man again, and curiosity is deep within me. He is nothing like the 'friends' of Alex's I met at that party. Nothing like sleazy Tom, or pink-hair. Graeme is serious, and a man of substance. Another time, I would like to get to know this man that Alex considers such a good friend. But not now.

Now there is work to be done.

I move to Alex's other side. The screen is filled with gobbledegook. Alex leans over and types some words into the prompt. The screen goes black and then an image begins to render.

I am tempted to squeeze my eyes shut and yet I don't want to miss this moment. I need to know. This is the person who has discovered the truth of my identity.

I reach down and grab Alex's hand as a grainy image slowly begins to clear on the screen.

We realise who it is at the same time.

"That fucking bastard," he groans, reaching for his phone.

"Carlton? That doesn't make any sense." The next frame loads. He's knocking at the door, looking up and down the hallway.

"Carlton." He turns around to face me but he's on the phone. "I need his home address."

"Alex." I shut my eyes, thinking back over our conversations. "This is a mistake. He would never hurt me."

"This guy?" He points at the screen. "This guy who's suddenly in your life and all over you like a rash?"

I resist the urge to point out that the same description could be used for Alex; that if attentiveness is a marker for guilt then surely Alex is by far the guiltiest.

"He would never hurt me," I repeat. "I'm telling you."

"Come on, Sasha. Don't be so naive," he snaps, draining his coffee quickly. His phone buzzes. "Stay here."

He's walking fast, moving out of the office and I have to jog to keep up with him. "Don't. Alex, don't do this. Let me talk to him."

"You? Hell, I wouldn't let you within a mile of him. Not until I know what he's playing at."

I'm shaking again. I grab his wrist and pull him to face me. He's strong but he doesn't fight me. "Please."

Realising his superfluousness to matters, Graeme moves past us. "I'll be in my office."

Neither of us acknowledge the statement. "Please don't do this."

"I will not let him harm you."

"There's more than one way someone could do that though." I wrap my arms around his waist. I need him to understand. "You're not the only who's been falling in love." He looks confused. Does he think I'm referring to Carlton?

"I love you too. I'm not going to let you put yourself in harm's way for me. And if you really love me, you have to understand that I have to do this, that it's important to me." I put my head on his chest so that I can hear his steady, fast heartbeat. "We'll go together. We'll speak to him side by side. Okay?"

He wants to say no, but I think he is as afraid of what he's capable of as I am. "Fine. But you stay behind me and you do what I say."

I nod, even when I know I would run into a burning building to save Alex. "Deal."

———

The second his front door opens I am afraid for Carlton's life. Not mine. He looks terrible. And not in the sexy, tousled Alex way. But I feel Alex's anger and it is a force in pursuit of Carlton. He clearly believes Carlton is a threat, even when I just know in my gut that it's not true.

"Sasha!" He exclaims, his eyes moving quickly from Alex to me. "Where the hell have you been? I have been calling you all night."

I frown and reach for my phone. It's not in my pocket. "You don't have my number. I never gave it to you."

"I got it from faculty support."

"Why?" Alex demands, wrapping his hand around mine. I inhale deeply, trying to reconcile the man in front of me with a threat. I just can't make sense of any of it.

"Because I've been worried." He steps back, opening the door a little wider. Alex won't simply let me walk past though. He pushes a hand against Carlton's chest, holding him tight against the door frame.

"Is anyone else here?"

"Here? No. Why? Who would be?"

Alex still doesn't make an effort to move into the elegant townhouse. Nor does he release his grip on Carlton's shirt.

"Start talking," he commands through gritted teeth. "Begin with the note."

Carlton reaches up to push Alex's hand away but Alex is like stone.

"Don't test my patience."

"Sasha," Carlton looks at me with obvious frustration. "What the hell is going on?'

"That's a question for you," Alex retorts, his voice like steel.

Carlton looks genuinely confused, worried and more than a little pissed. "Sash, can we talk privately?" His eyes flit to Alex. "No offence, but this guy's..."

"Watch it," Alex cuts him off, the warning emanating from his words, his voice and his very stance.

I know I have to get control of things. "Carlton, why did you leave that note?"

He shakes his head. "I didn't leave a note, but I do need to speak with you. It's really important. Can you come in a minute?"

"Why?" Urgency turns my voice to a whisper. Apparently, he realises I'm not going to come into his apartment willingly.

"Someone is following you. It's been going on for a week now."

Ice sledges through my veins. Is he lying? Covering his own stalking? Or is Alex completely wrong? But why was Carlton at Alex's? And why does Carlton think this? Nothing makes sense. My world has spun completely off its axis. "I don't understand."

"I came to tell you yesterday. Ally said you'd be at his place."

I look from Alex to Carlton, waiting for sense to form from his words.

"Ally? You brought my mum into this?"

Alex speaks over me. "Tell us about the note."

He expels an angry breath, his eyes pierce Alex. "I already told you, I don't have a single clue about any goddamned note. I knocked on the door, and waited. You didn't answer. I left."

"Okay," I instinctively believe him—I do trust this guy and I'm pretty sure my instincts have been honed finely over the years. "But my parents?"

His eyes search mine, looking for something I can't provide, because I am at a total loss.

"What do my parents have to do with this?"

Alex pushes at Carlton's chest. "Answer her."

"Don't," I cry, no longer in any doubt about Carlton's innocence. "I just want to understand."

Carlton speaks softly, calmly, helping me understand. "I first met your parents a few months before you turned eighteen. They wanted to know what legal options were open to them to keep you in a program."

I shiver. I don't believe it. I don't want to believe it. The idea of my parents knowing Carlton and not having told me feels like some kind of betrayal. I need to understand. "Why you?"

"I've helped several victims move into Witness Protection in the states. I've written papers on it. I worked on the taskforce that reshaped the whole damn thing. I know it inside and out. Your parents wanted ways to keep you safe. Secrets we use. Ways to bury your identity again if it became necessary. They were afraid what your life would look like once you aged out of the programme." He reaches for me but Alex is there, a wall between us. Carlton expels a shitty sigh. "It's a coincidence that I ended up teaching at your university."

"Like hell," Alex snaps angrily.

Carlton speaks as though Alex hasn't. "But when I realised, I contacted them—just to touch base, really—and they asked me to look out for you."

"I don't need a babysitter," I whisper.

"Someone is following you."

"You said that already." My heart is firing but I'm determined not to show just how fucking terrified I am. "I don't buy it."

"I wasn't sure at first either," he speaks slowly and gently, as though I'm a witness again, about to break down and run away. "But yesterday I was in your bookstore after class and he came in asking about you. Pretending he'd bought a book you'd recommended and saying he wanted to thank you. I recognised him from the back of a class a few days earlier—at the time, I recognised he was new, but didn't think much more of it. But this guy is looking for you, and I don't get a good feeling off him."

Questions jumble through me. I don't know what to say. "And you told this to Ally?" I think of the conversation we've just had with my parents. They sounded as shocked by the note as I am. Is Carlton lying?

"Are you kidding? No. Not yet. I wanted to speak to you first."

I shake my head, my lips compressed. "So who is this guy?"

"I have no idea. I got a picture on my phone but it's not good quality."

"You took a picture?" Alex sneers angrily. "Was it a little too hard for you to pursue him?"

Carlton's look is laced with ice. "I said a man is following her. I have no interest in attacking him without more evidence…"

"Isn't that just a perfectly insipid response from someone like you?" Alex's eyes drag over Carlton with fury. "You had him within arm's reach and you took a photo."

"What would you have had me do?" Carlton snaps. "Beat him to a bloodied pulp because I think he's following your girlfriend?" He makes an effort to calm himself. "Witness Protection is full of things like this. People get paranoid whenever anything is even remotely awry. Simple, easy to explain incursions become massive man hunts without any real reason. For all I know, you know this guy, or you knew him at some stage. I wanted to talk to you before we decide how to proceed."

A muscle works overtime in Alex's jaw. He doesn't like the use of the word 'we', but I do. He's another person on my team and that can only be good for me. Especially because he's kind and intelligent and he seems to genuinely care for me.

I'm impatient now. Every discovery leads to a bunch of questions. I want to know the truth and yet it has a frustrating ephemeral quality.

"Show me the phone."

"It's inside."

"Go and get it," Alex commands darkly, guiding me back out of the townhouse onto the street. I realise he is still acting under the belief that Carlton might be planning to hurt me.

Carlton wants to say something to Alex but he holds himself back. "Fine."

He reappears less than a minute later and hands his phone to me.

A fist of suspense is slamming into me. I am going to see this picture and the missing piece will slide into place. I lower my gaze, my breath is held, my stomach is in knots. But when I look at the grainy image I see only the back of a man I do not recognise. There is nothing familiar about him. He looks to be of average height and build, with dark blonde hair. He is wearing generic clothes.

Disappointment is threatening to swallow me. What small hope I had is fading. "I don't know who this is." My eyes ricochet from Alex to Carlton.

"Look again," Carlton urges, propping his hip on the door jamb.

"It's no use." I hand back his phone. "I could look at it for ten hours and I still wouldn't know who it is."

They are talking about me. I cannot hear their words but I sense the tone from across the street. She is afraid. Her boyfriend is furious. And the other one – the teacher who loves her – is a tangled crucible of emotion. He is jealous, and he is incensed by his impotence, and he is afraid for her. He wishes he could be the one to keep her safe from discovery.

Don't they get it?

It's too late for that.

Do you wonder why I didn't just take her? I could have, you know, so easily at any point in this last month. I could have grabbed her quickly and avoided all this.

But this – this panic I see on her face – this is her reward for what she did to me.

We are sitting in the front lounge of Carlton's house. It overlooks the street and I take comfort from the regular passage of cars. "What did the note say?"

A shiver runs down my spine. "*Sasha, we need to speak. Meet me after your last class tomorrow. It's about Bianca.*" I repeat it from memory—a memory file I suspect will be forever imprinted on by this piece of paper.

Carlton nods slowly. "So it's a fair bet that this guy is going to be on campus later today." His eyes drift to Alex's. "Right?"

"Genius. Well done, you."

"Alex." I spin around to face him, my expression holding a silent warning. "Leave it. This isn't his fault."

Alex's lips compress with impatience but his eyes soften and he holds a hand up in a conciliatory gesture—or at least an acknowledgement. I turn back to Carlton.

"So you've got two choices, Sash."

Alex bristles beside me at the easy diminutive Carlton employs. No, worse, he tenses his hand into a ball, squeezing a fist. I put a hand reassuringly on his leg. "Which are?"

Carlton, sitting opposite us, leans forward. He speaks only to me. "You either face the music. Or you go into hiding."

Alex makes a groan of frustration. "Thanks. That's really helpful."

Carlton shoots him a withering glare. "You know how I feel about you. I want you hidden away from any danger, forever." I feel Alex's temperature spike. "But I know you. You won't be happy leaving this mystery unsolved."

Having reached the same conclusion a matter of hours ago, I can only nod.

"And this is your best chance to find out who's after you." He shifts a little in the seat. "You are being hunted, make no mistake about it. And whoever is after you will not go away softly simply because you fail to turn up to class today."

Nausea is a wave I am now skilled at surfing.

"Stop it," Alex grunts, dragging a hand through his hair. "I can keep her safe."

"Sure you can. By making her your prisoner?"

Alex stands up and prowls to the other side of Carlton's lounge room. "So what do you suggest?"

Carlton moves to take the seat just vacated by Alex. He sits beside me, placing a hand on mine. "You haven't done anything wrong. You are the victim. You saw a terrible, terrible thing when you were still a child. You lost your family and went to live with strangers. You do not need to run from them."

"Hang on a second." Alex holds up a hand, his eyes boring into mine. "Sasha is not your latest innocence project. The fact she is a victim will have very little impact on whether or not these bastards want to hurt her."

Carlton speaks as though Alex hasn't. "What kind of life do you want to lead?"

I roll my eyes. "Alex is right though. It's not that easy."

"Nothing good is ever easy. You know that."

I shake my head but Carlton leans closer, so that our eyes are level. "You told me that you want to fight for those who have no voice to speak for themselves. You told me that intelligence and education are the hallmarks of true power and yet you are surrendering all of yours to men who seek to cower you and diminish those qualities. Men who have strength of weaponry and guile but nothing more."

Alex is incensed. He moves to stand behind me; his fingers curl around my shoulders. "Beautiful words, but would you kindly shut the fuck up now?"

His touch gives me strength. "It's okay," I promise him.

"I don't know what your stake is in this but my only interest is Sasha's survival," Alex continues menacingly.

"I have the same wish," Carlton's words show what a brilliant litigator he is. They are soft and persuasive, simply-couched and impossible to contradict.

"And Carlton's right." I murmur after a brief pause. "This is how we can find him. He's going to show up. I can do this."

"No." Alex squeezes my shoulders. "I have a better idea."

Carlton rolls his eyes. "Of course you do. But did it occur to you that this not your choice, nor is it mine? Sasha has to decide what she wants."

I look up at Alex. "What's your idea?"

"You stay in my office. Where I know you are safe. Carlton will go to your last class. He can fly under the radar without arousing suspicion. I will also go. When this man arrives, I'll handle him."

"No. Terrible idea." For all the reasons I didn't want Alex to confront Carlton I do not want him to be involved in apprehending this person.

"Actually, it's not," Carlton says softly. "It's low risk to you…"

"Yeah, and huge risk to *him*."

Carlton laughs. "You think he's in danger?" He sizes up Alex and I imagine what he must be seeing. The strength. The contained power.

"My dad was like that," I whisper. "No matter how strong someone is, *they're* stronger. They're dangerous, because they're willing to do things you never could."

"Want to make a bet?" Alex demands.

I shake my head. "Don't. You have to understand…these bastards shot a kid, a kid they *knew*. They will do whatever it takes to win."

Now it's Alex making a guttural noise. "And yet you seriously want to be the one to flesh them out?"

"No," I shake my head from side to side. "But I will not be stalked. I can't live like that. Wondering if each day, each time I go out, is going to be the time they finally catch up with me."

"Then let me handle this," Alex speaks decisively; I think he knows a part of me is tempted.

But I shake my head, because there are worse things than imagining my own death, and losing Alex is one of them. "No. It has to be me. I'm not willing for you to take that risk."

"It's my risk to take."

But I've made up my mind. "No." I stand up, and though my stomach is filled with butterflies and my knees are weak, I square my shoulders and assume a look that I hope inspires confidence. "It has to be me; this is the only way."

Sixteen

Like Wraiths the Night Forgot to Take

When expectation is heavy in the air, time conspires not to pass. The day is creeping as if it were a half-dead snail crossing a darkened passage. I am a curious mix of tired and alert – my mind is filled with questions and I think, for the first time in years, I may be on the brink of answering them. In the corridors of the university where I have spent so much of my time over the last four years I am surrounded by the smell of ambition and academia. I should feel worried, but I am oddly comforted by the familiar.

"Sasha." I turn when I hear my name being called and my eyes lock with Carlton. His grin aims to reassure me.

"Hi. Is everything okay?"

"Yeah. So far as I know. Look, I wanted to talk to you about something else. Something that's literally just come across my desk. I would have flagged it with you sooner had I known about it." He pauses and my interest is sparked. "And it's probably not something you can even think of today, but maybe you need to hear this, right now. Maybe what I'm about to say will lead you to a different decision about your life and your future."

I'm instantly sceptical. "Go on," I urge, my eyes skimming the hallway behind him. There are still hours before my last class. Where is Alex? Is he watching us via the cameras that pepper the halls? Guilt, misplaced or not, shimmies over me.

"My firm's taking on a new case. We're defending six children from being deported. They were trafficked into the States and they've been there for a few years. The crimes against these kids will make a part of you wither up. They need care and help, not criminal proceedings."

I feel my face crumple with sympathy. The cruelty people are capable of enacting, and on children, mortifies me. "That's so sad."

"Yeah." He nods. "And there's a lot of work involved. We're taking on a team of interns to help with the background research. I want you to apply."

The invitation is instantly confusing. Am I wrong to be wary? I smile, but I'm sure it conveys my doubts. "Do you want me to apply as my law professor? Or as a man who's made it obvious he's interested in me?"

He props his hip on the wall and his eyes seem to be staring at me in a soulful way. It reminds me, just a little, of Alex. They are in no way alike and yet now their intensity almost matches. I don't want Alex to see this and I know he must, because we are so in tune with one another.

I'm grateful that the Closed Circuit cameras recording the university hallways don't have microphones. "I want you to apply for the role because you're brilliant and passionate and it would guarantee you your pick of jobs once you graduate." He moves infinitesimally closer. "Plus I think it's where you should be."

"Why?" I push, my voice husky.

"For one? It's dangerous for you here."

"You're the one who told me to stop running…"

"And I think that's the right advice." When he swallows, his Adam's Apple moves visibly in his hair-roughened throat. "But this is an incredible opportunity. It kills two birds with one stone. You could start a new life."

I swallow and shake my head. I imagine walking away from Alex and my insides are agonisingly cold. "That's why I couldn't do it."

"You need to think about it," he says with a quiet urgency. "Think about the case. What it would mean to these children. You have talked about the power of our profession—so use it."

"I love Alex and he's here."

"And if he cares about you, he'll want you to make the right call for your future. Internships like this don't come along very often."

I bite down on my lip. Carlton's firm is astonishing. It would be a career-making move to intern there. I shake my head from side to side, and sigh. "And there's not a part of you that wants me to come because you're..." I blush, not sure how to say it.

"Go on?"

"You don't think something's going to happen between us, right?"

"No," he laughs and shakes his head ruefully. I remember how much I like him, and why. "I think you're great. And if you weren't with Alex, who knows? But I'm not looking to incentivise you into my life. This is not personal. I value my firm and my reputation too much for that. I want you to apply because you'd be amazing at the job."

"You don't think it would be kind of awkward, me working for you?"

His eyes meet mine. "No." He is powerful when he speaks, and I remember that he is an incredibly successful lawyer. His prowess has been created from his strength and passion. "Here, we're friends. We talk like equals. There? We wouldn't be that. I would hardly see you at work. My office is up in the clouds. I'm sorry to say, you'd be based out of a cubicle in the basement, reporting to someone who's about seven rungs down from me."

"Right." How stupid can I be? My cheeks are on fire. What did I think? That I'd be sharing an office with the founding partner of the firm?

Sensing my pique, he leans closer. His face is making promises that I know he would keep if I gave him the chance. "Outside the office, you could see as little, or as much, of me as you want. I'd be happy to help you to settle in, obviously. Maybe even take you to a few Broadway shows? Matilda?"

"I just want to be friends," I say softly.

"Ah. What happened to being naughty, sometimes?"

I shake my head but a smile is flipping across my mouth against my own better judgement. "I'm more nice than naughty, you know."

"We'll see." He smiles and again I am reminded that he is beautifully handsome, and that I used to have a huge crush on him. I don't want to remember that. I cannot ever revive those feelings. "Will you think about applying?"

I bite down on my lip. "I need to talk to Alex…"

"Fine, do that. But Sasha? Imagine yourself in five years' time. Is he in your life still? Will you regret turning down an opportunity like this for him? Can he offer you what I am?" He pauses. "Professionally, I mean."

I am torn; I am a medieval prisoner being dragged over the rack. "I'm not turning down the opportunity," I whisper finally. "But it's a big deal. I just need to give it proper thought."

"Well, think quickly. I've asked them to hold the process up by a day for you, given everything that's going on, but beyond that they need to start interviewing and we've already got a shedload of CVs from the last intern application . Our workload is groaning."

"I just don't think I can do it. Moving to America, leaving my parents, especially in the midst of all this…I'd be too worried."

"I'm pretty sure Ally and Rick would want you as far away from this mess as possible."

"Let me think about it." I blink up into his face and he smiles down at me.

"Sure. I'll give you as long as I can."

"I should think so, given it's your company."

He laughs. "It's been a long time since I've interested myself in matters of staffing though." He presses a finger into my shoulder. "But for you? I'll try."

I flash him a small smile that I hope serves to bring our *téte a téte* to a close. "I'm really pleased you thought of me."

"How are you going? With the other stuff today?"

I shake my head. "I'm impatient. I want it to be over. I'm not afraid. I'm angry. You know? Like who is this guy and what does he want?"

Carlton nods. "Only a few hours. Have you had lunch?"

I nod, but it's a lie. I just don't want Alex to have to see us together for a moment longer. "I have to get to class. I'll see you later."

"Last class."

I'm sitting in an empty classroom a short time later when he finds me. I feel him before he makes a sound and I spin, my heart hammering so hard against my ribs that I fear it might make an early exit from my body.

There is a bag in one hand and he wears a serious expression.

I am unutterably, indescribably pleased to see him. A lump forms in my throat; a stupid lump that warns me tears may be right behind so I swallow furiously to clear it.

"Lunch," Alex says by way of explanation, lifting the bag a little higher. "You haven't eaten."

"I think I'm too nervous."

He nods and places the bag on the desk between us. He is dressed casually today in jeans and a sweater. I think it's an attempt to blur into the background of university students but Alex LaMar is incapable of blending in anywhere.

The silence between us prickles with a tension I do not want to acknowledge. I close the distance and stand right in front of him, silently willing him to wrap his arms around me and make me feel better. He doesn't. He lifts a hand and cups my cheek, staring down at me with a look of curiosity I haven't seen in his eyes before.

It's that fucking conversation with Carlton.

He saw it, and he's pissed. And damn Carlton because he knew Alex would be watching and I think he banked on being able to set the cat amongst the pigeons for us. What can I say to him? Should I tell him the truth? Should I tell him part of the truth? Should I dress it up as an exciting opportunity?

"I ran into Carlton a minute ago," he says softly, his eyes raking mine, sending goosebumps and shards of awareness over my body.

I nod silently.

"He told me about the internship programme."

Temper spikes a fever in my blood. "He shouldn't have done that."

Alex's jaw moves, like he's grinding his teeth together. "Why not? You think I don't have a right to know?"

"I think it's something I should decide," I say with a shake of my head. "And of course I was going to talk to you about it."

"He was concerned you would dismiss the idea out of hand." He strokes my cheek and I shut my eyes on the wave of pleasure and rightness. "That you would use our relationship as an excuse."

I am angry but anger risks pushing Alex away and I need his closeness in this moment like I need air. "Nope."

His smile is distracted. "Nope? Not even a little bit?"

"Would you want me to?" I wrap my hands around his back, holding him tight.

He expels a soft breath. "I want you to keep your head in the game today. We can talk about this tonight. Afterwards."

I bite down on my lip. He's right, but I want to reassure him. "I meant what I said this morning. I love you."

Something clouds in his expression a little. Doubt? Disbelief? He covers it quickly but I see it and uncertainty immediately flares within me. It is a sensation that only grows when he doesn't say the words back to me. "You should eat. I know you aren't hungry, but you'll focus better."

I disentangle my hands from around his back and reach for the bag. Peering inside, I see a sandwich and a coffee. There's a biscuit too, chocolate chip. "It's for luck," he says with a smile.

I hope I don't need luck. Then again, can you ever have too much? "Have you eaten?" I ask, unwrapping the sandwich and holding a triangle out for him.

He shakes his head. "I'm fine."

I have to force myself to chew and swallow. My stomach is in knots and food is complicating that landscape. But he's right. A few mouthfuls of chicken and lettuce sandwich and I begin to feel somewhat calmer.

"I told Carlton I wanted to speak to you before I would make a decision," I say when I've finished the first triangle. I see Alex is torn; he wants to talk about this now, because he's impatient and his habit is to cut straight to the point. But he also wants to know my mind won't be clouded with distractions all afternoon.

"So we'll talk tonight."

I don't like being fobbed off, even if he believes he's doing it for my own good. "I don't want to leave you."

His eyes blink shut and a muscle works overtime in that beautiful face of his. "Tonight."

I'm missing something. "No, now." I lift the other sandwich from the box and settle myself on top of a desk mainly because I think my knees are going to give out.

"It doesn't matter now."

"So you don't care one way or another?" I push, my eyes lowered, as though the sandwich is the most interesting thing I've ever seen.

"Care?" I hear him swear under his breath and his eyes show the strength of emotions that he is carefully containing. "Of course I fucking care. But it's a decision that only you can make. It's your career, not mine."

I nod slowly. "So if I went, how would it work? What would that mean for us?"

He guards his words carefully. "Hard to say right now." His smile aims to reassure me but falls wide of the mark by several degrees.

"Then I'll stay," I respond firmly. "There'll be other opportunities."

He makes a guttural sound and comes to stand between my legs. He grips my face hard now, his fingers splayed across my cheeks. "You can't stay for me. I won't let you. I won't be the person who does that to your future."

You are my future, I want to shout but I don't see enough in him to encourage those words from my lips. My expression is a weak imitation of nonchalance. "This is delicious."

His eyebrows crinkle as he knits them together for a moment and then he nods. "Good." He drops his hands to my thighs and rubs them through the fabric of my jeans. "I'm watching you, okay?"

I laugh because it's one of those cheesy, slightly menacing lines from a bad movie but he means it to be reassuring. "I know."

My heart schisms and yet I nod. He's walking away from me and it doesn't feel like it's just for the afternoon. I put the sandwich down and move quickly after him. The hallway is busy and I bump into someone not paying attention as I weave through the halls. I catch him at the old stairs. "Alex?"

He turns to face me, and he is a ruthless CEO again, all powerful self-control and emotional distance.

I know of only one way to get through that barrier. I stand on my tiptoes so that I can whisper in his ear. "I don't know what I'll tell Carlton; I don't know what I'll do, but I do know I need you, with all my soul."

And I do. I need him now as I think I always will. I will not leave him, ever.

———

And I'm here. In the final class of the day, listening to Carlton, my eyes glazed as every single instinct in my body is trained on observing the room. I am near to the back, but in the middle, so I cannot easily turn one way or another without arousing suspicion. I know all of the students by sight, which means that if the guy is here he's been coming to my classes for a long time. That thought makes me cold.

Halfway through Carlton catches my eye and shakes his head. Has this all been for nothing? The class continues and I am barely listening, but that hardly matters.

As it draws to a close, my sense of outrage is a powerful, all-consuming beast. How dare this jerk stuff me around? He did say 'after' the last class, so it's possible he's waiting for me. Before Carlton has dismissed us I stand up and slide my way along the row of seats, my fingers curling around the cold metallic door handle of the room.

Carlton watches me go but I don't see him.

The hallway is more or less deserted. A few students moving slowly across the linoleum tiles like wraiths the night forgot to take. I stand outside the class, waiting for a sign from whoever it is that hunts me. There is not one. With a sense of bewilderment, I focus my eyes on one of the security cameras and shake my head.

It has all been for nothing, then. And I am no closer to the answers I so desperately need.

SEVENTEEN

LIKE BATMAN WITH A SPECTACULARLY NARROW VIGILANTE FOCUS

His hands move over my flesh, spreading goose bumps and desire with his light, sensual touch. I arch my back, silently inviting, impatiently wanting. He runs his hand lower, over my abdomen, to the apex at the top of my thighs and I groan.

The day is over, and though I am frustrated by the lack of answers; and indecision about the internship swirls through me, I care for nothing in that moment except this. The perfection that comes from being with Alex.

It is a cool night yet my body is hot; mercury is in my blood, boiling it in the fine casing of my veins. His mouth on my nipples is the most exquisite agony. I trace lines across his back, digging my nails into his hips, pulling him towards me with a single-minded desperation.

His throaty laugh sends arrows darting across my spine. It is so perfect.

My hair is dark against the pillow. He bunches it in his fist and then releases it; his mouth lifts to mine with punishing intensity. I sob, though it is not from sadness so much as a sense of being utterly overwhelmed. My legs wrap around him and still he doesn't come inside me. I am desperate to feel him.

"Please," I cry out, as he moves close, tantalisingly close, but doesn't enter me.

His hands lift to my breasts, he holds them in his palms and teases my nipples with his finger and thumb. I sob again. My need for him is making me ramble incoherently.

When he takes me it is not hard and fast, it is a gentle, tender encroachment and I moan, low in my throat, at the way my muscles expand to welcome him. It is like being brought home. He presses my wrists to the bed and kisses me. I feel like he is about to say something and I drag my lower lip between my teeth, waiting, feeling, hoping.

But he doesn't. He thrusts into me again, hard now, making me his in an inimitable way. I cry out into the silence of his apartment.

He plays my body like a musical instrument; it is so easy for him to drive me to orgasm now that I almost wonder if something is wrong with me. I can barely hold on; each thrust is tipping me over the edge. He knows it too. He runs his hands reverently over my breasts as he moves inside of me and it happens. I am flying, soaring through the heavens, screaming his name, my body quivering with the pleasure that he provides. But I know even as those sweet waves subside that more is to follow.

He waits just long enough for me to catch my breath and then he's right there, his body rocking mine. He pulls me up from the mattress so that I am in his lap and now I am moving, taking over instinctively, hard and slow, deeper inside of me until I feel his muscles bunch and I know he's working to hold onto his own control.

I don't want that, though. I want him to be as lost to this thing as I am. I need to see him as powerless as I. So I don't let him slow me down. I move faster, taking him deeper and I kiss him like he kisses me—with a desperation that comes from the very centre of my soul.

We explode together, as close as two humans can be. Our bodies are wrapped together, our mouths bonded, our souls as one. Even our breath comes out as a single husk. I love this, and I love him, and it is such a relief to be able to say that I do; I whisper it into his ear but my heart is shouting it.

He squeezes me tighter, and kisses my shoulder, but says nothing.

That tiny seed of doubt is being watered. Does he regret what he said earlier that day? God, was it only this morning? No wonder I am so tired.

But no matter how tired I am, he must be more so. From what I can tell he didn't sleep last night at all, and he has been at the university with me today. Now that my first need has been answered, I stroke his arms. "You should sleep."

"Sleep is the last thing on my mind," he assures me, and I have no idea what he's referring to.

He dislodges me from him neatly, placing me on the bed before standing and walking to the ensuite. I hear the water from the shower and stay in bed, staring up at the ceiling. I love this man so much it hurts. And I know he loves me now. But he's fighting it again. Fighting me.

My tummy makes a grumbling sound of complaint. I stand gingerly. As always, after making love to Alex, I feel like I've enjoyed a bit of a work-out. I pad through to the kitchen where there is a worrying lack of food available.

My tummy grumbles again and I grimace. But then…the cookie! I remember it with far more gratitude than it deserves. I have a vague memory of jamming it into my handbag after finishing the lunch Alex brought me. My bag is on the kitchen bench. Peering in I see the usual assortment of things I always mean to clean out. Pens that no longer work, lipstick, notebooks, and the cookie.

As I lift it out a piece of paper is stuck to the glue of the packaging. I dislodge the paper and am about to throw it back into the bag when my eyes rest properly on the writing.

"Bianca."

The cookie is forgotten as my fingers tremulously unfold the piece of paper.

"*This doesn't concern anyone but us—I told you that. Meet me tonight, outside your apartment. 9 o'clock. Don't bring Carlton or Alex* (He's under-lined that three times)."

I feel sick. I feel hot. I feel cold. I feel…everything. My body is reverber-ating with the entire spectrum of emotion. Fear emerges, but is quickly swallowed by determination, and weirdly, relief, because he *did* come. Somehow, he came, he realised I wasn't alone, and so he left this note.

I stuff the note back into my bag and flick my eyes to the microwave. It's already almost nine. "Shit." I am shaking like a leaf and I look like I've just rolled out of an orgy. I run my fingers through my hair, trying to tame it into some form of neatness. My clothes are strewn over the apartment, a physical testament to our impatience to be together. I slip my jeans on and then a sweater. I don't bother with a bra or shirt. I know that if I don't get out the door before Alex emerges from the shower I will not be able to go.

I know that I will weaken and tell him.

I know that I will see fear in his eyes and that it will stop me from doing what I must.

What I owe my parents—my real, dead parents.

And so I grab my handbag from the kitchen. The water stops running; my heart is in my mouth. I pad towards the door but quickly, like a pantomime artist. I pull it inwards, casting a quick glance at the security camera and then I swear softly.

I run back into the apartment and scrawl on the notepad he keeps near the fridge, *Gone for food. Back soon. S.x*

Rustling noises come from the bathroom; I have hardly any time. I return to the door, pulling it open and clicking it closed again quietly. The lift arrives almost instantly—thank heavens for small mercies—and I am in it and descending before I can question the wisdom of this.

I am falling in with this person's plan despite the danger. I am sick of danger.

I don't want to die.

Of course I don't. I have seen death and I have lived with the gratitude of the survivor. I have spent more than a decade honing my skills for survival but in this moment I choose to face death rather than to walk beside fear and doubt for the rest of my life.

I contemplate catching a tube but time is not on my side. I opt for a cab. One pulls in almost as soon as I raise my hand. I feel that there are Gods or guides shepherding me towards my fate. First my hunger pangs, then the lift, and now the speedy arrival of a carriage to my destiny.

My driver is chatty but I don't mind. I am able to smile and nod appropriately while my mind is absorbed in my own matters. My birth parents and brother are with me the entire way there. And so are Ally and Rick. I think about them all and I wonder what they would say if they knew I was ignoring all of the safety protocols and moving straight into the heart of drama.

They wouldn't understand the visceral need that runs through me to face my family's attackers head on. They took my family but I will not let them have my pride and dignity.

Only Andrew would have understood my need. He would have gone anywhere with me. I smile as I remember the sweetness of having his chubby little hand curled inside mine. The trust of that boy was the most beautiful thing.

And Alex? He must have found my note by now. And my phone, which I have left in the apartment to stop him from being able to find me. It's not that I think he's some kind of crazy stalker, but he's a tech billionaire and I'm pretty sure locating me through my phone signal would be a walk in the park for him. I've seen his office now, I know what tools and people he has at his disposal.

The cab pulls up near Marylebone station and I step out, my head bent, my senses tingling. Is he watching me now? Does he see that I am alone? My flat is a short walk away and I want to approach it on foot. I need the time to scope my bearings. I move quickly, slicing through the crowds like a ghost.

It is just past nine when I arrive. I stand, my breath burning from my lungs, my eyes tearing across the night sky. It's freezing but I don't feel it. It didn't occur to me to grab a coat.

I wait. And I wait. And when nine thirty slips past I am a tangle of emotions. Anger, frustration, grief, impatience, and in contradiction to that, gladness, because I was brave and took risks but didn't have to fight for my life tonight after all. I spin around, my eyes chasing figures in the dark. Though there are the usual late night types around, I cannot see anyone approaching me.

I am tempted to leave. But what does that say about me? Will he know I came?

"I had to be sure you were alone."

His voice is dark and throbs with a strength of emotion that terrifies me. I have heard crazy and I have heard unhinged and I think he might be both. It comes from right behind me. Every bone in my body is alert. I have heard this voice before and though I cannot place it exactly, I know it is from my deep past—that which I prefer to forget. There were voices that night; angry voices, like this, shouting, trying to find me.

I turn slowly. My eyes scan for detail but he is in the shadows and wearing a hood over his head. I cannot tell his age, nor can I see his face. I couldn't even say with certainty if this is the same man from the photo Carlton took.

His body is large though. He towers over me and he's broad shouldered and obviously very strong. Fear threatens to unbalance me but I fight against it.

"I am."

He nods again but says nothing so I take the lead.

"Who are you?"

He angles his head away from me; his chest moves rapidly. Up and down. Up and down. "You are Bianca DiSotto."

I think my agreement is a little redundant but I nod anyway. I do not know until that moment that I am proud to claim that part of myself. I have been waiting to own her, to speak her name aloud and hear it voiced by others, to recognise her once more as a part of this world. She is me, as I am her. No more running. "Guilty as charged."

"And yet you don't know who I am?"

My eyes narrow. "You remind me of someone," I say honestly. Fear is subsiding. The men who killed my parents were not talkers. If he wanted to kill me, surely I'd be dead by now. Unless…unless he wants something else first. Information? I have none to give. I said all I knew on the witness stand at the trial. "What do you want from me?"

"I want…" He takes a deep breath to compose himself. Fear is back. "I want you to tell me about that night."

It is not what I expect but I am grateful to be alive. The longer we talk, the safer I will be. I understand this and so I comply. "How did you find me?"

"That's not important," he snaps and I remember that I should be afraid still.

I nod jerkily. "Everything that happened that night is a matter of public record. It was in the papers at the time."

"I've read the papers," he says, and his voice sends tingles across me. His anger is palpable. "But they only tell me so much."

"So what do you want to know?"

"You were hiding in a closet in your parents' room?"

I nod. The street is no longer cluttered by other people. A sole bus drifts past but it is an orphan, a single shuddering beacon that is rapidly fading into the distance, alone, just like me.

"Why did you hide?"

A furrow crosses my brow. "My mother told me to." The past is swallowing me. "We used to play hide and seek. She and I. The wardrobe was one of the best spots. She told me to stay there, and to stay there no matter what happened." I swallow. "So I did."

"Even when you saw your parents being stabbed? Their throats slit?"

My face pales. I feel the colour fade from it. "My mother spoke to me as she was dying." I sob now, lifting a hand to my mouth. "She told me to stay. You don't know what that felt like. To see the life leave their bodies. My father, so strong, fading into bones and pale flesh before me."

He jerks his face away, and I know he feels my description.

"Who are you?" I ask again.

"I am asking the questions." His accent is different to mine; spiced with the far north. "You had a brother."

I nod. Pain is a fresh ache inside of me. "Yes."

"Why didn't he hide with you?"

I swallow a sob. "I didn't know where he was. It all happened so fast."

"How did it happen?"

I don't want to relive it but I need to keep him talking. My instincts tell me that is what will make me safe. "There was a noise."

"What noise? Where were you?"

The memories are playing out in my mind like a film. "I was watching my mother set her hair in curlers." Bizarrely, I smile. "She was beautiful; like a film star. Dad was working in the study because he had an important trial the next day and mum was going out with friends." I lift a hand and toy with my necklace. "I used to love watching her get dressed up. She would wear a silk robe while she did her hair and make up and then, at the last minute, she'd slip on a dress and step into heels and it was like a Fairy Godmother had transformed her." The words drip with nostalgia and I know I am being self-indulgent but he doesn't hurry me along.

"And?"

I nod. "There was a loud noise. I didn't know at the time, but I learned later, through the police, that they'd driven a stolen police car through our gates." I swallow. I am saying 'they' but in my mind I imagine he is one of them, somehow. "Our property was high-security but it wasn't fortified for something like that. They drove the car to the house and through our entrance way. My father called out. I still remember the sound of his voice as he shouted at my mother to get to safety."

I swallow. My throat hurts.

"And she saved you? Did she care about you more than your brother?"

"No!" I shout the word as a loud protest. "Andrew was our angel. We all doted on him." I sob, remembering his sweetness in a way that hurts so much. I want to hold him. "He was the most amazing kid. So smart and funny and he was full of love. He was beautiful."

"Yet she chose to save you."

"Why do you keep saying that? She saved me because she could. There was no chance to save Andrew. She went for him," I say slowly, remembering that she had hidden me and then gone out of the bedroom. "But they caught her at the top of the stairs and dragged her back to the bedroom. My father was with them."

"You couldn't do anything to help them?"

I shook my head. "I was only ten." I groan. "I wish I could have. I have spent every day since then wondering how I could have acted differently. But these men were intent on killing my family; they would have killed me too, even though I had grown up with their children."

"Yes, you had. You were close to the children."

It makes me wary because I am forced to recall that he and I are enemies. He is involved in this somehow, and not in a good way. "My father trusted those men. So I did too."

There is a tension from him at that statement. "Go back to the night. Your parents were stabbed in their room?"

I nod. "The rest is well known."

"But I want to hear it from you."

"Why?" I am emboldened by my grief. "Do you want me to relive it before you kill me?"

He is silent for a long time.

"Who are you?" I shout. I should be more afraid; no one is nearby. He could strike at any moment. And yet I no longer care. Perhaps this is my fate—to end my life while memories of my parents and brother are thick in my heart. Their lives and deaths are flooding my mind. I am with them and I feel them with me, too.

"I am your retribution," he responds angrily. His voice—where do I know it from? Why does it make my skin crawl?

"My retribution? For what? What did I do to you?"

"You did nothing!" He is furious! His voice is raised and his hand shakes as he waves it through the air. Is it good for me that he is unsettled? Or is he more likely to snap and hurt me out of blind rage?

"You told me you would always keep me safe and you did nothing! I hid and I waited and I waited and you never came! I was shouting your name and you stayed in the closet, hiding to save your own life, with no care for mine!"

His words are odd little daggers, perforating all of my certainties. I am sucking in breaths but I cannot push the air into my lungs. It makes no sense. None of it makes sense. "I don't...I..."

"You fucking coward," he shouts, and I see tears glistening on his face. His face. It is still mostly covered by the hood of his shirt.

I am no longer afraid. Not of him, but of the truth, that is finally, finally dawning. I step towards the man and when I am close enough to touch him I reach up and push at his sweater. He is there; it is him.

My brother, but not my brother. His face is scarred. I stare at the damage and he lifts a finger to it. "Two bullets. One narrowly missed by brain, the other sliced through my ear."

"Andrew?"

"You should have come to me! I was so scared. I kept calling your name, over and over. And you survived. You served only yourself."

"No!" I need him to understand me but I feel as though I can hardly breathe. I speak quickly—too quickly. The words hurt. "I wanted to go to you. But these men, they...I was so afraid, Andrew. Every bit as afraid as you. I was only ten." I cry now, openly, uncaring. "I wish I had acted more courageously, but I know I would never have gotten to you. They would have killed me."

"How do you know that?" He demands and his eyes are red-rimmed. He hates me. It is almost as bad as when I believed him dead, for he is voicing all of the recriminations I have levelled at myself over the years.

"They wanted my father to understand what he had done," I explain carefully. "They slit mum's throat in front of him. Her eyes were looking at me through the slats in the closet door. I had to stuff one of her nighties into my mouth to stop from screaming. Blood spurted everywhere. She was limp for a long time but they were so careful—they made sure that they gave her a slow, agonising death. It was the same with dad. They shot him, but in a way that would mean he lay beside her for a long time. Andrew, I tried to save them when the men were gone, but I tried to save you first. I went to you." I lift my hands and stare at them and they are red in my mind. "But you were already dead. I'm sure of it." A doubt sears into my mind. "You were dead. You were dead." The words are tumbling out of me but I can't control them. My mind is fading to black.

I am incapable of holding myself upright. I feel the ground racing towards me. I am powerless to stop the faint and he does not react quickly enough, though he tries. My head crashes to the sidewalk with a thump. But I am not unconscious for long. This is far too important for that. I blink my eyes, focussing on his face, which now hovers a little over mine. His eyes. I would never forget his eyes; it is like they have been poured with melted caramel and gold-dust. "I don't understand."

"You're bleeding."

"I'm fine." I put my hand on his chest and feel his heart. "It's not important."

"How did you survive?"

He is angry with me but there is concern too. He leans forward and inspects the matted hair at the back of my head. His fingers run gingerly over my scalp before he lifts his other hand in front of my eyes. "Follow my finger."

I do so for a minute and then dash his hand away impatiently. "Stop. Ignore it. I faint all the time."

"You always did."

"I just don't understand how you survived. I held you. You weren't breathing...I saw you. You were...I don't..." My sobs are leading to hyperventilation.

"Take it easy, Bianca. You're going to faint again and I don't want to play nurse maid."

"Then tell me! Tell me how you're here!" I squeeze my eyes shut. "I relived the worst night of my life because you asked it of me. Now tell me how the hell you survived that."

"You should go to a hospital," he says out of nowhere and I groan.

"I'm not going to hospital."

"My car's just down here. I'll tell you as we drive."

"I said I'm not going to hospital."

"Then let me drive you back to his place. We can talk on the way."

And because I am freezing cold and starting to shake, I nod. I am also still a tiny bit afraid and the idea of being returned to Alex glistens before me like an oasis on my horizon. Andrew helps me up. Touching him is like reconnecting with the past, only there are miles of barbed wire between here and then. He leads me across the street. "You died," I whisper. "We had a funeral."

"I know." His profile, illuminated by moonlight and golden street lights above, is hard and angular. He looks so much like my father I am almost unable to breathe.

"So what happened? Please tell me. I need to know."

He stops walking besides a black Maserati.

"Hop in."

I briefly take in the luxurious car and wonder at his current circumstances before doing as he's said. There is a tiny part of me, and it is only tiny, that wonders if I am being foolish to go so willingly into a car with a man I do not know. A man who says he is my brother, but who could plausibly be anyone from the past.

It is a stupid thought and I brush it aside. I have looked into his eyes and they are the same as the beautiful little gaze that used to follow me around the house as a child.

He throbs the engine to life and pulls out into traffic. It is not a long drive and I want him to begin talking immediately. "How are you still alive?"

"I don't remember much from that night." His fingers grip the steering wheel until his knuckles glow white. "I remember the fear. A fear that paralysed me. I remember hiding under my bed and I remember calling for you."

Guilt is a slick inside of me. "I heard you," I whisper. "I heard you. But mum was watching me." I sob again and I want to touch him, to reassure him, to tell him I love him. But I am not worthy of saying that to him. I let him down. I failed him.

"I was pulled from under the bed and shot." He shifts his gaze to mine for a moment. "The man who shot me was never found."

A frown pulls at my brow. "How do you know?"

"Let's just say putting this right has become a bit of an obsession of mine."

A shiver runs down my spine at the dark intimation. "Andrew...Is that still your name?"

"No." He enters the roundabout at Hyde Park Corner like a pro and it causes me to wonder if he lives in London. He knows the roads so well.

"I want to understand this. I can't believe you are alive. If I had known..."

His face is harsh. "It is one of the reasons I needed to see you."

"Why? You have stalked me. You've *terrified* me. Why didn't you just approach me?"

"I have been so angry with you," he says honestly. "I wanted to understand your life. They saved you. Why? Why did our mother choose you?"

"It wasn't like that."

He is quiet and finally, he shrugs. "Maybe."

"You should have just talked to me."

"I had no idea I could trust you. You left me to die. You were in the room when they died. I am cautious, Bianca, because it is how I am going to stay alive."

"God, Andrew, if there had been a flicker of life in your body I would have stayed with you. I wouldn't have left you. I thought only I had lived. And that's what everyone told me. It's how it was reported. Those men were charged with your murder."

"Yes." Brompton road is full of traffic. He slows to an almost-stop.

"So? What happened?"

"I know this only from what I have been told, you understand. My memories of that night are not complete."

I nod, my breath held.

"I did die, technically, in the ambulance on the way to the hospital, but I was revived. I died twice more that night and they were sure I would be brain dead. But children...I suppose there was a lot of sympathy for a tiny gunshot victim. Three teams of surgeons worked around the clock and eventually I stabilised. I was admitted under a false name. One of the detectives—a man named Russell Swan—contrived to cover up my survival. He felt that, if I were to live, I would be a target of future attacks. Given the involvement of dodgy cops in our parents' murder, he was right to be so cautious."

I shiver. "So you were put into PPU as well?"

"Yes. Very deep into PPU."

"And you knew about me?"

"Not at first." We are close to Alex's apartment. He pulls into a park and idles the car; now he can face me and I study his face in more detail. "Around the time I turned ten things started to come back to me. Memories of you. Mum, dad. Our life. Our house. That night. I nearly had a fucking breakdown trying to make sense of it all." My heart aches for this young man. "My PPU mother told me the truth. I went into therapy to help me deal with it. It was like this poisonous bomb that kept detonating. The discovery of our family—the fact my parents weren't my real parents. The fact that this," he runs his fingers over his face, "wasn't a birth defect as I had been told."

I swallow. "You must have been completely lost."

"Yes."

"And me? When did you find out about me?"

His smile is lopsided and so like my own that I find myself returning it instinctively. "When I could google. I became obsessed with it. I read everything. Everything."

"How did you find me?" The question is not simply self-serving and yet I must know. If he found me I am vulnerable to discovery by others.

"That's a long story." He reaches out and puts his hand over mine. "But you're my sister. The only relic of our family. I had to find you."

Tears clog my throat. "What can I call you?"

"My name is Ben now."

"Ben."

"Ben Campbell." He nods.

"You must be eighteen?"

"Yeah."

I am floored. He seems so grown up, like a man. Is it because he is so like dad that I see our father instead of the child?

"Where do you live?"

He shakes his head, declining to answer. "Old habits die hard."

"Don't I know it?" I smile, despite the circumstances. "Andy...Ben. I will never forgive myself for failing you as I did that night."

He presses back against the chair and squeezes his eyes shut. "I have been angry with you for a long time," he mutters. "You were my sister. Some of the fragmented memories that first came back to me were of us playing together; of you telling me to trust you, of you holding my hand, making me feel invincible, and then when I needed you, you weren't there."

"I was afraid," I whisper, ashamed of letting my own fear contort my obligations.

"I want to get to know you again."

His breath leaves his body in a weary gesture of resignation. "I want that too, but not yet."

"Ben ..."

"No one can know about me." His eyes are full of intensity. "Not Alex. Not Dr Carlton. Not your parents. Not Meera."

"You know so much about me." I shiver even though this is my little brother.

"I've been watching you," he says softly.

"You broke into Meera's apartment. You took the picture of us."

He nods.

"But why?"

His eyes glitter with determination. "Information is my power. She's your best friend."

I am so angry with him and yet I understand as no one else could. We have been raised to operate on a different playing field. We are cut from the same cloth and we have been through the same machine. We are one. "But I took the picture so that I would have it. You are not much older in it than you are in my memories. And I have no photos of you back then."

It is sweetness—an island of normal human instinct that I can cling to in the midst of this raging ocean of ancient anger.

I imagine keeping all of this from Alex and though I know I am capable of it, my stomach squirms. I am so sick of lying. So sick of secrets.

"I started something, Bianca. It's important and I need to finish it. I don't want you getting caught in the middle of it. The fewer people that know I'm alive the better."

A new sledge of fear runs through me. "What did you start? What do you mean?"

"Not all of those who hurt us have been punished for that night."

I close my eyes on a wave of disbelief. Incredulity colours my words. "You're going after them."

"Yes."

"That's foolish. You have a new life." I run my finger over the dashboard of the Maserati. "A good life, by the looks of it. You have PPU parents who love you..."

"My parents died last year." Grief perforates the simple sentence. "Holidaying abroad. They were caught in a suicide bomb attack."

"That's awful." Woefully inadequate description of such a harrowing event, I know.

"I came to you as a warning. I had to be sure you deserved to be warned, that's all."

"Warned about what?"

"I'm stirring up a hornet's nest and there's every chance it will lead them to you, as well as me. I found you. They will too."

"How did you find me? Was it that photo in the paper?"

He shakes his head. "That was stupid of you, but no. I found you six months before that."

"How?" I beg, confusion making me feel targeted and isolated in equal measure.

"Facial recognition software." He scans my face. "You are just the same as you were then." He lifts his fingers to my hair. "Even with the dye job."

"What are you? Some kind of spy?"

He laughs. "No. I'm more like Batman with a spectacularly narrow vigilante focus. My parents left me with enough money to fund this little quest of mine for the rest of my life. I will not stop until I have exterminated the men who did this to us, to our mum and dad."

I feel the determination of his words but I am loathe to encourage them. "I don't think our parents would want that," I say slowly, finally. "Mum would want us to live our new lives. To be alive."

I squeeze his hand. "Please just leave this all alone. It's in the past."

"You say that and yet you're still in hiding. You live in fear of being discovered. When will that stop? Will you one day fear for your children? Will you drop them at school worrying that they might be taken as a final enactment of this tragedy?"

"No. I...No." But my voice wretches with the emotion he's invoked. "I never plan to have children." I never plan to get married, I add silently. To love is to risk losing, and I cannot go through that again. Nausea rises through me, because those determinations are completely at odds with what I feel for Alex, for the future I desperately want with him.

"I'm going to end it." He skims his eyes over my face. "And when it's safe, I'll come to you. Then we can get to know one another."

"What if you don't? What if they're stronger than you?"

Another lopsided smile. "Then I'm dead, and it's just the same as it always has been for you. But it won't come to that."

I squeeze my eyes shut.

"You have to keep a low profile now. Go away somewhere. Disappear. Vary your routines. Move out of your flat. If they find you, it will weaken me."

"How? What do you mean?"

His smile is so familiar that my heart stutters. "Because I would do anything to keep you safe. Even risk exposing myself. My life is now linked to yours again, Bianca." *Don't fail me.* I hear what he's not saying. The accusation he doesn't want to level at me again. Because I did fail him then. I did.

"I don't want to lose you again."

His eyes pierce mine. "You won't. I'm going to be fine."

"How can you say that?"

"Because I'm very, very good at what I do."

And I don't, for a second, doubt him.

Eighteen

The Truth is a Black Hole

"She's here." Alex's eyes lock to mine and there is relief and accusation within him. "I don't know. I'll find out." He disconnects the call he's been on.

I have no idea how I look, but going by the way his face changes it is not pretty. He stalks quickly across the room, his eyes dragging from my messy hair to my blood-streaked cheek, down to jeans which are scuffed with sidewalk dust. "Jesus! What the hell has happened to you? Where have you been?"

His hands on my shoulders are interrogatory. He spins me, checking me over, probing me first with fingers and then with eyes.

"I'm fine," I don't want to lie to him. "I fell over."

"Your hair is thick with blood."

"I know." I lift my fingers to it self-consciously. "I landed backwards."

He turns me to face him and his expression shows disbelief. His hand is in the small of my back, propelling me out of the door again.

"What are you doing?"

He doesn't say anything; I can feel anger emanating from his body. "Alex?"

"Just...don't speak." He presses the button for the lift and the doors open instantly. We are inside and moving quickly to the garage. His driver is waiting for us. He too visibly blanches when he sees me.

"What is it?" I snap, wishing I had my phone so I could at least look at myself in the camera app.

"Where to?" The driver ignores my question. Alex waits until we are in the car before responding.

"A doctor. Now."

"Alex," I groan, unwilling to take a seat in the car. "You're overreacting."

"Like hell. Get in."

I shake my head but one look at his face and I decide my revolt can wait. He's not just furious, he's also worried as hell and I don't want to put him through that. "I'm really okay," I reassure him as I lower myself into the car. He takes the seat beside me then reaches over and clips my belt into place. His hand lingers on my hip but it's not sensual: it's the smallest contact—as though he's reassuring himself.

We move quickly out of the car park. I crane to look from the window. Andy's Maserati is gone and another vehicle has taken its place. So where is he?

My brother. I swallow a small, disbelieving sob.

It is enough, for now, to know simply that he is alive. I could never have hoped he would survive that night; for years I have believed the opposite.

I want to know more; I want to get to know him better. Will there be a time for that?

I can feel Alex's tension as we drive. He is hardly moving, his eyes fixed out of the window. Only his fingers shift, drumming impatiently against his jeans-clad knee. I am getting tired. The car slows at traffic lights and I feel my head fall forward. I must have drifted asleep and been jerked by the momentum.

"Fuck. Go faster." He unbuckles my seatbelt and lifts me onto his lap. I'm too tired to object. Besides, it feels nice to be held by him. His arms around me are moving gently, slowly, but I'm still freezing cold.

He feels the goosebumps on my arms and speaks again. I feel his words, rather than hear them. His chest rumbles. "Heater, Mav."

Mav. Who's Mav?

"Got it."

His driver, of course. Maverick. I remember thinking it was a funny name when we first met. Had his parents been Top Gun tragics?

"I feel the speed for need...no...spleed..." I laugh at the way the words are coming out all mixed up.

"Don't talk." Alex presses a kiss against my hair. I smile. It feels nice.

"I love you," I say, nuzzling in closer to his chest. He smells so good. Like shower gel and sex. I yawn and close my eyes. The sense of tiredness is delicious. Like the best kind of exhaustion.

"Don't shut your eyes," he says, lifting my chin with his thumb. His eyes scan my face and I can see he's really worried now.

"I'm sorry," I mutter, looking away.

He kisses me gently then, on my lips, then my forehead.

The car slows to a stop and when Mav opens the door I see red lights forming glowing puddles on the bitumen. Alex pushes me up gently, guiding me to the door of the car.

"Mav."

His driver hardly lets my feet touch the footpath before he scoops me up, holding me against his broad chest.

"I clan walk," I laugh and shake my head. "I *can* walk," I correct. "And you are seriously strong." The 's' sounds are slurred, as though I've been drinking.

Alex strides ahead. I watch his beautiful body disappear through sliding glass doors and am tempted to cat call or shout 'nice butt', but I'm really tired now and I don't know if I can get the words out.

There is white linoleum everywhere, pale green chairs and fluorescent lights, and out-of-date posters along the walls implore me to 'Get Vaccinated for 'Flu!' and 'Practise Safe Sex!' and 'Always Wash Your Hands'.

The man Alex was speaking to steps out from behind the counter and pulls a bed from his back. Okay, even I can see how silly that sounds. He's not a magician and a bed is not a rabbit and his back's not a hat. I'm rambling, even in my head.

Mav lays me down with surprisingly gentle hands, arranging my hair on the pillow. Wait. There's no pillow. He's just making sure it's not caught up around his watch, I think. Alex's face is above mine, grim and worried. And furious.

I remember wondering what it would be like to feel his wrath. To be the object of his displeasure. Now that I am the recipient of it, I am wishing to be anywhere else.

"Don't be closs," I whisper.

He swears so quietly I don't hear him. He bends down so that his lips are right by my ear. "I'm not closs."

I frown. That doesn't make sense.

"Sir? We should go now."

"Right." Alex straightens up and I am being pushed away. I sit up to see him, and have a vision of his face wracked with such emotion that I shiver. Then, the man Alex was talking to puts a hand on my shoulder. "Stay still, miss. It's Sasha Lewis, right?"

I nod, flopping back against the bed. Damn the lack of pillow. My head is killing me.

"This iffn't sholt."

"Very true. Watch out." We push through some doors and he disappears. I can hear his voice but not the words he's speaking.

A woman appears now, her face pleasantly lined around her eyes and mouth, as though she's smiled a lot in her time. Her hair is slightly greyed around the temples and clipped back into a barrette that leaves some of it falling over her shoulders. It's nice hair.

"Hi Sasha, I'm Melinda. I'm going to have a little look at what's going on, okay?"

I nod but she shakes her head. "Stay still, thanks."

She's shining a light in my eye. It hurts like a mother-fucker. I close my eyes against the pain and she makes a murmuring sound which I think is a good sign.

"Open up," she says, tapping me on the shoulder.

I blink up at her cautiously but the light assault is over and now she's holding a finger in front of my eyes. Just like Andrew did. Andy! My brother. I haven't thought about him for at least twenty minutes. A smile curves my lips.

He's alive.

"Who's alive?" She asks and I bite my lower lip. I didn't mean to speak out loud.

Something odd is in my mouth. And my neck. Melinda's hands are on my shoulders, rolling me gently and the man who pushed me into this room is holding something.

Oh. I'm vomiting. Right. That's nice, isn't it. It's covering me. My hair now has a sludge of blood and vomit and I must stink worse than I think I look.

"Sorry."

Her smile is amused. "You're not the first person to be sick in an emergency room, love."

"Soft's slong…" I close my eyes and take in a deep breath, focussing all my attention on the words I want to get out. "What's wrong me?"

"What's wrong with you?" She repeats, her eyes scanning my face. "You have a nasty concussion." I hear her snapping gloves on and again she's lifting me slightly so that her fingers can run over the back of my head. After a minute of probing she nods, satisfied apparently. "I'm going to send you for an X-Ray, Sasha. It's just a precaution to rule out anything more serious." Her face hovers closer to mine. "I'm almost positive that you just need a good rest and a quiet few days to come right though."

I nod, too tired to argue.

I am x-rayed and then a female nurse who must have drawn the short straw gently changes me out of my clothes and runs warm water through my hair and over my shoulders, cleaning away vomit, blood, and family reunions that must stay secret.

My clothes are put into an orange bag and tied to the side of my bed; for clothes I am provided with a hospital gown, though at least it's not like those ones you see on telly. It's completely closed at the back so no risk of showing off my arse.

Sometime after her ministrations, before I can thank her, I fall asleep. And I sleep all night, except for the several times I'm shaken awake so that they can shine a light in my eyes. It's torture, truly it is. Don't they know I just want to sleep?

I think it's around four o'clock when I first notice his shadowed frame, hunched in a chair. At first I think he's asleep and I drift off again. But at six o'clock, more light is permeating my little room, and I realise he's in the exact same pose, dead still, his eyes locked to my face. There is fear slicking his body. I can smell it.

I smile to reassure him. And I do feel a lot better. Aside from a God awful headache, I'm more or less myself.

"Hey." My voice is croaky but no longer slurred by confusion.

He stands immediately and comes to the side of the bed. He doesn't touch me. His hands are thrust deep in his pockets. "Hey yourself." He clears his throat. "How do you feel?"

"Fine," I lie. I reach for him. I want to touch his flesh. He is worried and I hate that it is because of me.

He nods. "Good."

"I'm sorry," I say after a beat of silence has passed without either of us speaking.

He shakes his head. "Don't. It's not your fault." His Adam's Apple jerks as swallows. "Hell, Sasha." He drags a hand through his hair. "What happened?"

My eyes shift away from him in what I know must be a tell-tale sign of guilt. "I told you last night, didn't I? I fell."

It is obviously a lie and I sense it is the moment. A turning point for us. A withdrawing from him, a distancing that I may one day learn to live with.

I hate lying to him.

It feels like I am peeling my skin off, layer by layer. I have felt this way before, and I feel it again now, more keenly. It has grown in proportion to my love for him, and his love for me.

But the truth is a black hole.

I trust Alex. I trust him with my life. But with my brother's? No. I will never betray Andrew again. His secret will stay with me, always. It's not even a decision.

"When can I go home?"

A frown tugs at his lips. "Melinda wants to check you out personally. After that."

I shake my head. It twinges and I pull a face. He notices. Concern flashes in his eyes.

"This is so silly. It was just a clumsy accident," I murmur.

"I don't believe you." His statement hangs between us. A silent challenge. Though he hasn't phrased it as a question I know he's asking me. He wants me to tell the truth, to contradict myself.

My eyes drop to the waffle weave blanket covering my legs. "I know."

I feel his breath breeze over my head. "Were you with him?"

My eyes startle guiltily to Alex's face. "With who?" The question is breathy.

"Carlton. Who else?"

"Oh." It's absurd; a ridiculous notion. "No."

"Sash..." He sits down on the side of the bed. His weight depresses me towards him, so that my legs curl a little around him. Or maybe that's just me, wanting to be as close as possible to his warmth and strength.

"I wasn't." I put my hand on his arm, squeezing it. "We're just friends."

He nods. I know how unusual it is for him to feel this insecurity and I hate that it is because of me.

Things are weighing on his mind. I can see his worries as surely as he can see my web of secrets. "Close your eyes. It's early."

I don't want to. I want to talk to him. But this secret is so much worse to keep than the first. It will be our undoing. And the realisation makes me weep inside. I close my eyes and try not to think about the unravelling of our love. The dismantling of what we have come to mean to one another.

When next I awake, Melinda and Alex stand side by side at the foot of my bed.

"And flying?"

"Not for a week or so," she says with a shrug. "But that's just being cautious. Head injuries are funny things; it's better to be safe than not."

His hair flops over his brow and he rakes it back. "Anything else I need to know?"

"Just keep it easy for her. Let her rest. No stress."

His lips are a grim line. "Fine."

Melinda turns to study me and notices my eyes are open. "Ah! The patient of the hour. How do you feel?"

My headache is easing. "Okay, I guess."

"Good. I've given Alex strict instructions to call me if you start speaking gobbledegook again. But that's not likely."

I smile at her and wait until she's left the room then turn my focus on this enigmatic man. "So? What next?"

"You come home." He clears his throat.

"I don't want to put you out." I look down at the bedding. "I mean, I know how busy you are and you've already lost days because of..."

He lifts a hand to silence me. "I've hired a nurse."

"Oh." It smarts. My cheeks flush, though I don't realise how badly I had been lacking colour. "Right. Thank you."

I move to stand from the bed, but he's there with me, his hands gently, impersonally, helping me. I run my palms over the gown once I'm standing, looking to fill the silence. "How glam is this?"

His smile is just a ghost of a thing. "You ready?"

I nod. What's going on? A familiar figure is standing in the lounge area.

"Has he been here all night?"

"Who?"

"Mav."

"Yeah."

I feel worse, if that's possible. So much inconvenience for everyone, just because I couldn't keep a level head when I most needed it.

It is strange coming back to Alex's apartment. I walk in with the knowledge that things have shifted fundamentally between us, and also just for me. I have a brother. I am no longer a sole survivor, the only one left from our family. We are orphans, but we live.

We.

Plural.

Two DiSotto children.

Everything is just as it was when I left the night before.

Everything, that is, except Alex.

He links his fingers through mine and pulls me slowly behind him, leading me to our bedroom. Our? When did it go from being solely his to one we share?

"I'm not tired."

His eyes are laced with frustration. "I don't particularly care. Get in."

He's bossy to a fault, and I've kind of come to accept that. But I want to provoke an argument and I know why. When we argue, our tension builds to an inevitable climax. I don't think he'll sleep with me in my current condition, but I don't know if I have that discipline myself.

"No."

His eyes run over me appraisingly as he draws in a deep breath. "Fine," he says slowly, and I know he's going against every bone in his body by not telling me to stop being so fucking stupid. "Where would you like to be?"

I bite down on my lip. "The lounge."

"Okay." He puts an arm around my waist, leading me back through the apartment.

"But first I want to shower. And get changed."

He groans. "Sasha..."

"Just quickly," I demur.

"Fine." He studies my face. "That's fine."

I can't help but smile. "That seems to be the word of the hour. Why do I get the feeling it's not the F word you're really thinking?"

He doesn't look at me. "Because you know me."

In the bathroom, he lifts the hospital gown off me carefully and then begins to strip his own clothes. My surprise is evident so he explains, "I'm not going to risk you falling over again, knocking your head through the glass screen."

He starts the water running and holds the door for me. It is such a pleasure to experience that first jet of water, soothing my body. I let it flush my hair, and am surprised to see dark brown running towards the drain. The last vestiges of blood are coming out.

He fills a loofah with shower gel and begins to rub my body, cleaning me, caring for me, tending to my needs, and stirring new ones. "Alex?"

His eyes meet mine. His chest is wet. Beautiful, wet, sexy. I drop my mouth to his nipple and flick it with my tongue. He draws in a breath but steps backwards. "Don't."

"I can't help it."

"Yeah, well, you have to." My hands run the length of his torso, teasing his abdomen until I find his shaft. I wrap my fingers around its firm length. He's pretending he doesn't want me but our bodies are responding as they always do.

"Why?" I push my body closer to his, so that my soft curves are flattened against his angles and planes. "You know there's only one way to make me feel better again." I grab his wrist with my spare hand and bring it to the heart of my arousal. I am throbbing with heat. I know, I know, sex should be the last thing on my mind. But I'm craving reassurance and I know that's a pretty messed up thing to need at a time like this but hey, I'm only human, and a pretty fucked up one, I'm coming to realise.

He pulls his hand away and moves it to my shoulder. He's going to push me away. So I lower my own fingers to my sex and begin to move them while my other hand runs the length of his strong shaft.

"Sash." It's a guttural cry. "Don't do this." Now his hands are stronger as they curl around my wrists and stop me from seriously enjoyable exploration.

I bite down on my lip and he kisses me gently. Water runs over us.

"I want you," I say simply.

"Yeah, I know." He swears. "That's mutual. But I want you to get better more. I want to be able to look after you, not just fuck you." He kisses me again, so tenderly that my knees feel weak. "Let me do this."

"Do what?"

His eyes are haunted; there's sacrifice and inevitability in his gaze. "Let me do what's right for you."

Nineteen
Every Molecule on Earth has become Dull and Leaden

The seasons are merging, bringing with them a coldness that is impossible to ignore. It has been five days since I met my brother and Alex hasn't pushed me for details on what happened that night.

This is uncharacteristic.

He likes to know everything, and especially everything about me, and yet he takes my lead on this. Ally and Rick are less content with my reassurance that I'm taking extra precautions. They want me to go to the police. But I would never do that. I can't do anything that might lead to Andrew's discovery.

So I am quiet on the matter, happily ensconced in Alex's flat, watching autumn bleed into winter.

The first real sign I have that the seasonal shifts are bringing other changes with them is the arrival of Carlton at Alex's apartment.

I hear Alex welcome him and realise this is by pre-arrangement.

Though I feel completely well now, I am enjoying my invalid's position on the sofa, surrounded by a duvet, pillows, and a never ending supply of cups of tea and chocolate, not to mention: Alex.

I straighten a little self-consciously, tucking my hair behind my ears and stand when Carlton approaches.

"Hey." His eyes are scanning me, as though I'm an *object d'arte* he intends to buy. "How are you feeling?"

"Much better, thanks."

"What happened that night?"

I hear Alex clear his throat and lower my head. Apparently Carlton hasn't got the memo that we aren't talking about my stalker. It is as though he has disappeared into thin air; which, I suppose, he has. "I've been worried about you," he pushes. "Have you heard anything else from whoever it was?"

"No," I say honestly. "I guess they gave up. Or maybe I got the wrong end of the stick."

His frown shows that he thinks that's a big load of bullshit. "I haven't seen him back on campus."

And he won't. Andrew is gone, I'm sure of it. I have no way of contacting him, and yet I suspect he's watching me still. Not to scare me, but to protect me. He is my brother, and we are linked—now more than ever before, even when we cannot speak as normal siblings do.

I drop my gaze to the stack of books Carlton is holding. "What's that?"

He places the books on the coffee table then takes the seat opposite me. Alex is nearby, hovering, his presence dark. "Research."

I wrinkle my nose. "For an assignment?"

"Sort of." He leans forward in the chair, pinning me with his earnest, intelligent eyes. "It's background for the internship."

The internship. I'd completely forgotten about it. I don't dare look at Alex. I don't want to ignite this issue between us. "I'm not going to apply." I don't look at either of them when I say it.

Carlton responds first. "Why not?"

Why the hell does he think? I am so in love with Alex that the idea of being separated from him by an ocean and a considerable continent makes me want to vomit. "It's not the right time for me," I say.

You have to keep a low profile. Go away somewhere. Disappear. Move out of your flat.

My brother's words are a ghost in the room that I alone am aware of.

"You can't pick and choose with things like this," Carlton responds.

"This is the case. It's big. And it's important. Do you want to be a part of it? Of great justice? Or doesn't any of that matter anymore?"

"Of course it does." I am angry. I don't think he has any business questioning my commitment to justice.

He reaches into his pocket and pulls out his phone. The photograph he shows me is of two girls, probably about the same age I was when my parents died. "These girls have been trafficked for sex across the States almost their whole lives."

Bile claws at my throat.

"They are terrified of adults. Look at the fear in their eyes and try to imagine how it got there." He lets the words hang between us. "Who will empower them if people like you decide it isn't convenient?"

"Stop it," I say softly, closing my eyes on the wave of sadness that is deluging my certainties. "That isn't fair."

"Yes, it is. It's a perfectly fair assessment of this situation. You have a brilliant legal mind and I need your help. They need your help. What reason can you possibly have for not going?"

"Because," I mutter. My eyes lift to Alex, but nothing flickers in his face. No hint of recognition or relief; no look of pleading or remorse. Nothing. As though my decision is completely inconsequential to him. "I have all this stuff going on..."

"Isn't that more of a reason to get away from here?" Carlton points out pragmatically. "Who in LA is going to care about something that happened a long time ago, a long way away?"

I resist the urge to make a Star Wars joke. It's not the time. He wouldn't appreciate it.

"It's not that easy. I'm halfway through the term."

"So? I told you, you'll get credit for this."

"And my parents are here. My best friend. And Alex." I practically whisper his name, so ashamed am I of having to enumerate him as a reason. Why do I feel like that? I can't say.

"Alex agrees you should do this."

The words hit me over the head like a board. I stare at Carlton, but my ears are screeching and my eyes are itchy. "Does he?" I murmur softly. "How nice of him to fall in so neatly with your plans."

I hear Alex shifting a little. He's right behind me. His hand on my shoulder is encouraging me to be calm. To listen.

"I need to know today, Sash."

"Today?"

He nods. "I'm flying out tonight to start work as soon as possible."

"God, I can't make this kind of decision that fast." I want to brush Alex's hand away. It's mocking me; mocking us. What we are to each other.

Carlton's eyes move higher, to the man who is the reason I am hesitating. We all know it. His smile is perfunctory. "I don't know this for certain but I *think* Alex is in a financial position to afford to come over often. Don't you have offices in LA anyway?"

Alex squeezes my shoulder again; panic grows.

"You can't," I murmur, the words hollow, thinking of Alex's life, before me, of his business, sure, but also his mother. "You can't relocate."

Carlton shakes his head. "So? I don't mean to be insensitive but do you really want to jeopardise everything you've worked for? Do you know how rare this opportunity is? You are crazy to even think of passing it up. That's before you factor in whoever your crazed stalker is."

Alex's hand lifts of my shoulder. "That's enough." He walks towards the door and pulls it open. "You've said your piece. Sasha will contact you today with her decision."

Carlton lifts his phone up in front of me as he stands. Their eyes. The girls in this photo have eyes that completely lack life. A shiver runs down my spine. I recognise their fear.

"What are their names?" I ask when he's about to leave.

"They go by Britney and Casey," he said quietly. "We don't know what they were christened. Britney was sold when she was only two months old. Casey, from what we can tell, was kidnapped at six months. There are four more. Some younger, some older, their stories just as tragic."

"Fuck." I shut my eyes and lean back against my wall of cushions.

I hear the door click closed and then the approach of Alex's footsteps. My face shouts a silent but furious reproach. "What the hell?"

I feel bombarded and trapped. And now I also feel like a rather selfish first-world lawyer who preaches about equality from the middle of her billionaire boyfriend's Knightsbridge penthouse.

Alex crouches at my feet. His body language is intimate but he's completely closed off to me. I can't tell what he's feeling. This silence is unfamiliar. It is being weighed down by sadness and confusion.

"Do you want me to go?"

"Of course I don't," he says, only I'm not convinced. *But.* He hasn't said it, yet the word is there, jutting into my brain.

So I say it, prompting him to continue. "But?"

"If you hadn't met me, and Carlton offered you this, would you even be hesitating?"

My breath is hurting me. My lungs burn with the pressure of trying to inhale and exhale. "I'm not going to speak in hypotheticals," I mutter lamely. "I have met you, and I love you."

He nods, but says nothing.

Doubt, sharp and painful, begins to rip through me. He has said he loves me. And he's not the kind of man who would make that up, or lie about it. But since that day in his office, when we were both afraid for my life, he hasn't said it to me even once.

I say it often. I litter our days with little mentions of love.

Panic spreads; it is wildfire in my veins, superheating my skin from beneath.

"I love you," I say again, baiting him, jiggling the fishing line, waiting for a response that will allay my worry.

It doesn't come. He sighs instead. "Listen, Sash." He sits up on the sofa beside me and it takes every single bit of my will-power not to tell him get stuffed and storm out of the room. Indulging a fit of histrionics would definitely feel good but I want to hear what he has to say. Hope is not completely lost.

"Yeah?"

He curls my hair behind my ear. "You should go to America."

It floors me. "Why?"

A muscle jerks in his cheek. His eyes don't meet mine. Something bad is coming. "What happened to you that night?"

I frown and then shake my head as I comprehend what he's asking. "I went out for a walk. To clear my head."

He nods, standing up and walking towards the windows that look towards Harrods. His back is ramrod straight. "I don't trust you. You're lying to me. You've been lying to me all along."

"I had to," I say, surprised to hear the words are saturated by tears. "I hated lying to you but..."

"You're still lying to me," he interrupts coldly.

Fuck. "If you don't want to be with me, then have the fucking balls to say that. Don't try to ship me off to America on the pretext of my career."

He drags a hand through his hair, pushing it back from his face, but he doesn't look at me. "Your career isn't a pretext."

"But the fact that I've had to tell lies of self-preservation? That's a deal-breaker?"

He spins around, his eyes lock to mine. "Is that what this is? A lie of self-preservation?"

I open my mouth, realising the trap but only now it's too late. "It's... yes." I look away. "I can't say anything else."

"Because you don't trust me either."

I shake my head. "That's not true. You know I trust you."

"So tell me."

I open my mouth and close it again. I'm gaping a little like the Mexican walking fish that made a bid to freedom when I was fourteen, leaping out of its bowl and landing in the middle of the carpet. Funny that even now I can feel shame at my reaction. I was too squeamish to lift him up and touch his soft, slimy body; too afraid of those odd, mutated looking limbs and the way they might hurt me. So I'd looked around ineffectually for something to use—a tool to help me get him back into water. By the time I'd manoeuvred his body onto a piece of cardboard, he was dead.

"I don't know jack about healthy relationships." Alex's voice runs through me "I've never seen one. I've never had one. But I know plenty about the fucked-up kind. And I think that's what we are."

I'm suffocating. Is this what my fish felt like? I can't draw breath. It's agony. "You don't love me."

His eyes scan my face. And I know exactly what this silence means.

I shake my head. Tears are falling down my cheeks; I don't bother wiping them away. "Don't say it," I beg, shaking my head. "If you don't say it, I can at least pretend..."

"America is your decision," he says instead. He moves around me, walking towards the door of the apartment. "But don't make it based on me."

"Where are you going?"

"Out." He turns around once, and his eyes are haunted with all of the things he hasn't said. "When you let Carlton know, tell me too."

"Are you kidding me?" I storm after him, my body shivering with rage. "That's what you want to say to me? Why are you treating me like someone you hardly know?"

"Isn't that what you're doing to me? You keep saying you love me but you keep everything walled up inside of you."

"You have secrets too."

"Which brings us back to what I said. We can't make this work. Neither of us has what it takes. Let's just accept it."

"So you want me to go?" I murmur softly.

"I want you to decide what's right for you."

"And if I stay?"

He frowns. Now it's his turn to go all fishy, gaping over words that don't fit what he wants to say. "You should go," he says finally. "We both know it's the right choice."

My anger is a beast in my chest. I push at him and sob simultaneously and then spin away, stalking through the apartment to the room we have shared. I half-expect him to follow me, but when the door clicks shut, he is gone.

———

It takes me two days to wrap up my life in England. To do my last work shift, to arrange things with the university, to have one last dinner with Meera, back from Mumbai and full of love for the world and everyone in it after taking part in such a special family wedding. She doesn't know anything about what I've been through and I keep it that way. Alex is right. I'm great at lying. I lie so naturally that I glide through dinner with

Meera without mentioning anything. Not my broken heart or my broken brother.

I farewell my parents who are, obviously, thrilled that I am moving away from what they perceive to be a now-dangerous existence. I must lie to them, also. Andy's secret is not mine to share and so I hold it close to my chest, right in the spot beside my broken heart.

And it is broken. With every moment that passes without word from Alex, it becomes more and more so.

I left a note for him. *I'm leaving. Thanks for everything.* I presume he got it, it was right on his kitchen bench. But I haven't heard a word from him since.

His absence is indescribably enormous in my life. As though every molecule on the earth has become dull and leaden. I am waiting for something to happen to make me feel more alive.

Perhaps this is it. I stare at the plane, and in the small part of my brain that still has cognitive function, I wonder at the miracle of human-kind. That at some point, someone decided to build an aircraft, something that would defy all of the laws of gravity and torpedo through the air.

A little girl walks past me, her eyes, like mine, locked to the vehicle beyond the windows.

"Wow. It's huge." She speaks with an American accent.

"Yeah. A double decker."

She looks up at me curiously. "I'm going home. How 'bout you?"

I wrinkle my nose. "Nope. This is my home."

"So you're going on holiday?"

I shake my head. "Sort of. I'm going to do a job. But it'll take a little while."

She nods, her expression pensive. "My daddy does that. He goes every-where for work."

"Does he?" I smile gently. "You must miss him."

"Yeah. Kinda. But he brings me back awesome toys. And this time I got to come with him."

"That's nice."

"This was my first time in London."

"Was it?" Subtly I scan the airport, looking for the grown-up who belongs with this kid. Oh, she's sweet and I don't mind her talking to me, but nor do I want anyone suspecting me of something sinister. Sad, isn't it, that these are the times we live in? "Did you like it?"

"Guess so. Kinda cold."

I smile knowingly. "Compared to California, I guess."

"Alison?" A man is behind us, and the little girl looks up with a huge grin.

"Oh, hi, daddy."

"Honey, how many times have I asked you not to wander off like that."

She—Alison, apparently—rolls her eyes in an exaggerated fashion. "He's always on his cell phone. I don't wander off. He's just not looking."

The man looks suitably chastened. "It was an important call."

She stands and brushes her hands down her jeans. "Aren't they all?" It's such a mature observation that I gather it's an impersonation of someone in her life. Perhaps her mother? "Nice talking to you," she smiles.

"You too. Enjoy the flight."

I settle back down in my seat, resuming my brooding. It's hard to believe this is actually my life. A week ago, Alex was at its centre, and now he's not. Or he is, but not in a real way. Not in a way where I can reach out and touch him, where I can have him to look forward to. I don't know how long I've been sitting, waiting, when the first announcement is made, asking the passengers of my flight to form a line.

I don't move.

What's the point when seats have been assigned? Is there any advantage to racing to get to the seat you're going to be wedged into for hours and hours?

I watch the line move in the reflection of the windows. People shuffle. Noises. Children crying. Crinkling of crisp packets. I close my eyes, tuning them out. For a moment, I'm back at Alex's, in my favourite spot, by the windows that catch the afternoon sun, warmth in my hair, across my skin. I open my eyes, willing the dream to have become reality, but it's not. I'm still here, in the impersonal airport waiting area, surrounded by strangers. A lump forms in my throat.

I've always known that our separation was inevitable. It was one of the first things we agreed to. And yet here I sit, denial coursing through my veins, because the idea of my existing without Alex is abhorrent.

There is another noise. Closer than the others. Deep breathing. I look out of instinct, curiosity sparked. I turn my head slowly, not sure what I expect. Definitely not him.

Alex.

His chest is rising and falling as though he's run a marathon and, for once, he looks properly dishevelled. Delicious.

Shock sears me. Am I hallucinating? Did I conjure him up?

His hands wrap around my wrists, pulling me to standing. The magazine I'd been saving for the flight drops between us. He doesn't speak. Another silence; another mystery.

"What are you doing here?" Damn it, I'm trying to remember that I'm angry with him. That he's fucked me around royally and broken my heart, but all I can think about in that moment is how badly I want to kiss him. To feel his arms wrap around me and hold me tight.

"I messed up," he says thickly. "I was so angry, so fucking terrified but I should never have said what I did."

I feel the eyes of people behind us and cast a glance over my shoulder. Yes, curious gazes abound. I pull my hands free self-consciously and move a little closer to the window. He follows, protecting me from the curiosity of passers-by with his broad frame. "What do you mean?"

His hands cup my face, as if making sure I'm real. "These two days without you, I just...I can't do that. I can't live like this."

Confusion and doubt hamper my ability to form words. I am angry with him, I am hurting, and I am aching. But I have lived with hurt and loss and my instinct is to protect myself from more of both.

"You don't trust me," I remind him stiltedly. "And you're right. We can't do this without trust."

His nostrils flare as he breathes out, long and slow. When he speaks, his voice rumbles. "I trust that you are good and kind. I trust that you are honest and well-intentioned. If there is a secret you need to keep from me, I have to learn to live with that, if the alternative is letting you walk away."

I shake my head and then switch to a nod. I don't know how I feel. My lips are quivering unstoppably. He rubs his thumb over my lower, and then drops his hands, linking our fingers together.

"When you disappeared that night, I faced a fear I have never known possible. I believed you had been kidnapped. For the hour you were gone I imagined the very worst happening to you. And then you came back looking like an extra from The Walking Dead, with blood all over you, scratches on your arms. If you are in that kind of danger and I can't protect you from it, it will kill me. Don't you see that? How can I keep you safe if I don't know what threatens you?"

I am sorry for what he felt. "I don't want you to protect me," I whisper. "I'm not your mother."

His head jerks away as though I've flicked him hard against the jaw.

"You grew up wanting to save her, but knowing you were too small, that you couldn't." Though he has never said as much, I am sure I'm right. "It's only natural that you would have a hero complex."

"Never before," he said with a gruff rebuke. "Only with you."

"So I bring it out in you," I say softly. "But I have spent my life running, hiding and being protected. First by the programme, then by my parents, even by Carlton though I didn't know it. It's time for me to be brave and face the world on my own, don't you think?"

His expressive eyes show a thousand and one emotions. "I want to be with you," he says thickly, finally. "I want to stand beside you while you fight your own battles. Don't tell me whatever secret it is you need to protect, but let me stand with you when you need me."

It's too much. It's so close to being exactly what I hear that my resolve crumbles. "Why?" I whisper.

"*This is a final boarding call for flight AA 720 to Los Angeles. Would all remaining passengers please proceed to the boarding gate.*" The disembodied voice shatters the intimacy of our conversation. I blink as if waking from a dream and turn my eyes to the line. It's disappeared. There is only me, and Alex.

"I have to go."

He nods but his hand squeezes mine. "Just wait, a moment."

"I can't wait," I shake my head, frustrated and angry and broken all at once. "You told me to go. You said you don't want this. You don't want me. I'm going. Literally, now."

"I know, I just need to say something before you do, something I have regretted not saying since I last saw you."

I stare into his eyes, waiting, breath held.

"I love you. I love you. I love you. I love you as Bianca or Sasha. I love you in my bed, in my shower, at my table, in a restaurant, in my car, in my head, on the phone, all the time. I love you." The words rain over me like tantalising pleasure. But the timing...It couldn't be any worse.

"God, Alex. This is a shitty thing to do." I shake my head, even as my heart is soaring. "I accepted this internship. I've signed a contract. People are counting on me. I can't not go."

"I know that." He wraps his arms around my waist. "I still want you to do this. It's obviously important for your career. And for you personally too. But don't go to America and close the door on us."

"You did that," I shoot back, my mind swinging from one extreme emotion to the other. "You're the one who did that."

He strokes my face. "Seeing you hurt and out of it that night I realised I would do anything to know you are safe. Even give you up. But I don't want to. I don't want this to be over."

"Excuse me, ma'am?"

I blink at the interruption, wiping away the tears that are covering my face. A pretty flight attendant is watching us with apologetic interest. Her make up is layered on thickly so she looks like a beautiful porcelain doll.

"We really need to board the flight for take-off now."

I nod, breaking away from Alex and reaching for my bag. "Why are you doing this now?"

"I couldn't let you leave..."

"But you couldn't arrive ten minutes earlier?"

"I had to buy a fucking ticket and the security line was monstrous. And I only found out an hour and a half ago that you were leaving today."

I see fear in his face as I hoist the bag over my shoulder. It is a powerful experience for me having spent the last two days feeling as though I have been walked all over. But the desire to gloat is quickly usurped by a fervent need to wipe away the worry I see on his features.

"I have to go." I look towards the attendant. Three of them are watching us now.

"I love you." He says it so simply; does he realise how badly I needed him to say that days earlier?

"So? What do you want? How does this work?"

"I would come with you if I could..."

"I'm not asking you to do that."

"My mother…"

"I know." I interrupt him. "I know. And I get it."

"I'll visit."

It's two simple words but they burst over me like a glitter bomb. My heart thumps and rolls.

"Ma'am?"

I nod jerkily. "I'm coming."

"I'll visit," he repeats, wrapping his arms around my waist.

What can I do but surrender? At one stage, Alex was all that I wanted. And while I still want him, just as much, I also want other things. My future, salvation for those being treated unjustly, and a chance to prove to both of us that I can exist without him in my daily life.

I lift up onto the tips of toes, not caring about our audience. "And I will come back yours, as much yours as I have been since the first night I met you." I kiss him as though we are alone in our bedroom and he is going to make love to me. I kiss him with all of my love and all of my need.

"Visit soon," I breathe the words into his mouth.

I feel him watching me walk away and so I sashay my hips a little more. I love him, and he loves me. And for right now, that's as good as it's going to get.

I turn around once I'm through the doors. The attendants are already locking them behind me. Seeing him on the other side of the glass feels a thousand kinds of wrong but I lift my hand and quiver my fingers in a silent farewell.

My heart is breaking.

I have just taken my seat when my phone buzzes with a text message. I check it quickly, before I can be told to switch to flight mode.

If you ever doubt my love for you, read this message: without you, I am nothing. My strength is tied to you. I am not a perfect man, and I am not a perfect boyfriend, but I will never stop trying to make you happy.

And as the plane takes off, I smile.

Because I believe him.

I trust him.

And yes, reader, I love him. With all that I am and I rather suspect for all time.

THE END (FOR NOW)

Alex, Sasha and Carlton will be back in Book 2 of The Redemption Series by Clare Connelly, HAND ON HEART - preorder now so you don't miss out on the steamy second instalment (where Sasha goes to LA and joins forces with Dr Carlton. Can they survive a long distance relationship?).
Sign up to Clare's newsletter for more information.

Books By Clare Connelly

HARLEQUIN TITLES

Bought for the Billionaire's Revenge

Innocent in the Billionaire's Bed

Off Limits

Her Wedding Night Surrender

Burn Me Once

Bound by the Billionaire's Vows

The Season to Sin

His Innocent Seduction

Bound by their Christmas Baby

Her Guilty Secret

Shock Heir for the King

The Greek's Billion-Dollar Baby

Spaniard's Baby of Revenge

The Bride Behind the Billion-Dollar Veil

Dare Continuity

Cross my Hart (Notorious Harts Bk 1)

SINGLE TITLES

Her Guardian's Christmas Seduction

Stolen by the Desert King

In the Hands of the Sheikh

His Nine Month Seduction

The Sheikh's Contract Bride

Seduced by the Vengeful Tycoon

The Sheikh's Stolen Bride

The Sheikh's Secret Baby

The Sheikh's Million Dollar Bride

The Tycoon's Virgin Mistress

The Sheikh's Virgin Hostage

Bartered to the Sheikh

The Sheikh's Arranged Marriage

Marrying for his Royal Heir

The Greek's Marriage Revenge

The Velasco Love Child

The Sultan's Virgin Bride

Bound to the Sheikh

The Medici Mistress

His Loving Deception

The Sheikh's Convenient Mistress

The Princess's Forbidden Lover

Marrying her Enemy

Rakanti's Indecent Proposition

Seducing the Spaniard

The Italian's Innocent Bride

The Greek Tycoon's Forbidden Affair

The Terms of their Affair

A Second Chance at Love

The Sheikh's Christmas Mistress

At the Sheikh's Command

The Billionaire's Christmas Revenge

Seduced by the Italian Tycoon

Raising the Soldier's Son

Warming the Sheikh's Bed

The Tycoon's Christmas Captive

The Brazilian's Forgotten Lover

Betrayed by the CEO

The Billionaire's Ruthless Revenge

The Italian Billionaire's Betrayal

The Sultan's Reluctant Princess

Love in the Fast Lane

Bought by the Sheikh

The Tycoon's Summer Seduction

All She Wants for Christmas

One Night with the Sheikh

A Bed of Broken Promises

Tempted by the Billionaire

The Sheikh's Christmas Wish

To the Highest Bidder

The Tycoon's Secret Baby

Bedding His Innocent Mistress

The Sheikh's Baby Bargain

The Greek's Virgin Captive

The Sheikh's Inherited Bride

Claiming His Secret Baby

Blackmailed by the Spaniard

Her Surprise Baby Christmas

COMPENDIUMS

Casacelli Brides

Mediterranean Tycoons

Desert Rulers

Billionaire Bad Boys

Too Hot to Handle

Desert Kings

Happily Ever After

The Darling Buds of May Café

Royal Weddings

The Evermore Series

Join the Club

Never miss a new release or give away!
Sign up to Clare's newsletter to stay in the loop.
Check out a full list of books and bio at
www.clareconnelly.com
Follow Clare on Social Media as @Clarewriteslove (because she does)
And if you loved this book, please take a moment to leave a review once you're done. Thank you!

If you love listening to your happy endings, then don't forget, you can catch THE EVERMORE SERIES as Audiobooks, with new titles being released all the time.

Available on audible.com and iBooks.

Following is a full list of Clare Connelly's titles - more than 80 romances to fall in love with, again and again. Happy reading!

Printed in Great Britain
by Amazon

42676071R00138